THROWING THE CURVE

PLAYING FOR KEEPS SERIES- BOOK 2

LAUREN FRASER

First edition

CONTENTS

BLURB

Nothing is more important than the team. Until her.

How is this her life? Peyton Sharp prides herself on being a good person and doing the right thing. So how the heck did she end up at a party with a married man? Sure, she hadn't known he was married, but still. Apparently, all her life experience didn't prevent her from being an idiot when it came to men. And don't even get her started on Ryan Graves.

Being a good teammate has been drilled into star pitcher Ryan Graves' head since he first picked up a glove. Somehow, he never thought that would extend to helping his cheating teammate out of a jam. he avoids relationships for a reason. Now he's fake dating a woman who hates him. Thinking about her more than he should and questioning everything he thought was important. This was not what he signed up for.

Falling in love with his fake girlfriend was never part of the plan. *But when life throws you a curve, sometimes all you can do is swing for the fences.*

Throwing the Curve can be read as a stand-alone

CHAPTER ONE

W as it too soon to be meeting his teammates? Peyton glanced over at Simon. Did she even want to meet his friends? What if she didn't like them? God, she wasn't even sure how she was feeling about Simon, let alone his friends. *Gah.*

He winked and reached across the center console to place his hand on her knee. "Relax babe, they're going to love you."

"Remind me whose party this is again?" she asked as she slid her hand nervously down her lap, smoothing out her skirt. She clasped Simon's hand, hoping it would calm her nerves. Going to a party with him felt like a big step. One she wasn't sure they were ready for.

"It's a housewarming for Sanchez. He's new this season and plays left field. He just bought this place. It should be pretty low key, just a few of the guys from the team and their dates."

"Does he have a first name?"

Simon chuckled. "Yeah, Tony."

The car pulled up in front of a sprawling rancher in Mission Bay. Peyton scanned the front of the house, her eyes lingering on the beautiful old rose bushes beneath the front windows. Just like the ones at her grandma's house. She could almost smell them from here and it instantly transported her back to making rose water on summer break as a kid.

She pushed open the car door and rounded the front of the vehicle.

Simon stopped beside her and made a rough noise in his throat, and she turned toward him. "What?"

"Nothing. I thought he would have bought something a little newer. This thing looks like it was built in the eighties."

Peyton rolled her eyes. "It doesn't look that old." She once again scanned the front of the house. "It's lovely and the location is fantastic. There's a great public beach right down the street." She'd love to live in a place like this. Who wouldn't?

"Yeah, a *public* beach," Simon scoffed.

"Oh my god, could you be a bigger snob? Seriously, there's nothing wrong with a public beach. That's where most of us common folk go to swim."

He wrapped his arm around her waist and pulled her closer to him. "Yeah, but you're not common anymore, baby. You're with me now. I don't do common."

She tensed at his tone. They'd only been dating for a few weeks, and she'd never dated someone with money before. She wasn't sure if the slight jabs at her economic level were normal, or his way of trying to brag, or what it was, but it grated. "Let's go inside."

He placed his hand on the small of her back as they made their way down the side of the house. Laughing and splashing sounds drifted toward her as they rounded the corner and into the large backyard. Peyton stopped as she looked around to get her bearings. Holy cow. Older home or not, this backyard alone was worth buying the house. A large in-ground pool with several people splashing around took up the right side of the yard. A sweeping decorative cement patio curved around the pool. Off to the left was a beautiful, covered area with a fireplace and a large flatscreen tv hanging above it. Who had a TV outside? This was whole other level stuff than what she was used to.

"Andy," a deep voice yelled, drawing her attention toward the barbecue.

Simon walked toward the man working the grill. "Hey Tony, thanks for having us."

"Glad you could make it." Tony glanced over at her. His dark brown eyes scanned her from head to toe. He smiled and stuck out his hand. "Hi, I'm Tony, you must be Carmella?"

Ouch. Peyton's shoulders tensed. Who the hell was Carmella?

Simon laughed. "Nah, man, this is Peyton."

"Oh sorry, my mistake. I'm new, so still trying to figure out who everyone is."

She glanced over at Simon, and he rolled his eyes like Tony was an idiot for getting her name wrong. He smacked Tony on the back. "No problem, man, it happens. We're going to grab a drink," Simon said.

"Sure, help yourself. There's beer and wine in the fridge there," he said, pointing to the small stainless fridge in the outdoor kitchen. "And I think Saunders is in the kitchen watching Kendall make margaritas if you want one of those."

"What'll it be?" Simon asked.

"A margarita sounds great, actually," she replied.

They wove their way inside to the kitchen. "Hey hey, looks like this is where the party is," Simon called out.

Five heads swiveled toward them. "Hey Andy."

Peyton scanned the group. Good lord, she had not been prepared for the testosterone flowing off these men as she they all swung their attention toward her.

"Can we grab a couple of those, Kendall?" Simon asked.

"Told ya if you stood around talking instead of blending you'd be stuck making these all night." A brown-haired guy she was pretty sure was the shortstop Pete Saunders, smacked the woman making drinks on the butt.

Peyton glanced over at Simon. Was he going to introduce her?

Instead, he stepped up to the island and grabbed a tortilla chip from the bowl and dipped it into the salsa. Okay, apparently manners weren't his strong suit. She stared at him.

Wow, he was like a different person when he was alone with her than he was in front of his teammates. The Simon she knew had pursued her hard. He'd been sweet and attentive. This 'Andy' as his teammates called him, was a bit of an arrogant jerk. She eyed him speculatively and wondered which one was the real man.

She stepped up to the counter. "Hi, sorry. Looks like Simon isn't going to introduce us, so I'm Peyton."

Simon glanced over at her. "Sorry, babe." He placed his hand on her hip. "Peyton, this is Gonzo, Smitty, Zip, Kendall and—" He paused and turned to the man standing on the other side of Peyton. Wow, he was gorgeous and looked seriously pissed. She sucked in a breath as ice-blue eyes drilled into her.

Simon snorted beside her. "The guy glaring at us is Undertaker."

"I told you not to fucking call me that," glaring guy growled.

Apparently, there was no love lost between these two.

"Why not? It's perfect." Simon glanced around at the other men around the island. "Don't you guys think it fits him perfectly?"

"Ah, not really, no," Pete answered.

Gonzo wrinkled his nose and shook his head. "I think Ryan is good. No need for a nickname, really."

"Ace works," Smitty piped in.

"Come on, you guys, just because Ryan has no sense of humor doesn't mean the name isn't perfect," Simon said as he picked up another tortilla and dipped it.

She turned to Simon. "Sorry, why would Undertaker be perfect?"

"Come on, babe, I thought you were a ball fan."

She bristled at the mocking tone of his voice. She definitely was not a fan of Simon with the boys. "I am. I just have to agree with them that Undertaker sounds more like he's a wrestler than a pitcher."

"How'd you know I was the pitcher?" grumpy guy asked.

She glanced over at him and again was struck by his piercing blue eyes. Sheesh, she'd seen all these guys on TV when she watched the games and the interviews, but she hadn't been prepared for them up close. The TV did not do Ryan Graves justice. "Like Simon said, I watch sports. It's kind of a job requirement to understand the game."

Ryan's eyes ran down her body, and she fought the urge to cross her arms over her chest. He wasn't looking at her like she was a desirable woman, but like something he found on the bottom of his shoe. What the hell was that about?

"Yeah? What kind of job is that?" he mocked.

"Oh fuck," Smitty mumbled.

Ryan's stare whipped off her and over to Smitty. "What?"

"Incoming," Smitty muttered and nodded toward the doors behind them.

"Fuck," Simon groaned and took several steps away from her just as the sliding glass door opened and three women walked in.

"Surprise," the curvy brunette called as she sashayed toward Simon and leaned in for a kiss when she reached him

Peyton felt like she'd been kicked in the stomach. He had a girlfriend? What the heck? She looked over at Simon and the beautiful woman now wrapped around his side. He refused to make eye contact with her. Mother F'er. She shook her head as a sick feeling swept through her stomach.

"Hi everybody," the woman called.

"Hey Carmella," Ryan said from beside her.

Carmella eyed Peyton up and down. "Who are you?" Carmella asked.

"That's Peyton. She's Undertaker's date," Simon said.

"No," Ryan growled.

"Right, right, sorry we agreed I wouldn't call you that." Simon laughed. He looked down at Carmella and made a face. "He has no sense of humor."

Carmella squealed. "Oh, my gosh, I've never met one of Ryan's girls before. This is so exciting. I'm Simon's wife, Carmella."

"His wife?" Peyton asked. Her ears buzzed, the noise getting louder and louder. She looked around the room, trying to get her bearings. Her mind raced to catch up with what was happening in front of her. Was she being punked? This was like some bad movie.

Carmella smiled and waved her hand in the air. A huge diamond sparkled on her ring finger. "Seven years."

Oh my god, she was a home wrecker. How had this happened? He was married? Her eyes flashed to his bare ring finger. Why didn't he wear a ring like a normal person?

"Who's watching the kids?" Simon asked his wife.

"You have kids?" Peyton squeaked.

"Yep, three of them," Carmella replied to Peyton before turning to her husband and patting his chest. "Don't worry, when Chelan called and asked me to come, she'd already okayed it with her nanny, so they are all at our place."

Peyton placed a hand on her stomach. Oh, my god she was going to be sick. She needed to get out of here. Her eyes flashed around the room. "Where's the bathroom?" she asked.

The woman across the island from her, Kendall possibly, pointed to the staircase on the right. "It's upstairs at the end of the hall. You can't miss it."

"Thanks," she murmured before making a beeline out of the room.

Once inside the washroom, she leaned her hands against the counter and dropped her head. How had this happened? How could she be dating a married man? She'd asked him about his relationship status, and he'd told her he was single. She cringed. No, he'd said there was no one she'd needed to worry about, and she'd stupidly thought that meant he was single. Paired with the naked ring finger and she'd figured it was fine. Sure, she'd expected he might be a bit of a player because he was a professional athlete, but she'd thought that meant more he wouldn't get serious about her, which is why they still hadn't officially slept together despite several weeks of dating.

She covered her mouth and groaned. Ew, she'd had oral sex with a married man. Gross.

She sat down on the edge of the tub. Oh my god, she was the other woman. Nausea rolled in her gut. No, no, no, no, no. This was not happening. She couldn't be the other woman.

An affair had ripped her parents apart. There was no way she was going to be that person. She'd done everything right. How could this happen?

She looked around the washroom. Great and now she was stuck in a stranger's bathroom with the guy she was having an affair with downstairs with his wife. She was a home wrecker. *Oh my god.* She was no better than the women her dad had been with.

She had to get out of here. But how?

With trembling hands, she pulled her phone out of her purse. Her vision blurred as she tried to pull up her contacts. *Great, and now she was crying.* She wiped her face, took a shuddering breath, and dialed her best friend Rayne. The second Rayne picked up, she whispered, "He's married."

"Who's married?" Rayne whispered back.

"Simon," Peyton whispered louder.

"Holy shit, he's married," Rayne yelled. "Sorry. He's married?" she whispered.

Peyton chortled, making a weird half-laugh, half-snotty-crying sound. She wiped her nose with the back of her hand. "Why are you whispering?"

"I don't know. You were whispering so I went with it," Rayne answered.

"Well, I'm hiding in the bathroom at a party. That's why I'm whispering," Peyton replied. She looked over at the small bathroom window. Shoot, there was no way she could squeeze out of that little thing.

Oh god, she couldn't breathe. Why was it so hot in here? She grabbed the edge of her shirt and fanned herself.

"Pey, you still there?" Rayne's voice cut through the buzzing in her ears.

"Yeah, just trying to figure out how I'm going to get out of here. Can you come pick me up?"

"Sorry sweetie, I'm at work and have a client coming in ten minutes."

"Fantastic," she grumbled. Getting an uber all the way out here and back to her place would cost a month's rent.

"How the hell can he be married? Didn't you ask?"

"Of course I asked. I'm not an idiot," she snapped. "Sorry, you didn't deserve that. I'm just...god. I don't know what I am. Pissed off. Embarrassed." She rubbed her hands across her face. Gross, why was she so sweaty? She glanced at her flushed face in the mirror. This day was just getting better and better. Now she was having like a hot flash or something. She flapped her arms to try to cool herself down. "Rayne, I've got to get out of here," she whispered as the panic roared in her chest again.

"Just breathe, it'll be fine."

"It's not going to be fine. The jerk told his wife I was Ryan Graves' date."

"Is he cute?"

"Are you freakin' kidding me right now? "

"What? I'm just asking. I mean, clearly you can't date Simon now, and it's been a hot minute since you got laid. So..."

"Not helpful, Rayne. Like at all."

"Okay, so maybe your new date could give you a ride or something?"

"Yeah, sure, the guy who glared at me like he hated me on sight is going to give me a ride."

"Seriously, he glared at you?" Rayne asked.

"Yep, but totally makes sense now since he thought I was the other woman." She groaned. "Which I totally am." Tears welled up in her eyes and she looked up at the ceiling. "God, Rayne, help me. What am I supposed to do? I can't keep hiding in the bathroom forever. People will start to think it's weird."

No sooner had the words left her mouth than there was a knock on the door, followed by a deep male voice. "You okay in there?"

"Crap, Rayne," she whispered. "Umm yep, fine, be out in a second," she called to the stranger at the door. Could this day get any worse? "I gotta go," she whispered to Rayne.

"Call me when you get home," Rayne said.

Peyton hung up the phone and glanced at herself in the mirror. Perfect, she looked like a hot mess. She splashed some cold water on her face and looked at herself again. Awesome that made it worse. Now her face was all blotchy. *Oh god, kill me now.*

Taking a deep breath, she grabbed the doorknob and pulled the door open. Of course, it had to be him. Icy-glare Graves.

"It's all yours," she said as she tried to step by him.

"You okay?" he asked.

"Not really." Laughter drifted up from downstairs. There was no way she was going back down there. "Do you know the address so I can get an uber?"

He smirked at her. "Didn't sign on for meeting the wife today, hey?"

"Didn't know there was a wife."

"Yeah right," he scoffed.

Peyton's shoulders tensed. Who the heck did this guy think he was judging her like this? "Obviously I didn't, or I wouldn't be here."

"Come on now, that's not entirely true. There are at least two women in the pool out back that are dating guys they know are married, because they are fake dating other guys on the team. I just have no intention of being one of those guys."

"Are you kidding me?"

"Nope." He looked her up and down and shook his head. "So what? You didn't google Andy before you started dating?"

"No, why would I?"

"Right, you expect me to believe you started dating a professional athlete and didn't look him up online? Please."

"I didn't," she snapped. Although now she really wished she had. "I didn't think I had to."

"Sure." He laughed. "Sell that one to someone else, sweetheart."

"Are you calling me a liar?" She glared at the man in front of her. What an arrogant prick. How dare he stand there judging her when his friends were the kind of guys who behaved like this?

"Just calling it like I see it, sweetheart."

"Screw you," she seethed.

"Not really interested. Thanks."

Peyton's jaw clenched. This guy was unbelievable. "I'm going to need you to move out of my way."

"What, so you can join the party? I'm not having you go down there and embarrass Carmella in front of everyone."

"Embarrass Carmella? Right." She took a deep breath. "You have no reason to believe me, but I have no intention of hurting Carmella. Simon might be a jerk, but his wife did nothing to me. I need to get out of here. Can you help me do that? Please?"

He stared at her for several minutes before finally nodding in agreement. "Sure come on." At the top of the stairs, he paused and glanced back at her. "What was your name again?"

"Peyton."

"Peyton. Got it." He looked down the stairs and sighed. "Alright Peyton, let's do this."

Why did he have to make it feel like they were facing a firing squad instead of his teammates? This didn't bode well for her getting out of here unscathed.

The moment they stepped into the kitchen, the women descended on her like a pack of hyenas. "So, Simon said you run the sports program for kids that he volunteers at. Is that how you met Ryan?" Carmella asked.

"Uh... how... uh... Ryan and I met?" she stammered.

"Yes, how did you two meet?" Carmella prodded.

"Umm..." She looked around the room at all the people staring at her expectantly, waiting for her response. She didn't want to lie. God, she didn't want to be here at all.

A hand brushed across her shoulder and she glanced back at Ryan. "Peyton isn't feeling very good, so I'm going to run her home and come back. So maybe we can save the inquisition for another time, hey, Carm?" He smiled at Simon's wife.

Carmella wrinkled her nose at him. "It wasn't an inquisition. I'm just curious about how you met." Carmella's eyes warmed as she smiled at Ryan. "You never bring women to these things, so of course when you do we know she must be special. I want to make sure she deserves you."

"Thanks, Carm, I appreciate it. You don't have to worry about me."

"Of course I do. You're the sweetest guy I know." Carmella turned to Peyton. "You better be good to him."

"Jesus, Carm, he's a grown man, not a puppy dog. Maybe he brought her because she's hot and he wants to fuck her," Simon said.

Peyton sucked in a breath. Did he really just say that?

Carmella elbowed Simon in the gut and he let out an *oomph* sound.

"You're such a dick," Ryan growled. His entire body was tense against Peyton's side, like it was taking everything in him to stay in place. This stranger was more protective of her than the man she was supposed to be dating.

"What?" Simon asked.

It was official, if they hadn't been done before she found out about his wife, seeing what a douche he was around his friends would have solidified the deal for her. Peyton stared at the man in front of her. What had she been thinking dating him?

"Carm, I will never understand what you see in this guy. But it's always a pleasure to see you," Ryan said then turned back to Peyton. "You ready to go?"

"Yeah, definitely," she replied.

Ryan pressed his hand against her back and guided her toward the door. Who knew her knight in shining armor would be the one person at the party who hated her?

CHAPTER TWO

Ryan slid behind the wheel of his SUV and glanced over at the woman in the passenger seat. How the hell did he get himself into these situations? He'd give it to Andy. He had great taste. She was gorgeous.

"So where am I taking you?" he asked.

"What?" She slowly turned her head toward him and blinked her blue eyes like she was just waking up. "Sorry, what did you ask?"

"Where do you live?"

"Oh, um, Little Italy, but you really don't have to take me home. I can grab an uber or something so you can stay at the party."

A hand rapped against the window of the car, drawing Ryan's attention away from the woman beside him. He rolled down the window. "Hey Johnny, what's up?" he asked the relief pitcher standing at the car door with a buxom brunette who was definitely not his wife. Ryan scowled. What the fuck was wrong with all these guys bringing women who weren't their fucking wives to this party? Jesus. Why the hell did they get married if they wanted to keep sleeping with other women?

"Where you going Graves? The party is that way." He pointed toward the house.

"Yeah, I know." He gave a fake chuckle. "But Peyton isn't feeling great, so we are cutting out early."

Johnny bent down and gave Peyton a solid once over and a smile slid across his face. "Yeah, I'd probably head home too." He winked at Ryan before saying, "I'm sure Ryan will take good care of you Peyton." Johnny stood and rapped the top of Ryan's car with his knuckles before walking off.

God, why couldn't half the guys on the team keep it in their pants? It sure as hell didn't say much about the ability to sustain a marriage with their schedule. And what was wrong with these women that they were willing to accept being the other woman simply to date a ballplayer? He glanced over at Peyton. She was a beautiful woman. Surely she wanted better than being Andy's side piece.

"Seriously, you don't have to drive me home. You can go back to the party." Peyton's voice cut through his thoughts. "I mean, we just met, and I know Simon put you on the spot with the whole fake date thing, but you don't really have to play it out any further than what you did inside."

He glanced in his rearview mirror and watched Johnny and his date walk around the side of the house with Johnny's hand firmly on his date's ass. Fuck. He really had no interest in going back in there in the mood he was in. "It's all good. I'm kind of partied out. So Little Italy?"

"Yeah, thank you. I really appreciate you taking me home."

"Sure." He put the car in gear and carefully navigated backing out of the line of cars in the driveway.

After several minutes of silence, he glanced over at Peyton, who sat staring out the side window, wringing her hands anxiously in her lap. "So how long have you and Andy been a thing?" he asked.

She wiped her hand across her eyes before turning toward him. "Umm, I met him about a month ago. But clearly..." She waved her hand in the air and let out a loud breath.

"I'm sure he'll be showing up tomorrow with a big bouquet of flowers and some bling to apologize for his wife showing up on your date."

She shifted in her seat. The sadness in her eyes quickly turned to anger. "And you think some jewelry is going to make up for what happened in there?"

"I have no idea? I'm just saying I'm sure he'll try to smooth things over. He seemed pretty into you when you showed up."

"Yeah, well, there's no amount of bling that will make up for that," she muttered.

"No?" Ryan asked, unable to keep the skepticism from his voice as he looked at the gorgeous blonde beside him. She was like the poster girl for what every ball player was looking for in a trophy girlfriend. Long legs, killer body, and perfect smile. Yeah, there was no way Andy wouldn't be buying out the jewelry store to get this one back.

"No." She scowled at him. "God, he's married."

"Come on, are you still going to pretend you didn't have a clue he was married?"

"What is your problem?" she snapped. "I told you I didn't know he was married, and I didn't."

"Right."

"You know what? You can let me out here, and I'll figure out my own way home."

"Don't be stupid. I'll take you home."

"Honestly, if you are going to keep being a jerk, I'd rather walk."

"Fine. You didn't know he was married." Ryan glanced over at her. Could she really be that naïve? "So, how did you say you met Andy again?"

"He came in with your press liaison and a couple of other players to discuss the team volunteering where I work, and we kind of hit it off."

"Where do you work?"

"I'm the coordinator at Kidsplay."

"Like the kids' sports program the team is partnering with?"

A smile split across her face. "Yeah, I found out this week that we were chosen. It's going to be so amazing for those kids."

"And I guess hooking up with Andy was a nice perk. He must have really gone to bat for your program for them to pick it. Nicely done."

"Okay, seriously, you need to stop the car now."

"What? Why?"

"Are you flipping kidding me? You just called me a whore."

"No, I didn't?"

"Oh my god, are you serious? Stop the car."

"Don't be ridiculous. We're almost there."

"I said stop the car. Now."

"This is so dumb," he muttered. "Don't you think you are being a bit dramatic?" He pulled the car to the side of the road and stopped.

"No, I don't. What I think is you are a judgmental jerk. You just met me, and yes, I'll admit it wasn't under the best circumstances, but you don't know me. So you can take your ride and your holier than though attitude and shove it." She pushed open the car door and slammed it shut behind her.

The cars behind him honked its horn to get him to move. He watched Peyton storm off down the street and debated going after her.

"Move your car, asshole," a voice yelled from a vehicle behind him, followed by a long horn that quickly was matched by several other vehicles following suit. Fuck it. He glanced over his shoulder and threw the car into gear.

He looked over at Peyton stomping down the street as he drove past. His chest tightened. Was she right? Was he being a judgmental asshole? Probably. But what did he have to go on? She was sleeping with a married man.

In this day and age when you started dating someone, it was just common practice to look the person up online. There's no way this woman hadn't done the same thing with a *professional athlete*. Come on. Before his sister had dated Pete, she'd practically cyber-stalked every guy she ever dated to make sure he wasn't some kind of weird serial killer. Then and only then would she consider meeting him in a very public place for coffee. Peyton couldn't tell him she didn't do the same thing.

She might try to play the victim now, but there was no way she hadn't done her research. He wasn't buying it.

He rubbed his hand against his chest. So why did he feel like such an asshole?

Fuck. Because he'd been a dick.

Whether or not he had that opinion, he shouldn't have voiced it out loud. He'd been raised better than that. Shit. And now that the team had agreed to partner with her organization, it's not like he'd never see her again. They were going to have to work together at some point.

Guess he was going by the youth center to make amends. Apparently, Andy wasn't the only one needing to buy some flowers for a certain gorgeous blonde.

Monday morning Peyton pulled her car into a spot outside the youth center and got out.

"Pey—ton," a voice called from the group of teens resting against the side of the building. "Morning, what are you all doing here so early?" she asked as she walked up to the five boys.

"School was canceled. Some threat or something, so we're hoping we could mess around in the gym," Jesse the ringleader of the group replied.

"Mess around? No. Use the weights appropriately? Yes."

"Ah shit, Pey, you know that's what I meant."

"Oh, I know." She made eye contact with each of the boys and smiled at the group. "Depending on who else shows up today, maybe we can get a pickup game going later or something."

"You going to play?"

"I think we've established basketball is not my game."

Jesse laughed. "Yeah, but is sure if fun to watch you try."

Peyton narrowed her eyes and mock glared at the youth. "Ha-ha and that right there," she said, pointing at their mocking faces. "Is exactly why I won't be playing. I have other gifts I bring to the table."

"I'll say you do," Tyson mumbled.

"Ew, Tyson. Just... no... that's inappropriate on so many levels." Peyton stared the teen down and he dropped his head.

"Sorry, Peyton. Won't happen again."

"Thank you. I appreciate your apology." When Tyson looked her in the eye, she saw his remorse. He'd come a long way since he started coming to the center. The first few times he'd come, they'd had to ask him to leave for breaking rules, and she hadn't been sure he'd come back. But he had. And over the past several months, he'd really made strides toward being a different kind of kid. There's no way the Tyson who had shown up here six months ago would have apologized for his comment let alone meant it. The fact he clearly did warmed her heart and gave her hope for his chances. This was why she did what she did, because this place mattered.

"Give me a couple minutes to unlock everything," she told them.

"Cool," Jesse replied.

She unlocked the front door of the center and punched in the code for the alarm, and flipped on the lights in the main area. She walked down the hall and unlocked the gym, turned on lights in the weight room then turned back around and opened the front door to call the boys in. "Alright, come on in. Enjoy your workout. James should be here in about five minutes, so he'll be out front if you need anything."

"Thanks, Peyton," they called.

"No problem. I'm glad you came by when school was canceled."

"Yeah well, Cy's arms look like little chicken wings so…" Jesse poked the other boy in the arm.

Cy spun and wrapped Jesse in a headlock. "Chicken wing this, motherfucker."

Peyton rolled her eyes as the two boys wrestled to the ground. Why was it boys loved to play that way?

"Hello?" a male voice called from out front.

"Sounds like James is here. Make good choices, boys," Peyton called as she walked out of the weight room.

Peyton turned on the coffeemaker in the kitchen, then wandered out front to say good morning to James.

"Soo, how was your weekend? How'd the party go?" James leaned his elbows on the counter and watched her expectantly. "Give me all the tea."

"Well, he's married, so there's that."

"Holy shit, he's married?" James stood up straight and stared at her. "Didn't you google him?"

"No, why does everyone keep asking me that?" Peyton grumbled.

"Well, because that's dating 101, sweetie," James replied. His nose wrinkled up as he looked at her sadly.

"Seeing how I haven't had a date in three years, I wasn't aware that was like a rule."

"Honey, it's been a rule since the internet was invented."

"Yeah, well, it's been a hot minute since I had to worry about any of that. And I kind of thought it would be nice to get to know someone with no preconceived ideas." She blew her bangs off her face. "Why didn't you tell me to research him online first?"

"I figured you knew. You've helped me deep dive before my dates."

"Yeah, but that's before you hook up with some rando you met online and you want to make sure you aren't going to end up a skin suit."

"True, but the concept is the same, sweetie."

"Well, I figured I was pretty safe that a professional baseball player probably wasn't going to turn me into a nice ottoman cover. I mean, I'm sure that kind of thing would have made national news and I don't think his team would have him down here trying to organize volunteering with children."

James snorted. "You'd like to think."

"Yeah, you would." She plopped down onto the sofa. "God, I'm so stupid. I mean, I looked for a ring. I asked. I honestly thought if he was taken, his teammates or publicist would have said something when he was flirting with me since that kind of seems like a PR nightmare." She dropped her head against the back of the sofa. "How can I work in this field and be that naïve?"

"Oh honey, who can blame you, really? We see some shitty things. You just wanted to believe in the fairytale."

"*Fairytale,* right. Well, he definitely wasn't that. And the sixteen voicemails he left me over the weekend proved it."

"Sixteen? Yikes, that's a bit excessive."

"You think?" She snickered. After the first half dozen calls, she'd turned her phone off. Unfortunately, with his team volunteering, she hadn't been able to delete his number, but lord knows it had been tempting.

A giant black SUV pulled up in the parking lot. She stood up to get a better look. Four women dressed in designer clothes exited the vehicle.

"You've got to be freaking kidding me," she mumbled.

"What?" James asked.

"That's his frickin' wife," Peyton squeaked. Oh god, why was she here? She eyed the back hallway. Did she have time to make a break for it before they walked in?

"Go to your office, honey. I'll see if I can figure out why they're here. Go," James ordered.

"Are you sure?" she asked.

"Yes, go, quick." James pushed her in the back, and she stumbled toward her office.

She paced around the small space, waiting for James to come tell her it was safe to come out. Several minutes later, James walked in and winced. "Apparently they are here to volunteer?"

"What? What do you mean they're here to volunteer? Doing what?" She looked around the office. This couldn't be happening. Why? Why? "What did you tell them?"

"I asked what they had in mind. She said something about adding some flare to what the guys were doing, whatever the hell that means?" James shuddered. "They scare me, and that's hard to do. You have to go out there."

"What? No, I don't!" Peyton grabbed her friend's arm. "Seriously James, I can't. I'm not cut out for this kind of thing. I'll confess and I don't want to ruin this woman's life with some frickin' Bill Clinton moment of what constitutes cheating in their relationship."

James' lip quivered as he tried not to laugh.

"It's not funny," Peyton growled.

"Clinton moment? Really? Come on, that was good."

"James, seriously." Peyton widened her eyes and stared at him. "Help me."

"Okay, okay. Call shithead and tell him to get his ass down here and tell his wife she can't volunteer because it's fucking ridiculous."

"Oh god, I don't want to call him, but it is ridiculous. Do these people not talk? I mean seriously. She just rounds up a bunch of other wives, comes on down, and no one thinks to tell them it's a bad idea. What is wrong with these guys?"

She took a deep breath. "Okay, first things first. I'll call sleazeball and tell him to get his wife. Then I'll try to encourage her not to volunteer." She picked up her phone and turned back to James. "Can you go back out there and make sure no one is going to steal her car or try to rob them or anything?"

James squeezed her arm. "It'll be okay, honey."

"Sure it will." If only that were true.

James closed the door behind him as she stared at the phone in her hand. She could do this. After one deep, fortifying breath, she pulled up Simon's number and hit dial.

"Peyton, baby. I'm so glad you called me back."

"Nope, we aren't doing this. The only reason I am calling is because you wife is here with some of the other wives, and they want to volunteer. You need to fix this, Simon."

"What do you mean Carmella is there?" Simon's voice raised several octaves.

"I mean, your wife is out front with her friends, and they want to volunteer because the team is volunteering here, and apparently that means so do their wives."

"Shit. I'm on my way."

"Hurry," Peyton snapped and hung up.

She dropped her phone down onto her desk. God, she hadn't even had her first cup of coffee yet. This day sucked. She wanted a do over.

The intercom on her phone clicked on. "Umm, Peyton," James said.

"Yes, sorry I'm coming."

Okay, she could do this. *Just put on your big girl panties and go out there.* She adjusted the waistband of her pants and smoothed down the front of her shirt. Her hand trembled.

How was she supposed to face this woman when she knew what a sleaze her husband was? And how did she not say something to her? But how could she do that? It would ruin this woman's life and those kids... God, those poor kids. She knew what that felt like. Her dad was the same kind of cheating jerk. She'd thought she could spot them a mile away. Apparently not.

She took a deep breath. "Big girl panties, big girl panties," she muttered to herself. Who was she kidding? There were not panties big enough to handle this situation. This was some supersonic Spanx kind of deal. Another deep breath and she pulled open the door and walked down the hall.

Each step closer, the nausea in her stomach grew.

"Peyton, hi," Carmella gushed the moment she saw her.

"Carmella, what a surprise." She forced a smile that felt so fake.

"Sorry, we showed up unannounced. The girls and I got talking yesterday over brunch and we just had to come down and see the place where our fellas are going to be volunteering."

"Right, sorry, unfortunately, umm... there's not really a nice way to say this, so... umm... I'll just say it. This is a safe place for kids, so it's not really a place where we want people to come and look around as they please. Sorry, if that sounds harsh, I just have to really protect the kids."

"Oh, no, of course we totally understand." Carmella put her hand to her chest. "We aren't here to just be looky-loos. I thought because it was a school day, it would be okay to come down now because you'd have fewer kids around. I was hoping we could talk about some ways the girls and I could help out."

"Help out?"

"Yes, put us to work," Carmella said.

"Well, until I see what this program with the Hawks is going to look like, I don't really know what we'll need in terms of volunteers. So, it's a bit premature to even consider a meeting," Peyton replied.

A curvy blonde stepped toward Peyton. "Any chance we could sit down and have some coffee and chat?"

"Umm..." Peyton stammered.

"I'm Lisa Knight. My husband, Johnny, is one of the pitchers on the team. He's no Ryan but..."

"Johnny Knight? Right, yep, I know who he is." Crap, that was not the woman he was with at the party. How the hell could Carmella be here with her when she'd been at the party and seen Lisa's husband with someone else? She glanced over at Carmella, who smiled sadly at her like she knew what Peyton was thinking. Oh, hell no, she was not cut out for this crap.

"So coffee?" Lisa prodded.

"Why don't you go sit down in the boardroom, and I'll bring some coffee to you all, Peyton," James said.

Peyton glanced over at James and gritted her teeth. "Great." So much for being helpful.

"If I'm being honest, we really all just wanted to get to know Ryan's girlfriend a little better, so prepare to be grilled," Lisa said as she linked her arm with Peyton.

"Ryan?" James mouthed and Peyton rolled her eyes.

Could this day get any worse?

CHAPTER THREE

Ryan fought to stay focused on the PowerPoint presentation flipping across the screen as the PR team laid out the upcoming volunteer commitments they had planned for the players. This off season was going to be busier than the regular season. So much for down time.

Phone in hand, Andy walked back into the room and rounded the table, crouching down beside Ryan. "We need to head down to Kidsplay."

Ryan leaned back in his chair and crossed his arms over his chest. "Why do *we* need to go there?"

"Because Carm and a bunch of wives just showed up and if I know them, they'll be grilling Peyton about you."

Kirsty paused the PowerPoint presentation and leaned across the table toward them. "Why would they be grilling Peyton about Ryan?"

"Fuck," Ryan muttered. Of course, this had to happen in the middle of their team PR meeting with Kirsty there.

Why had he agreed to this? It was one thing to save Andy at a party, but come on, did he honestly expect him to keep up this charade?

"Because Ryan and Peyton are dating," Andy piped up.

Apparently so. Ryan glared at Andy, and the bastard just shrugged like it was no big deal.

"Seriously?" Kirsty sat forward in her seat. "When did that happen?" Her eyes lit up like they just told her they had a box of puppies. She pinned Ryan with her stare, anxiously awaiting his answer.

He shifted uncomfortably in his chair. "I don't know umm—" Fuck, he hated lying. How did this come so easily to Andy?

"I introduced them a few weeks ago, and it was inevitable" Andy looked at Ryan, then back at Kirsty and waggled his eyebrows lasciviously.

Kirsty propped her hands on the table. "Give me all the details." She grinned. "This is brilliant. Do you have any idea what I can do with this kind of information? This is a freaking goldmine. Ryan, you never bring women around, so you dating the woman who runs the youth program the team is going to be working with. This is a PR dream."

"Why's that exactly?" Ryan asked. Shit, shit, shit. He didn't want to be a PR dream. He purposely didn't bring women around the team stuff for exactly this reason. Ryan was fine doing any publicity that related to his playing, but his personal life? No, thank you.

"First, because she is gorgeous. The two of you will look amazing in photos, which is a win. Oh, my god I can already picture you two together in the press releases we'll be doing." She clapped her hands together. "You have just made my job so much easier."

"Why would he be in the press release? I was the one who went to the meetings?" Andy complained.

Ryan looked at his teammate. Unreal. He made this big production out of Ryan dating Peyton, screwed him into having to do extra PR, and then was pissed about it.

"Yeah, but come on, baseball player falls in love with the youth program coordinator and together they make kids' dreams come true. That is gold."

"Love?" Ryan croaked. "Umm, who said anything about love?"

Kirsty flicked her wrist. "Don't worry about it. It'll be awesome." She turned back to Andy. "So you guys are heading to Kidsplay now?"

Andy looked at Ryan and nodded.

"Perfect. I'll come with you." Kirsty turned to the rest of the team who were all watching the byplay like it was the world series finals. Ryan narrowed his eyes as he looked at his teammates. They were all just loving this. Nosey bastards.

"That's all for today, gentleman," Kirsty said. "We'll meet again in two weeks when I have a better idea of what the new youth program will be like for everyone. I expect all of you to make time to volunteer in some way with the programs. So get on board." She scanned the room and pinned the men with her stare.

Several groans sounded around the room before a few heads nodded.

"Great," Kirsty replied, before turning to Ryan and Andy. "Alright let's go."

Ryan pushed his chair away from the table. Pete caught his eye as he stood up. "Seriously?" Pete mouthed.

Ryan rolled his eyes and shook his head. "I'll call you later," he told his best friend.

He followed Kirsty and Andy out to the parking lot. "I'll drive," Kirsty said.

Christ, there was no way he was sitting in a car captive for Kirsty to grill him about his relationship with Peyton before he even had a chance to talk to her about any of this. "I'll follow you."

"Why?" Kirsty asked.

"Umm, I just thought I might want to stick around a bit and chat with Peyton after," Ryan replied.

"Ah," Kirsty sighed. "That's so cute."

"I'll ride with you," Andy said to Ryan.

He didn't want to be stuck in a car with Andy, either. It was taking everything he had not to lay into the smarmy jerk for putting him in this situation. "No, no, it would make more sense for you to ride with Kirsty. Don't you have that interview coming up later this week? I'm sure she'd love the chance to talk to you about that."

"I definitely would. That's a great idea, Ryan," Kirsty said.

"See you there," he replied with a wave as he strolled to his vehicle.

His mind churned as he followed Kirsty to the youth center. How was this all supposed to work out? He knew the importance of a program like this and he wasn't about to do anything that would screw up this program for the kids.

Why the hell had Andy put him in this position? He had to announce to the whole team Ryan was dating Peyton. Now there was no delicate way to back out. If Andy had just left it alone, it would have died a slow, silent death. He would have done his good deed getting her out of the party and he'd have been done. But no, now he was going to have to pretend to date a woman he didn't know, and from what he'd seen so far, he wasn't too sure he particularly liked. There was really only one reason a woman dated a guy like Andy and it, and it sure as hell wasn't his personality. The guy was a tool. Hell, if they weren't teammates, he'd have nothing to do with Andy. Even as teammates, his attitude made it hard to be around him most of the time.

Ryan pulled his car into the parking lot and inspected the old high school gym that had been turned into Kidsplay. The rest of the school had been torn down, and only the gym and fields remained. The basketball courts were in crappy shape, with cracks all over the concrete. It was amazing a kid didn't blow an ankle out there. When school let out, he could picture a group of kids running on the soccer fields and another on the ball diamonds.

The league was pledging money to the program and volunteer hours from the players to build morale in the community and get kids off the streets. It was the kind of program Ryan had always wanted to be a part of. Too bad it was all wrapped up in all this other shit as well, and he couldn't just enjoy playing ball with the kids.

Andy slowed down to wait for him as Ryan exited the car. "Don't fuck things up for me with Peyton," Andy told him.

"Seriously." Ryan stared at his teammate. "Your fucking wife is here, dude. Maybe you should focus on that rather than how to keep you side piece happy."

"Come on, you've seen Peyton. She's worth the risk, man."

"You've got issues," Ryan replied, then started walking faster across the parking lot to meet Kirsty at the door.

He pulled open the front door and waited for Kirsty to go inside ahead of him. Before he could step forward, Andy slid inside. Andy surveyed the waiting area like he owned the place. "Where's Peyton?" Andy rudely demanded to the man behind the desk.

"Sorry about him," Ryan said. "We are here from the Hawks and were hoping to sit down with Peyton."

"You're Ryan Graves." The man fanned himself. "Peyton didn't mention how much hotter you are in person."

Ryan coughed. "Umm, thanks."

"He really is, isn't he?" Kirsty agreed. "Hi, it's James, right?"

The man nodded. "Let me just buzz Peyton. She's in the boardroom with your wife and her friends," he said pointedly to Andy. Ryan bit back a smile at the look of disdain on James' face as he picked up the phone.

"I'll take you all back," James told them when he hung up the phone.

Ryan followed the other man down the hallway, past a gym where a couple of teenagers were lifting weights. Ryan stopped to peek through the window. All things considered it was a pretty decent setup. The equipment was older and well used, but it appeared to be maintained.

Continuing down the hall, he paused at the door to the boardroom, noting the group of women gathered around the table. Peyton glanced at the door and visibly sighed in relief when she saw Andy. Her eyes widened when they landed on Ryan. Then she appeared to relax even more. Interesting. He could just imagine the grilling she'd have gotten from Carmella and her crew.

"Ryan," Lisa squealed. "We've been getting to know Peyton. You did good snagging this one. She's a keeper."

"Good to know," he muttered. Peyton's eyes narrowed as she made eye contact with him. What was wrong with saying that?

"Ryan, can I talk to you for a minute?" Peyton asked.

Guess him showing up had given her the out she needed. "Ugh sure," Ryan replied.

"Excuse me for a minute, ladies," she said to the group before pushing away from the table.

"Hey Peyton," Andy said as she made her way toward them. She flicked a glance at him, then smiled at Kirsty. "I'm glad you could come down with the guys," she told her. She grabbed Ryan's arm and ushered him out of the room and down the hall toward an office.

She quickly closed the door behind them. "Oh my god, this is a nightmare," she groaned. "What are you doing here?"

"You mean besides saving your ass?"

Peyton scowled at him. "It's not like I asked for this to happen."

"Right, you're innocent in all this," he muttered.

Peyton pinched the bridge of her nose like she was trying to gather her patience. "Can we not—" She took several long breaths, then opened her eyes and looked at him. "Seriously, why are you and Kirsty here?"

"What you wanted just Andy? Cuz having him come down here alone wouldn't have raised some questions for Carmella?" Ryan stepped further into the room. He scanned her office, trying to get a better feel for the woman in front of him. Photos covered the walls. Most of them were of groups of kids playing various sports, but some were pictures of Peyton and her staff.

"Oh my god, I'm an idiot." Peyton paced around the room. "Of course that would have. Crap." She spun back around when she got to the wall. "Thanks, I guess."

Jesus, that sounded sincere. "Looks like our little fake dating thing is going to last a little longer."

Peyton's eyes snapped open wide as she gawked at him. "What do you mean?"

Ryan leaned his hip against the edge of her desk. "Andy announced to the entire team today that you and I are dating, and now Kirsty can't wait to run with it for the team promo crap."

"Oh my god, no." Peyton flopped onto the chair and dropped her head back. Her blonde hair draped over the back of the seat, almost touching the floor as she stared up at the ceiling.

"It'll be fine. We'll figure it out," Ryan said.

"You seriously want to do this?" Peyton stared at him.

"Not really, but I don't think we have much of a choice at the moment. There'll be too many questions if we say we aren't dating after all this shit today."

Peyton dropped her head into her hands. "How is this my life?" she groaned.

"Maybe because you fucked a married man," Ryan muttered.

Peyton's head snapped up. Her cheeks flushed with anger as she glared at him. "We never had sex," she growled. "And I didn't know he was married."

"Married or not, you can't tell me you weren't dating him for what you could get out of him," Ryan said. Look at her. She was a knockout, there was no way a girl that looked like her would date a guy like Andy if he wasn't an athlete.

"My god, you're a jerk." Peyton pushed her hair off her face, and Ryan scowled when his eyes followed the movement. What the hell was wrong with him? He was not supposed to be attracted to her. He hated women like her. Women who were relentless in their pursuit of athletes and didn't care who they hurt in the process. Been there, done that. And had his heart shredded for his efforts. He knew all about women who would use guys like him to get what they wanted and here she was again, willing to use him to help herself and her program.

"What is it you think I got out of dating him?"

Ryan glanced around her office. "I don't know. Maybe this nice little contract for your organization. I mean, you must have done something to sweeten the deal for them to choose you."

"Oh my god, you can go to hell," Peyton seethed.

"What? Are you honestly telling me that wasn't part of the draw of dating Andy?"

"So first I'm a home-wrecker, and now I'm a whore?" Peyton asked. He could practically see her vibrating with the effort to hold in her rage. He was surprised lasers didn't shoot right out of her blue eyes as she drilled him with a disgusted glare.

"Come on, I know the guy. Why else would you be dating him?"

"He was nice and sweet, which is more than I can say for you."

"Nice? Come on. Andy? He's many things. A sweet guy isn't one of them," Ryan scoffed. Andy was an asshole, through and through. Could this woman really not tell how fake Andy was when he was trying to get something?

"He was sweet to me, all right." Peyton sighed. "God, I was stupid." She rubbed her hand back and forth across her forehead. "Look, I get you don't like me any more than I like you but..." She wrinkled her nose like she smelled something off-putting. "This partnership means everything to these kids and now that we have it, I intend to do everything I can to keep it." She chewed her inner lip as she contemplated Ryan. "I hate to ask you this, but can you go along with the fake dating thing for a little while, so it doesn't screw things up because I really don't need any bad PR before this thing even gets off the ground."

A knock sounded at the door a moment before Andy stuck his head into the office. "What's taking you so long?" he asked.

"We were just working out some details. But I think we're done, right?" Peyton asked as she looked at Ryan pleadingly.

Shit. Looks like he was fake dating a woman who hated him. This was going to be awesome.

Peyton walked toward the door and Andy grabbed her arm. "It's good to see you, baby," he said.

"Don't call me that," Peyton snapped.

"Oh, come on, don't be mad. Now that Ryan here has agreed to be your fake boyfriend, we'll be able to see each other more often because you can come to the games and stuff. It'll be good," Andy crooned.

Ryan stared at his teammate. Holy fuck, was Andy seriously that obtuse? Read the room, man. Peyton looked like she wanted to kick Andy in the nuts, and he thought she was still his for the taking.

"Let go of my arm," Peyton snarled. "And if you ever touch me again, your baseball career will be done because you won't be able to catch with your dick in your throat."

"Baby, don't be like that." Andy pulled at her arm.

Ryan stepped forward and clamped his hand on top of Andy's arm and squeezed. "You heard her, Andy. Let her go."

Andy dropped Peyton's arm and turned to Ryan. "I knew she was good, but I didn't expect you to go down so fast, Ace," Andy jeered at Ryan.

"Don't be a bigger asshole than you need to be, Andy. Peyton told you that you were done. Respect it and go back to your wife." He turned to Peyton. "How about we just put the team and this program first and go back to our meeting?"

Peyton smiled sadly at Ryan and nodded before leaving the room.

Andy stared at Peyton as she walked away, then turned to Ryan. "Just remember, I had her first."

"Fuck, you're a dick," Ryan muttered. Unreal. The guy needed a good punch in the face. And if they weren't teammates who needed to be in sync, that's exactly what he would have done. Sometimes being a team player sucked.

CHAPTER FOUR

Tonight's loss had been hard. They'd won the first two games in the series handily and tonight it was like they forgot to even pick up their bats. As a pitcher, sitting on the bench watching your team lose was frustrating. Could he have done better? Maybe, maybe not. Who knows?

He couldn't play every game no matter how badly he wanted to. As much as he hated riding the pine on his rest days, sometimes losing was easier when he was on the sidelines. At least then he didn't spend the rest of the day picking apart everything he'd done wrong and feeling like the entire loss was on him, even though intellectually he knew it was always a team effort, win or lose.

And on a night like tonight when they'd only scored one run, it was damn hard to win no matter who was pitching, but that wouldn't have stopped him from blaming himself.

He followed the guys into the pub across from their hotel and sat down on the barstool at a four top in the middle of the pub as his teammates crowded into the remaining tables.

"That sucked," Pete groaned.

"No shit." Gonzo shook his head in dismay. "What the hell happened? We destroyed them yesterday and today? Fuck."

Ryan eyed the rookie Brandon Sims as he walked into the bar and glanced around. Waving him over, he watched as Brandon shuffled his way toward them. The kid looked dejected. Ryan had to give him credit for coming out at all tonight.

"Hey guys." Brandon sighed as he stopped beside Ryan's chair.

"You doing okay, kid?" Ryan asked.

"Not really. I don't know what happened." Brandon looked around the table. "Sorry, guys."

"For what?" Smitty asked.

"How shitty I played." Brandon dipped his head. "I don't know how the fuck I struck out every single time I came up. It was pathetic."

Smitty shrugged. "Eh, we all have nights where we can't hit."

"Yeah, but I had that fucking error too." Brandon stared down at his feet like the weight of the team was on his shoulder. Now that was something Ryan understood all too well.

"Bran, it happens. Last night you hit a home run and three RBIs." Ryan clapped him on the back. "We all have good games and bad games. One bad game isn't a big deal unless you let it be. What matters is what you do next."

Brandon looked up, his mouth pulled tight as he took a breath. "Thanks, Ryan." Brandon pinned his teammates with a resolved stare. The muscle ticking in his jaw was the only indication he wasn't as confident as he was pretending to be. "Believe me, I'll be showing up next game ready to kick ass. I won't let you guys down."

"Never thought you would," Ryan said. "Now go get a beer and let tonight go."

"Yeah, will do." Brandon nodded, then turned toward the bar. His shoulders still looked a little slumped as he walked across the room.

"Poor kid," Pete muttered. "I remember the first time the media roasted me after a game. Fuck, that sucked."

"It's never fun," Gonzo added. "But yeah, the first one was the worst."

"Kid's having a great season. He'll rally." Smitty picked up his beer and took a long, slow sip as he stared off toward the back of the bar. "Looks like Andy is in fine form again tonight."

Ryan watched Andy as he set a tray of shots down at a table of women. "He's such a tool."

"No shit, so why'd you help him out the other night with the girl?" Gonzo asked.

"I don't know. He's a teammate. That's what you do." Although when it was drilled into his head as a kid to always put your team first, he'd never pictured he'd have to rescue his teammate from getting caught cheating on his wife. It kind of seemed like that should be above and beyond. Except he kept hearing his dad's voice, telling him to do whatever it took to keep the team in sync. Unfortunately, that meant sometimes you had to take a bullet for a teammate.

"I guess," Gonzo said. "So, you are going to see the sexy blonde again?"

"I kind of have to since Kirsty thinks we're dating."

"I can't believe Andy did that to you at a team meeting," Smitty mumbled. "What an asshole. Please tell me blondie was smart enough to dump his ass."

"Her name's Peyton," Ryan said. "And yeah, she sure acted like she was done with him, but who knows?"

"Well, I guess if you're going to fake date somebody, she may as well be hot." Gonzo waggled his eyebrows.

"What's she like?" Pete asked.

"No clue really." Ryan pictured Peyton when she'd opened the bathroom door. She'd been a hot mess and as much as he disliked women who chased married men, he'd felt a little bad for her. "She said she had no idea he was married."

"What? She didn't google him?" Pete's brow raised in shock.

"That's what I said." Ryan shrugged. "But apparently not. Obviously, if she had, she would have seen what an idiot he is, but who knows?" Ryan looked back over at Andy, who now had a woman on his lap. "I seriously do not get it. What do women see in him?"

"No fucking clue," Pete replied. "I asked Kendall, and she said she didn't get it. She says he's smarmy, whatever the fuck that means, so I have no idea."

"Confidence," Smitty said. "Women like a confident guy."

"Nah, my sister nailed it. He is fucking smarmy." Ryan pictured Peyton, and his jaw tightened. The guys were right. She was fucking hot. It pissed him off to picture her with Andy. Maybe that's what his problem was with Peyton. He was jealous Andy had been with her. He honestly didn't get it. If she wasn't a groupie or trying to use Andy to get her company the contract with the team, then why the hell had she dated him?

"Damn." Smitty fake coughed into his hand, muffling his voice as a sultry redhead and her friend walked up to their table.

"Tough loss tonight," she said and trailed her hand down Ryan's arm. "You look like you could use a little cheering up."

"I'm good," Ryan replied. What the hell was that about? He'd said no with zero thought whatsoever. Not even a second glance at the woman. Now he was turning down a sure thing because of his fake girlfriend. This Peyton thing was messing with his head.

"You sure?" She pressed closer to him.

Ryan eyed the way her round breasts spilled out over the top of her shirt. She was hot in that obvious way while Peyton's sexiness was more subtle. Jesus, why was he even comparing them? Peyton wasn't here. He barely knew her.

Loud laughter erupted from Andy's table in the back and he grit his teeth. Here he was in a fake relationship with Peyton to save Andy's ass and the guy couldn't even be bothered not to cheat on his wife again the first chance he got. "Thanks, but I'm seeing someone," he told her, smiling to soften the rejection.

"I won't tell if you won't. She'll never know."

Ryan's spine straightened. That right there was a part of the problem. These women made it so damn easy for guys like Andy to cheat. "I'll know," he growled.

Gonzo leaned over to the brunette friend. "I'm single." He flicked his thumb toward Smitty. "So's he."

The red head slid closer to Smitty and away from Ryan. "Is that right?" she purred. "What's your name?"

"Jeff," Smitty replied.

Ryan hopped off his chair. "Here take my seat. I'm gonna go play pool."

"You sure?" the redhead asked.

"Absolutely." Someone may as well get lucky at this table, and it sure as shit wasn't going to be him.

Jesus, he needed to talk to Peyton and get this figured out because apparently he couldn't even cheat on his fake girlfriend. He didn't owe her anything, so what the hell was wrong with him? Would she even care if he slept with someone on the road? His jaw clenched. Was she dating people? Fuck. Why did he care? He really needed to talk to her and set some ground rules because there was no way he was going to be the only celibate one around here.

"I'll join you," Pete said, vacating his seat for the brunette to saddle up closer to Gonzo.

Pete draped his arm around Ryan's shoulder. "Look at us, just a couple of committed guys."

"Fuck you." Ryan picked up a pool cue and tested its weight.

"You seriously not going to date anyone else because the team thinks you're dating Peyton."

His gaze flashed over to the table with his friends and the women. "That's not dating."

Pete snorted. "Yeah, I'm aware. But it is part of the fun of being single on the road." Pete picked up his own pool cue. "You like this girl or something?"

Did he? He wanted her, that was for sure. But like her? He didn't have a clue. Everything Andy had told him said she was exactly the type of woman he typically steered clear of but the ferocious way she'd demanded he let her out of the car and how she'd stood up to Andy, she didn't behave like a groupie. The two pictures he had of her just didn't connect. Who was the real Peyton? The kind of woman who would date a guy like Andy. Or the kind of woman his dick kept trying to convince him she was.

"I want to fuck her. Beyond that, I don't have a clue."

"You really want to fuck someone who's been with Andy?"

Pete may as well have thrown a glass of ice water in his face. Ryan's stomach knotted. Why did she have to have been with Andy, of all people? "Just rack the fucking balls."

Peyton hadn't seen or heard from Ryan in a week. So much for their fake dating.

Unfortunately, after her last conversation with Kirsty, it had become abundantly clear that they needed to talk. Why had she agreed to this stupid idea? They didn't even like each other. The man was far too cocky for his own good, which made sense given how successful he was. She'd have to live under a rock not to see his face plastered on sports magazines in the grocery store. And after her horrifying experience with Andy, she wasn't ashamed to admit that she'd looked Ryan up online. For someone who claimed he didn't date much he sure had been photographed with some beautiful women.

She looked down at her phone. Kirsty had said the guys had a couple of days off before their next stretch on the road. Would he call? They weren't even dating, and the guy had her tied up, staring at her phone. She tossed her phone on her desk.

This was ridiculous. It wasn't her problem.

She sighed. Except it was. Who was she kidding? God, she wasn't cut out for all this cloak and dagger garbage. She prided herself on being honest. So why had she said yes?

She needed to get out of her head. Peyton grabbed her sneakers and threw them on before heading outside to see if she could find a game to join to take her mind off things. Outside, she eyed the basketball courts. A game was in full swing between several boys.

Cheering rang out from the baseball diamond. Peyton looked over as Markus threw the bat and started running toward first base. She scanned the field and pulled up short when she saw Ryan standing on the pitching mound with a grin on his face. What was he doing here?

"Nice hit, Markus," Ryan called out.

As Peyton walked toward the diamond, she could hear several kids trash talking Ryan. Amazingly, he took everything in stride, joking with the kids with ease. She stopped at the edge of the dugout.

"Hey fancy seeing you here," she called out to Ryan.

"Yeah, well, I had the afternoon off and thought I'd come see what this is all about. You were in a meeting when I got here, so..." He gestured to the surrounding field.

"I saw Markus just lit up your pitch there with a monster hit. That must be a bit of a bruise to the ol' ego to get schooled so hard on your first day."

"Ahh." Raucous laughter and cheers rang up from the kids waiting to bat.

"Ouch." Ryan placed his hand over his chest like he'd been hit. "I thought this was an anti-bullying place."

"If you think that's bullying, we clearly went to different schools," Peyton called back.

Ryan laughed. "That's fair." He tossed the ball in his hand up in the air and caught it. "You wanna hit?"

Peyton eyed Ryan, then the group on the field. It might be fun to see what Ryan was like in this kind of setting. See what he was really like around the kids. "Yeah, I could use a run around the bases."

"Cocky," Ryan said.

Even with the distance between them, she could feel his eyes lingering on her. A little zip of excitement rushed through her body. What that was about she had no idea. Apparently the sexy little banter had momentarily made her ovaries and her brain swap places.

"Confident. It's not cocky if you know you have the goods."

"Ho ho, alright, let's see what you've got," Ryan called.

Peyton picked up a bat from against the fence and felt the weight in her hand. *Please don't strike out.* That would be so embarrassing. She knew she was athletic, and the kids typically all wanted her on their team, but there was a big difference between playing with the kids and hitting the ball when you were being stared down by a major league pitcher. Even if he was lobbing in meatballs.

She walked up to the plate and took her position. Ryan stood confidently on the mound, smirking at her.

"Wipe that smile off his face, Peyton," Shonda called from behind her.

"Yeah, hit a homer," another voice, she thought might have been Darnell, yelled in encouragement.

Oh god, no pressure. She took a couple of practice swings.

"You ready?" Ryan asked.

She took her batting stance. "Yep, fire away."

The first pitch sailed toward the plate. She swung and missed. *Crap.* A chorus of groans sounded behind her.

"You sure it wasn't just cocky after all?" Ryan taunted.

Peyton narrowed her eyes and glared at him. "Keep it up," she called back. She dug her feet into the earth to get a better position. There was no way she was humiliating herself in front of this man. Striking out was not an option.

"You ready or you want to get the tee out?" Ryan mocked. The players in the field and some of her own team snickered. What a bunch of turncoats.

"Pitch the ball," she growled. She would not miss. She watched the ball and then, at the last second, chose not to swing as the ball soared beside the plate.

"Oh, getting picky now, huh?" Ryan teased.

"Well, I'm not gonna swing at garbage. I thought you were a professional. You're using a bigger ball and you still can't hit the plate underhand?" Peyton taunted.

"Ha-ha," Ryan said.

"We want a pitcher, not a belly itcher," her team began chanting.

"Geez, you all are vicious." Ryan laughed. "The pressure is on."

"Don't choke," Zander said from his place on second.

Ryan turned around and looked at his teammate. "Whose side are you on?"

Zander shrugged. "It's Peyton."

"Ah thanks, Zan," Peyton called across the field.

Ryan looked at her and shook his head. A slight smile curled up the corner of his mouth. A little flutter zipped through Peyton's stomach as she looked at him. The man truly was something to look at. She'd have to be blind not to see how gorgeous he was. Seeing him out here goofing around with a bunch of kids, trash talking and having fun, he was a whole other level of good looking. And not at all what she had been expecting.

She'd expected him to be a lot more like Simon had been when they'd first met. Simon had been willing to chat with the kids and toss the ball a bit the few times he'd been here, but there had always been a sense of separation between him and the kids. She'd assumed it was because the youth were a bit in awe of him and felt nervous. But now, seeing this group with Ryan she wondered if it was Simon who was stand-offish and gave off the vibe to the group that he wasn't really there for them.

She'd never seen her group embrace a newcomer the way they had Ryan. And in such a short period of time. Maybe she'd underestimated him and what he could do for this program. He'd been a jerk to her, but if he was good to these kids, she could forgive just about anything.

"Alright, you ready?" Ryan called.

"Yep," she yelled back. *Focus, Peyton, you can do this.*

The ball soared toward her, she swung and crack. The bat vibrated in her hand as it connected with the ball. Peyton dropped the bat and raced toward first as the ball soared over the second baseman's head and dropped into the gap.

Safe at first, she turned and faced Ryan.

He nodded. "Nice hit."

"Thanks." Peyton looked over at her team in the dugout, stuck her tongue out, and did a little dance. When she was done, she glanced over to find Ryan watching her with a strange look on his face.

Okay, not her coolest move, but who cared? The kids loved when she got in there and really played with them, and it was after games like these where she had formed her best connections with some of the tougher kids.

"Who's up next?" Peyton called. "I need someone to hit me home."

Half an hour later, they wrapped up the softball game. Ryan stood off to the side, surrounded by his team and half of hers, as the group peppered him with questions about playing major league baseball. Peyton made her way over to Ryan's fan club.

"Good game," she said to him.

"Yeah, you've got some good athletes here." He looked around the group. "By the time we get done with them, we might have some great ballplayers."

"Are you really going to come here again?" Darnell asked. There was a suspicious edge to the question, but the hopeful light in his eyes spoke of how badly he wanted to believe Ryan would be back.

"That's the plan. I'm sure Peyton has told you that my team will be doing some programs here in the coming months."

Marcus turned to her. "I thought you said that wasn't until their season was done, though."

"I guess we'll have to see," she replied non-committally. She wasn't making any promises she couldn't keep. But already she could see how much this would mean to the kids. How hungry they were for this kind of interaction.

"So how come you're here today when your season is still going?" Amy asked.

Ryan reached up and rubbed the back of his neck. "Umm, well, I came by to see Peyton."

"So, are you Peyton's boyfriend?" Shonda pressed.

"Umm.... ugh...." Ryan stammered.

"Stop being nosey," Peyton said. "Can you all grab all the gear and put it away for me, please?"

"Peyton's got a boyfriend, Peyton's got a boyfriend," Amy chanted.

She could feel the heat in her cheeks and mentally cursed that without a doubt, she was blushing brighter than Amy's cherry red shirt.

"Just put the stuff away," Peyton muttered.

Ryan laughed. "Thanks for letting me play today. I had fun," he told the group.

Peyton looked up at him. He honestly sounded like he meant it. She watched as he gave high-fives to everyone before they walked away to clean up.

Who was the real Ryan Graves? This sweet guy who played pickup ball with kids or the jerk she'd seen the previous two times she'd met him.

"Can we talk?" he asked.

She nodded. "Sure, we can go to my office."

Only time would tell who the real Ryan Graves was.

CHAPTER FIVE

Ryan followed Peyton down the hall toward her office. His eyes lingered on the way her ass swayed in her tight yoga pants as she moved. He shoved down the wave of lust that shot through him as he imagined what her ass would feel like in his hands.

Damn.

He definitely understood why Andy had chased after her. The reminder of Andy instantly erased the lust he'd been feeling. Everything about her physically was perfect. She looked like she worked hard on herself. And outside with the kids, he'd seen a side of her he hadn't expected. Normally the women he'd seen Andy with were the type who didn't like to get their hands dirty, but Peyton had been right in there playing ball with the kids, having fun and trash talking. Well, as much as you could trash talk when you never swore. What was that about?

"Why don't you swear?"

"What?" Peyton's brow knit with confusion as she sat in one of the two cozy chairs in the corner of her office.

"The way you talk. You never swear, even when you were pissed off at me the other night."

"I try not to." She picked at her fingernail rather than looking at him. "I'm trying to set a good example for the kids here."

"Not swearing is a good example?" Out on the field the way those kids had talked, there wasn't a word in the English language that would shock any of them. "I'm pretty sure they wouldn't care if you let 'er rip."

"It's not about that. I'm trying to show them that there are other ways of speaking. That words matter. They have power. When every other word out of their mouth is The F-word, it has no power. If they used other words, when that one came out, people would know they meant business. Plus, I'm trying to help them get ready for the real world, where they will have jobs and they can't talk like that to their boss or customers. So, I figure if they see I can get my point across without swearing, then they could to."

"Yeah, but sometimes you just need to say fuck."

"And when I need to, I will," Peyton replied. "So, what's up? Why'd you come by today?"

He dropped into the opposite chair. "I wanted to talk to you about us supposedly dating and what that means."

"Okay." Peyton pulled her right leg up onto the chair and wrapped her arms around her knee. "How long do you think we need to pretend to be dating?"

"No idea, a few weeks at least. I don't really want to pretend we broke up right away because that'd be weird."

"Why? You don't date casually?"

"No, I do." He shifted in his tiny chair. The thing seemed like it was a normal size when he'd first sat down, but now it felt like it may as well have been a child's seat. His knees were up in his throat. "Fuck." He winced. "Sorry."

"You don't have to apologize. I don't expect you to curb your language around me and as you said, the kids are certainly used to it, so you don't have to worry about it with them either." Her tongue darted out and he hungrily followed the movement. "So dating?"

"Right." He shifted again, trying to get comfortable. "The thing is, I don't do relationships, so Andy telling everyone you're my girlfriend has made this into something for people for some fucking reason."

Peyton winced. "Sorry, I didn't realize things would be this awkward for you. How long do you need me to pretend we're dating so you can save face?"

"I don't need to save face," he growled. What the fuck? He was doing this for Andy and her. This had nothing to do with him. If he had his way, he'd just fuck her and get it out of his system. But clearly that wasn't going to happen since Kirsty had told him she expected to get some photos of them at Coach Gill's anniversary party next week. "I stupidly allowed Andy to rope me into saying you were my girlfriend, and now we need to put on the act, at least for a few weeks. There's this team dinner next week. Semi-formal. It's for one of the pitching coaches and his wife's anniversary."

"And you need me to go with you?" She chewed her lip. "I didn't really think we have to actually go out anywhere together."

She sounded like she'd rather chew off her arm than attend a party with him. How the fuck could she have no problem dating Andy, but going out in public with him was somehow an issue? "That a problem?"

"No, I guess not, it's just..." She paused like she was weighing what she wanted to say next. "I wasn't really planning on being at events with Andy and his wife."

"You can't possibly still have feelings for the guy."

"Ew, no, I don't." She pulled her other leg up and wrapped her arms around both legs. "Honestly, I didn't have feelings for him in the first place. He seemed nice, but the spark wasn't really there for me as much as I wanted."

His gut twisted. She didn't have feelings for him in the first place. So why the hell had she shown up to a team party with a guy she didn't really like? "You hadn't fucked?"

Peyton's legs thumped on the ground. "What the heck? That's none of your business."

"Except it kind of is. Since I'm doing this fake dating thing with you, I need to know what Andy might say. He has a tendency to say stupid shit, especially when he drinks, and I'm not going to be embarrassed in front of my team."

"And if we'd had sex you'd be embarrassed?"

"No, I couldn't care less. I just don't want to be blind-sided if he says something." His gut clenched. The idea of Peyton fucking Andy made him feel sick.

"We didn't have sex I told you that before. We messed around a couple of times, but we didn't have sex." She looked down at her hand and started playing with her nails again. "The one night it kind of seemed like we might, I got a call from work and had to go. His reaction was..." She stopped picking at her nail and looked up. "It wasn't what I expected." She cocked her head to the side and watched him, measuring, assessing. "Do you want to know this? I mean, this is your teammate and you're all bros before hos."

Ryan snorted. "Andy and I are teammates, not bros."

"Whatever." She rolled her eyes. "Do you want to know this kind of thing?"

"Andy and I aren't friends. I'm trying to figure out what you saw in him because I don't have a read on you yet. And I need to if I'm going to play this game."

"This game... right." She took a deep breath. "I'm not normally someone who plays games like this, so this is pretty foreign to me."

"Can't say I've ever played either. So, Andy wasn't what you expected?"

"No, the night I had to go into work, he was a jerk, whereas every other time I saw him, he was really sweet. Cocky yes, but nice. I was actually debating breaking up with him, which is why I wanted to go to that party."

His jaw clenched. "What do mean why you wanted to go to that party? So you could meet some other players?"

"What? No, god." She shook her head "I wanted to go to the party to see him with his friends so I could figure out which one was the real Andy, the sweet guy I'd met or the one who got all pouty and moody when I had to go to work. He was angry because I picked work over him, and it wasn't like that. One of my kids got arrested and they couldn't reach the parents, so I needed to pick him up. I wasn't just going to leave a twelve-year-old kid in the police station. It boggled my mind that he couldn't understand that."

"Yeah, that sounds like Andy alright."

"That's what I was trying to figure out by going to the party." She absently shifted some things on her desk, lining up the pads of paper in a neat row. "And well, you know the rest."

"Was the kid okay?"

"What?" Her head snapped up. "What kid?"

"The one who was arrested."

Peyton blinked at him several times, like she wasn't quite sure what she was looking at. "He was fine, vandalism, stupid stuff. His mom was high, that's why she didn't answer the phone, so I ended up taking him to a foster placement for the night."

What kind of life must that be for a kid? "That happen a lot?"

"Which? Having to go to the police station or the finding temporary foster care?"

"Either, both, I don't know."

Peyton smiled sadly. "Unfortunately, both happen more than I'd like."

"That sucks." He had to give her credit. It took a certain kind of person to want to do this work. There was no way he could do it on a regular basis. Just thinking about a kid not having enough to eat or a person at home to care for them made his stomach knot. He wasn't sure if it was sadness or anger, but either way it wasn't a feeling he wanted to experience every day.

Peyton flicked her hair over her shoulder. The light from the window caught on the blonde highlights, making them glisten in the sun. He cursed to himself. This would be a hell of a lot easier if he wasn't so fucking attracted to her. How the hell was he supposed to fake date someone when all he wanted to do was dig his hands into her hair and pull her to him?

"So, here's the thing. If I'm going to be pretending, we're together you can't fuck Andy or anyone else for that matter."

"Excuse me. Who do you think you are telling me who I can and can't date?" Peyton snapped. Her eyes burned with fire as she glared at him.

What the hell was her problem? "You literally just said you realized Andy was a tool."

"He is and I have no intention of having anything to do with Andy, but need I remind you, this is fake dating. You don't get to dictate who I sleep with."

"Believe me, I'm very well aware this is fake. I'm not telling you who you can and can't sleep with. I'm saying fake or not, I'm not going to be humiliated because my 'girlfriend.'" He air quoted the term. "Is dating other people in public. So, for the duration of this so-called relationship, can you please not date anyone else publicly?"

"I have no intention of dating anyone else right now," she muttered. "But that goes both ways, buddy."

If he didn't know better, he'd say the idea of him sleeping with someone else pissed her off. He crossed his ankle over his knee and leaned back in the chair. "You jealous, honey?"

Peyton snorted. "You wish."

She was right, he did wish. Jesus, what was wrong with him? "So, we are agreed, for the duration of this little fake dating experiment, neither of us will be dating other people."

"You sure you're going to be able to go that long without sex, hotshot?"

He leaned further back in the chair and Peyton's eyes lingered on his chest. Not sure if he was reading things right, he spread his arms and leaned back further, like he was stretching out his chest. Peyton's eyes widened as she stared at him. She shifted in her chair and cleared her throat. Ryan bit back a smile. She was definitely not immune to him, despite how she wanted to play things.

"You could always help me out if you wanted."

"Dream on, buddy," she scoffed. Peyton adjusted the same pile of papers again for a third time.

"I'll be fine." He was currently in a dry spell, anyway. What were a couple more weeks?

"You sure?" Peyton raised her head. "According to Andy, professional athletes have a higher sex drive."

"Than what?" Ryan asked.

"I don't know, than the average guy, apparently."

Ryan threw back his head and laughed. "Please tell me you didn't buy that bullshit."

Peyton shrugged. "I don't know. You guys sure seem to have a lot of sex."

"We're guys. We like sex period." He watched her as her cheeks turned pink. Interesting. "It's just sometimes easier for athletes to get people to have sex with us than it is for the average guy."

"Oh, okay."

Enjoying the way, she seemed slightly uncomfortable with the way the conversation was heading, he couldn't help but add. "Besides, I'm a big boy. I can take care of myself if need be."

"Take care of yourself?" Peyton's forehead wrinkled as she looked at him. He smirked and she gasped. "Oh, got ya." She laughed nervously. "Good to know. Me too." She clicked her tongue and made a finger gun as she winked.

Fuck, she was cute. He laughed at the awkward exchange, then suddenly it registered what she'd said. "Hang on a second." He sat upright in his chair. "Did you just say you masturbate?"

Peyton looked at him blankly. "Doesn't everybody?"

"Jesus," he muttered. Now that was something he'd like to see. "And on that note, I'm outta here." If he didn't leave now, he'd be crossing all sorts of lines by asking her to show him what that looked like, and fuck knows that would be a bad idea.

Standing up, he pulled his phone out of his pocket, swiped the lock screen, and handed it to her.

"What?"

"Put your number in it so I can text you the details." He rolled his eyes.

"Oh, right." Peyton took his phone, punched in some details, and handed it back. He laughed when he looked at the screen.

"Best girlfriend ever, huh?"

"Well, you know if I'm going to be your fake girlfriend, I may as well be the best, right?"

"No point in doing things half-assed." He quickly fired her a text and hit send. "Now you have mine."

Her phone buzzed on her desk, and she looked down and sputtered out a cough slash snort sound unlike anything he'd ever heard. "Daddy? Really?"

"Well, you know." Ryan waggled his eyebrows. "Fantasy fake boyfriend."

"Daddy would not be the fantasy?"

"No? You ever had a daddy before?"

Peyton wrinkled her nose. "Ew, no."

"Then how do you know you wouldn't like one?"

"Some things you just know," she told him.

Ryan walked toward the door and without turning around he said, "we'll see."

Peyton stood in front of the mirror and debated her outfit choice for the millionth time. Behind her, the bed was littered with discarded clothing. How could she have gone through her entire closest and still feel like nothing was right? Maybe putting shoes on would help her decide since currently her wide legged trousers were bunched at her ankles, making her feel like she was playing dress-up. She slid on a pair of heels and eyed her reflection again. Definitely better.

She smoothed her hand down the front of her satin tank, loving the way the material felt against her skin. Forget it. She was just going to wear this. Whether or not it was the right outfit choice who cared? At least it was light and cool and she wouldn't be worried about being sweaty if the banquet hall was too warm. Pants was probably a terrible choice, but with the way she was feeling, she at least needed to be comfortable in her clothing since nothing else about the evening made her comfortable.

Tonight was her first official date as Ryan's girlfriend. Fake as it might be, to the rest of the world, it was real. She placed a hand against her stomach. The thing was going nuts. She should take another swig of Pepto before Ryan got here.

She picked up the pink bottle from her dresser and drank it straight out of the container. A spoonful would not cut it when her stomach felt like it was being trampled on by a herd of elephants. Peyton closed her eyes and took a deep breath, desperately trying to remember what her best friend Rayne had told her so she could pull some kind of relaxation into her body. She exhaled hard. Clearly, this wasn't working. So much for all the hours of yoga and meditation she had done over the years.

She opened her eyes. "Get it together, Peyton," she said to her reflection in the mirror. "It's a fake date, not an execution." She closed her eyes and drew in several more deep breaths. "You got this," she whispered.

Opening her eyes, her gaze landed on her dresser and the necklace her grandmother had left her. Peyton put it on and instantly a feeling of calm swept through her. This was exactly what she needed. She could still remember the first time she'd worn it. Her grandmother had been wearing the necklace when she'd come over to see Peyton after her dad left. She'd been crying and her grandmother had taken off the necklace and put it around Peyton's neck, telling her it would help her remember who she was and that she had strength she hadn't even tapped into yet.

Well, she sure needed that tonight.

Her doorbell rang. Peyton grabbed her purse off the bed and made her way to the front door. She paused, took a breath, then pulled the door open. Holy cow, Ryan looked hot. She gripped the doorknob tighter. Obviously she'd noticed how attractive he was the other times she'd seen him, but man, he cleaned up nice. His blue tie stood out against his black shirt and made his eyes pop like he had colored contacts in.

"Hey." Ryan smiled. His lips parted to show his white teeth.

My god, was anything on the man not freaking perfect?
"Hi," she replied.

His gaze trailed down her body slowly, his nostrils flared slightly as he looked at her. "You look great."

Her stomach fluttered at the compliment. Sheesh, she was being ridiculous. It was a simple compliment. She didn't need to go all gaga over it.

"Thanks, so do you." She grabbed her house keys from the bowl on the side table. "I'm ready if you are."

Ryan's deep chuckle drew her eyes. "What?"

"It's a party, Peyton, not a funeral."

"I know, I'm just not a very good liar, so this whole pretending we're dating thing is a lot, you know."

"I hear ya." Ryan stepped forward into her space and she stepped back. "Well, first of all, you can't be doing that if we want to convince people we actually like each other, let alone are dating."

"Do what?" she asked.

"Cringe, when I get near you."

"I didn't cringe. I just stepped back to give you some space." Unfortunately, he was way off base saying she cringed. Honestly, she wished that was the case, but she was attracted to him despite what a jerk he'd been to her.

"Yeah, well, if people are going to believe we're a couple, we can't be giving each other space."

"That's ridiculous. Of course we can give each other space."

He stepped toward her again and she held her ground. Power radiated off his body as he filled her space. "If anyone is going to believe you're mine, then I'm going to be touching you."

"Even if we were dating Ryan, I'm still my own person. I don't belong to anyone," she said. Egotistical jerk. Women weren't possessions.

"I know you're your own person, Peyton," he growled. "That's not what I'm saying." He stepped closer again, and she stepped away. Her back hit the wall, and he continued to move forward, crowding her against the wall. He pressed his body against hers, and she fought to swallow.

"Wha... what are you saying then?" she stammered.

He leaned down so his mouth was right against her ear. "I'm not a big PDA guy, but I'm not opposed to it." His breath brushed against her neck and she shivered. "And Peyton, anyone who sees you in this outfit is going to expect me to have my hands on you at all times to stake my claim." His hand brushed along her waist, his finger gliding against the silky fabric like a caress, making her nipples tighten. "Because honey, there's no way if I was fucking you, I wouldn't want every man in the room to know it."

She bit back a moan. "Okay," she sighed.

Ryan stood up straight. The lack of heat from his body was like a douse of cold water. When she looked at him, he smirked down at her. "You sure you don't like the idea of someone claiming you, Peyton?"

What was wrong with her? Why had she made that little breathy sound? She didn't like the guy. "Yeah, I'm sure. I don't need some guy manhandling me in a macho display of virility."

His gaze dropped and he stared pointedly at her chest. "Your body says otherwise."

She glanced down to see her nipples visibly standing at attention. The silky fabric provided no barrier at all. Dang. "Well, it's a good thing I have a brain then that makes all my decisions, isn't it?" She flicked her hair over her shoulder in a forced display of confidence and prayed he bought it.

"Good thing," he mocked.

"Why do you have to be such a jerk?" she asked.

"How am I being a jerk?"

"Oh, come on." She stared at him pointedly. "This whole 'I'm a big sexy guy and I can make you want me' crap."

"So, you admit you want me." The corner of his mouth curved up slightly in a ridiculously sexy half smile.

"Grr," she growled. "That's what I'm talking about. Whatever that just was." She wiggled her hand up and down in front of his chest. "That's chemistry. It has nothing to do with attitude."

"Oh, I don't know about that. Seems to me you kind of like the attitude just a little."

Darn it, he wasn't exactly wrong. Something about the way he'd stepped into her space and his voice had dropped into that dominant, confident tone had been really freaking hot, but that didn't mean she liked him. Because she didn't. "Don't flatter yourself, buddy." She rolled her eyes. "If we are going to do this whole fake dating thing, I can agree that yes, you will have to touch me and yes, I can't flinch or act like it's uncomfortable." She straightened her back and held his stare. "But that doesn't mean I like you or trust you or want to be friends." His jaw tightened as he stared back at her. "It just means we've both agreed to this charade, and neither of us wants to look stupid. The last thing either of us wants is gossip and negative PR. So, we do this thing. We play the doting couple in public, but beyond that? No."

"Oh, we're on the same page." Ryan leaned back against the opposite wall. "I agreed to play this game and believe me Peyton, I always play to win. Make sure you do too." His blue eyes sparked with warning. "I'm not going to let anything negatively impact my team and come back to bite me in the ass." He pushed off the wall. "You ready to go?"

"Ready as I'll ever be."

CHAPTER SIX

Ryan pulled his SUV up to the valet parking at the club and looked over at his date. Okay, so he could admit he'd been an asshole back at her place, but she got under his skin with her proper way of talking and holier than thou attitude, pretending whatever this attraction between them wasn't mutual. Maybe he'd pushed it a bit to prove his point, but it'd been worth it.

Unfortunately, now that he'd seen what she looked like on the cusp of arousal, he really wanted to see what she looked like full out. The way her body had slumped into his when he'd whispered in her ear. Would she like dirty talk? Would she be open to him taking control in the bedroom? Or would she fight him like she fought everything else?

He handed the keys to the valet and exited the car. As he watched Peyton round the vehicle toward him, he immediately glanced at her chest and could picture her nipples pressed against the fabric. Fuck. *Keep it in your pants, Graves.* This was a fake deal. Adding anything physical into the mix would be a bad idea.

"Alright, let's get this over with," Ryan said. He placed his hand at the small of Peyton's back and led her into the building.

"So whose anniversary party is this again?"

"Mark Gill, he's one of the pitching coaches. It's their twenty-fifth."

"Wow, that's impressive."

"Yeah, I guess so."

"You don't think in this day and age twenty-five years is a big deal?"

"I don't know. My parents have been married for thirty-two. My aunt and uncle, thirty, so I don't know, twenty-five doesn't seem that strange."

"Wow. Besides my grandparents, I don't know anyone who's been married that long."

"What about your parents? How long were they married?" Ryan asked.

"I was thirteen when they finally divorced, but my dad had cheated on my mom so many times over years."

"That sucks. Why'd they finally get divorced?"

"He got someone pregnant."

"Jesus, really? I'm sorry. That's fucked up."

"Yeah, it's kind of why I reacted the way I did when I found out Andy was married. I learned pretty early from my dad once a cheater always a cheater. I could never be as forgiving as my mom. I saw what that did to my her over the years." She shook her head slowly and exhaled. "I would never."

"Sorry, I was such a dick about all that."

"It's fine. You didn't know me and had no way of knowing what I was like."

"Still."

"Forget about it. Let's just get tonight over with." She stopped at the doorway to the ballroom and faced him. "Are you ready to fawn all over me because we're so in love?" she asked and batted her eyelashes at him.

"I don't do love, babe. But I'm ready to fawn all over you because I want to fuck you. Does that count?"

Peyton burst out laughing. "I guess it's gonna have to." She patted him on the chest. "You really are a sweet talker, Ryan. My heart's all a pitter pater."

He winked. "Just keeping it real." He threaded his hand through hers. "Show time."

Scanning the crowd, he spotted his sister and Pete sitting at a round table with a couple he didn't know. He gave Peyton's hand a slight tug and led her in their direction, weaving past people, nodding when necessary.

"Ryan." His sister Kendall jumped up from her seat. She threw her arms around him and whispered in his ear. "Thank god, save us, please."

Kendall released him from her hold and turned to his date. "Hi Peyton, nice to see you again. Love those pants. I wish I could pull off that style. My legs would look like little stubs."

"That's because your legs are little stubs," Ryan mocked.

Pete walked up behind Kendall and wrapped his arms around her waist. "I happen to love your legs," he murmured before placing a kiss against Kendall's neck.

"Thanks, baby," Kendall replied, then turned to Ryan and sneered. "See, he likes my legs."

"Among other things," Pete said as he nuzzled Kendall's neck.

"Yeah, I'm not even gonna—" There was no way he was touching that one. As happy as he was for the couple, the idea of his best friend and sister still wigged him out a little when he really thought about it.

"Who needs a drink?" Ryan asked.

"I'd love a glass of white," Peyton said.

"Me too," Kendall said, holding up her almost empty glass.

"I'll go with you," Pete said.

As they walked to the bar, he glanced back at Peyton and Kendall as they sat down at the table with the unknown couple. "Who were you sitting with?" Ryan asked.

"Some rich skybox guy."

"Coach is friends with someone who owns a skybox?"

"Doubt it, I think Kirsty invited all the bigwigs to make a show." Pete stopped in front of the bar and rested his elbows on the bar top. "So, how are things going with Peyton?"

How the hell did he answer that? "About as well as can be expected I suppose. We aren't killing each other."

"I thought you said she didn't know Andy was married, so what's the problem?"

Ryan looked back at the woman in question. Peyton threw her head back and laughed at something skybox guy said to her. "I don't know, nothing really. We just seem to rub each other wrong."

"I find that hard to believe. You can get along with pretty much anybody."

"Usually, yeah. I don't know, man, something about her turns me into an asshole."

"Seriously? You? Shit, I really gotta get to know this woman." Pete rubbed his hands together. "This is gonna be so good."

"What's that supposed to mean?"

"Oh, come on, I've been dying for you to meet someone who stirred something up in you. It's been a long time coming, man."

"What the fuck are you going on about? She's hot, I'll give you that, but she doesn't stir something up in me. What the hell does that even mean?"

"You'll see..." Pete waggled his eyebrows like an idiot. His mocking laughter drew the bartender's attention back to them.

Ryan just rolled his eyes. "Jesus, why is it every time someone gets into a committed relationship, they think everyone else is gleefully running into the same pit as them?"

"First of all, it's not a pit and second, because it's fucking awesome."

"What's fucking awesome?" Smitty asked as he walked up beside them and rested his hip against the bar.

"Being in love," Pete replied.

"Ah fuck, please tell me it's not going to be one of those nights." He turned to the bartender. "Can I get a rye and seven please?"

The bartender placed two beers and two glasses of white wine on the bar.

"Thanks." Ryan dropped a bill into the tip jar on the counter. Open bar didn't mean he had to be cheap.

"So, did you bring your date?" Smitty asked.

"Yeah." Ryan nodded toward the table when Peyton and Kendall sat.

"She is pretty hot, man. There are worse people you could be forced to hang out with."

"I think our boy is fighting the forced part," Pete replied.

Smitty stood up straighter and leaned in. His eyes lit up at the prospect of some fresh gossip. "What do you mean? He likes her?"

"Yep," Pete agreed. "He pretends he doesn't, but it's pretty obvious he does."

"So you *like* her, like her, not just fake like her." Smitty made a stupid face, like he was honestly expecting Ryan to say something.

"Holy fuck, what are you two twelve?" Ryan picked up his beer and Peyton's wine and strode toward the table. Those two were ridiculous.

He set the glass of wine down on the table, a bit rougher than he'd intended, and dropped into the chair beside Peyton.

"What has your panties in a twist?" Kendall asked.

"Your boyfriend is an idiot."

Kendall laughed. "What else is new? What'd he do this time?"

Pete slid into the seat beside Kendall and Smitty sat beside him. "I didn't do anything. He's just being all dramatic."

Ryan glared at his teammate as Pete batted his eyes, the picture of innocence. "You want to dance," he said, turning to Peyton.

She eyed the nearly empty dance floor. "Uh sure." She stood up and ran her palms down the front of her pants.

He placed his hand on the small of her back as he guided her toward the dance floor.

"I hope you aren't expecting me to be a wonderful dancer because that is not my gift to the world." Peyton chewed her lip nervously as she looked up at him.

Interesting. He never would have pegged her as someone who wouldn't like dancing. In the car, she'd been unconsciously bobbing to the music. He'd thought she would enjoy this. "We don't have to dance if you're uncomfortable with it."

"It's not that I don't enjoy dancing, I love it. I'm just not very good. And I'm not a huge fan of being stared at and judged."

"Who's judging you?"

"Are you kidding me? Every woman here is giving me the stare down, judging the woman you are finally dating."

"No, they're not," he scoffed. Where did people come up with these ideas?

"Um, yeah, they are. You weren't there when Carmella and her friends came into the center like vultures looking for any meat they could pick apart."

Okay, maybe she was right. Those women had been on high alert when he'd walked in.

Thankfully, a slow song began playing as they walked onto the floor. He wrapped his arms around her. "This okay?" he asked as he pulled her a little closer.

"Mmm hmm." She wrapped her arms around his neck.

There was something to be said for a tall woman. With her heels on, he barely had to bend his head to speak in her ear.

Scanning the room, he tensed when he spotted Andy and Carmella walk in. "Andy's here."

"Awesome," Peyton replied. "We knew he would be."

He spun her so she could see where Andy the asshole had sat down with several of the other players and their wives on the opposite side of the room from where they'd been sitting.

"We don't really hang out at these things too much if I can help it," he told her, hoping that it would put her mind at ease.

"If you don't like him, why'd you agree to help him out?"

And that was the million-dollar question. "I don't know. He's a teammate. Catcher. We need to be in sync, and that can't happen if he doesn't have his head in the game."

"Okay, I get that but still," Peyton pressed.

"It's just what you do for your team. Team comes first. Always."

Peyton pulled back so she could look him in the eye. "Always?"

"Kind of, yeah." How many times had it been drilled into him he needed to be the best, but at the same time not to get too cocky and think he was better than the team? That he was nothing without his team.

"That's kind of sad," Peyton said.

"What's sad about it?"

"I don't know. You should have a life outside baseball, don't you think? I mean, these guys do." She gestured to Andy and his table.

"Yeah, nice life. Every single one of those guys at that table cheats on his wife."

"Seriously, there's like five guys there."

"Yeah, why do you think Andy is friends with them? They're all the same."

Peyton looked around the room. "Are they all like that?"

"Nah, just that group. The rest of the team are cool. A lot of the guys are single, so they do whatever, but as far as I know, Andy and his buddies are the only ones who cheat."

"I sure know how to pick 'em," she mumbled.

"What are you talking about? To everyone here, you have great taste. You're with me."

"Ah, there it is, my other date, your inflated ego. I was worried he wasn't going to show up to the party."

"Ha-ha. I'm just saying. You dumped him and learned your lesson, and no one is any the wiser that this is fake."

"Your friends know."

"My friends have my back."

She chewed on her bottom lip. "What about the other people who saw me show up at that party with Andy?"

Ryan shrugged. "Honestly, I doubt they paid much attention." The guys were used to seeing random women arrive at a party and leave with someone else. No one gave it a hell of a lot of thought. He squeezed her hip reassuringly. "And like you said, no one wants bad PR for the team, so stop worrying. It's all good."

The music changed to some weird fast beat. "I don't know how to dance to this. You want to go sit down?"

"Sure." Peyton nodded in agreement.

He took her hand and led her toward their table. He eyed the table of coaches and wives off to their right and detoured that way. "I just need to say congratulations to coach."

"Okay." With no hesitation, Peyton tightened her grip on his hand and followed him as he wove around tables to get to where he wanted to go.

"Congratulations Coach, Mrs. Gill." Ryan shook his coach's hand and smiled politely at his wife.

"Thank you. Now Ryan, why do I have to keep telling you to call me Marlene?" coach's wife replied.

"Sorry, ma'am," Ryan said.

"Oh, now you just made me feel old," Marlene teased.

"Not a good idea, son. My wife feeling old is not the anniversary I was hoping for," Coach told him.

"No one could say you were old. Looking at you two, I can't believe you've been married twenty-five years. Were you high school sweethearts?" Peyton asked.

"Oh, I like this one, Ryan," Marlene said, as she patted his arm.

"Me too," Ryan said. "Peyton, this is Coach Mark Gill. He's my favorite pitching coach and his wife, Marlene."

"Nice to meet you both. I've heard wonderful things about you Coach Gill. Ryan said you've been a lot of help to him with homing in on things and making adjustments."

Ryan looked at her. How had she known exactly what to say?

Coach beamed at Peyton. "Is that right? Well, I'm honored. Your boy here is the best pitcher I've ever seen. It's been a real joy working with him."

"Thank you, Sir," Ryan replied.

"Peyton, have you met everyone?" Marlene asked.

"No, I haven't."

Marlene linked arms with Peyton and introduced her around the table to the team manager and the rest of the coaching staff. After several minutes of small talk, Ryan figured they'd put their time in. "Coach, Marlene, there are lots of people here who want to speak to you, and we don't want to monopolize your time. Congratulations again."

"Peyton, it was really lovely meeting you. Looking forward to seeing you at some games," Coach said to her.

"Me too," Peyton replied.

"You're coming to the one next week, I imagine."

"Next week?" Peyton asked.

Coach's brow furrowed. "The Make A Wish first pitch."

Peyton looked over at Ryan in confusion.

He reached for her hand and gave it a gentle squeeze. "Yeah, the one I was telling you about where Tommy will throw out the first pitch."

"Oh right, yes, the game with Tommy." She squeezed his hand back to let him know she'd caught on. "Of course, I wouldn't miss it. I just didn't realize it was coming up so quick."

"Well, I'll look forward to seeing you there," Coach Gill said.

Ryan placed his hand against the small of her back and eased her away from the group. "Thanks for that. You were great. Sorry, you just got roped into coming to a game."

"No problem, you're lucky I like watching baseball." She winked at him. "So who's Tommy?"

"He's this kid who had his wish granted to meet me. He's a cool kid, so I organized it with the team for him to throw out the first pitch when we play Texas next weekend. It'll be Sunday's game, so I'll get you a ticket."

"Sounds fun."

Out of the corner of his eye, he saw Carmella and Andy making their way toward them.

"Fuck," he muttered. "Incoming."

Peyton looked over and groaned. "Think we can make a break for it?"

"Nope, Carmella definitely has you in the crosshairs."

"That's what I was afraid of," Peyton grumbled. "It's going to be a long night."

He bit back a growl when he saw the way Andy was eye-fucking Peyton. Mother fucker. Asshole couldn't even try to pretend he didn't want Peyton.

Ryan wrapped his arm around Peyton's waist and pulled her up against him. "Just a heads up I plan to be handsy, so Andy gets uncomfortable and doesn't stay too long."

"K," Peyton said, her voice sounded all breathy. Did she like the idea of him getting handsy with her?

"Peyton, Ryan," Carmella gushed as they approached. "So nice to see you both. Peyton, you look beautiful."

"Oh thank you," Peyton replied. "So do you."

"You really do look beautiful, Peyton," Andy said.

Seriously? The guy was unreal. Ryan curled his hand into Peyton's waist, and she turned her body into his and pressed her hand against his chest and smiled up at him. "It's the first time Ryan and I have had a chance to dress up all fancy, so it's kind of fun."

"Oh Ryan, have you not been treating this girl right?" Carmella asked.

He ran his hand up her back, loving the way she shivered beneath his touch. "She hasn't been complaining, Carm."

Carmella waggled her eyebrows at them. "I'm sure she hasn't."

Peyton smiled up at him. Damn, she was either a better actress than he'd given her credit for or the little bit of touching they'd each been doing for Andy and Carmella's benefit was having the same effect on her as it was on him.

"I've got no complaints about dating Ryan whatsoever," Peyton said. Her hand trailed down his chest and across his stomach. His muscles rippled beneath her touch, and he bit back a groan. Placing his hand on top of hers, he narrowed his eyes when she raised an eyebrow at him, a glimmer of mischief in her eyes.

"If you'll excuse us," he said to Carmella and Andy. Grabbing Peyton's hand, he led her back toward the dancefloor. Somehow, he didn't think she'd appreciate it if he dragged her into the nearest closest like he wanted to.

Once on the dancefloor, he pulled her close, pressing his body against her. He wrapped one hand around the back of her neck, threading his fingers into her hair. She melted against him. Her body like a boneless puddle, putting him in control of their movement on the floor. He moved his other hand at her waist, and she practically purred. Jesus. His dick instantly pulsed to attention.

"That went well," he murmured against her ear.

"Mmm," she responded absently.

He smiled to himself. Definitely not the only one feeling this attraction. Glancing over her shoulder, he winced when he saw a number of rapt eyes on them. "Fuck," he muttered, as he put a little space between them.

"What?" Peyton asked.

"Nothing, I'm just thinking you weren't so off base saying there was a lot of interest in us." Why were they all looking at them? Didn't they have better things to do?

Peyton looked around the room and grinned. "Told ya."

It was one thing to be turned on by Peyton's touch. It was a whole other thing to have it happen with a hundred eyes on them.

"Just got a little too real for ya?" she asked.

"Mmm," he grumbled. "People should mind their own fucking business."

Peyton giggled, then threaded her hand through his. "Let's get you a drink."

The car pulled to a stop in front of Peyton's house. She turned to Ryan. "My god, that was exhausting. I don't know about you but I could use a drink."

Ryan's face glowed in the dashboard light as he turned to look at her. "You asking me inside?" His eyebrow quirked in that cocky way he had about him and dang if her stupid stomach didn't flip just a little. What the heck was that? She hated cocky guys, and Ryan was cockier than most. He knew he looked good. Women had been trying to fawn all over him all night. In an effort to use her as a human shield, he'd been touching her, running his hand up her back, whispering in her ear. And yeah, okay, she'd shivered a time or two, but it didn't mean anything.

"Don't read into it," she growled.

Ryan held up his hands. "No expectations."

"Mmm hmm," she muttered as she opened her car door and slid off the smooth leather seat.

Together, they walked up the sidewalk to her place "I can't believe I'm being given a look inside the inner sanctum."

"Don't make me regret this," she said pointedly.

His deep chuckle slid across her spine, and her body betrayed her by shivering again.

"You cold?" Ryan asked.

"Yeah, good thing we're here." She put the key in the lock and pushed open her front door.

"Good thing, cause these California summer nights are chilly."

She turned and glared when the little smirk on his face matched his tone. "I thought you wanted that drink, 'cause I can send you back to your car."

The jerk laughed again. "I don't know why you don't just admit you're attracted to me."

"I can admit you're good-looking, but you don't need me to tell you that. You had women telling you all night." She glanced back at him as her mind replayed all the conversations she'd had with various wives and girlfriends, who all seemed to have an opinion about how amazing Ryan was and how good looking. They'd certainly come out with the hard sales pitch on the importance of tying him down before some other woman sunk her claws into him. "I'm just so lucky to have caught the eye of such a handsome man." She batted her eyes at him mockingly. "How you chose little ol' me I'll never know."

He made a rough, semi-amused sound in the back of his throat. "Okay, you made your point." He pushed his hand through his hair. "I appreciate you being such a good sport tonight. A lot of the wives are uncomfortable with the single players on the team, so when they see a crack in the armor, they go in for the kill."

Peyton led the way into the kitchen. Digging into the freezer, she pulled out a bottle of vodka. "Moscow mule? Or you want a beer?"

"I'll have whatever you're having."

She grabbed a couple of copper mugs out of her cabinet and set them on the counter. When she turned toward the fridge, she bumped into Ryan. His hands settled on her waist. "Sorry, I didn't realize you were so close," she mumbled.

"No problem." He stepped toward her and her back hit the counter. Ryan rested his palms on the counter on either side of her. "I'm curious. How come you don't want to acknowledge this attraction between us?"

Her nipples beaded against her top, betraying her, so there was no point in denying it. "I already told you that you are undisputedly attractive. But I can think you're good-looking and still not be attracted to you."

"And you're saying you aren't attracted to me?"

"Mmm hmm." She kept her eyes pinned on the collar of his shirt, afraid that if she looked him in the eye, he'd see what a liar she was. She didn't even like the guy. Unfortunately, her body didn't seem to care. She'd been telling her body to get on board with the conversation all night. So far, it wasn't listening.

"So this attraction is completely one sided." His voice became dark and husky as he shifted closer to her. It took everything she had not to clamp her legs together to ease the instant ache that was created from his voice.

He traced his finger along her collarbone and held it there a moment while his thumb gently rubbed back and forth at the base of her jaw. His hand rested against her neck like a collar, but there was no pressure, so why was it so hard to breathe? It felt like the air had all been sucked out of the room.

"I can feel your heartbeat pounding." His finger pressed lightly against her pulse. "You can pretend you don't want me, Peyton, but your body says otherwise," he growled.

Two could play this game. She straightened and looked at him head on. "I don't have to like you to want to fuck you, Ryan."

At her use of a cussword, his eyes widened then darkened as the truth of what she said sank in. "That's very true." He licked his lip. "And point made on the power of words. Jesus."

He shifted his body, and she sucked in a breath at the contact. Heat radiated off him. The corner of his mouth quirked up in a sexy, confident way before he spoke. "I'd say the fact we don't like each other will make it even better."

Oh boy, maybe two couldn't play this game because the heated look in his eyes and that cocky smirk promised a whole lot more than she'd signed up for. She shifted against the counter. "How would us not liking each other make it better, exactly?"

He raised one eyebrow. "You really have to ask?"

Holy cow. Her mind instantly imagined how hot it would be to have sex with Ryan. Angry. A little aggressive. Phew. There was a reason make up sex was so hot because it always had that little bit of pissed off still in there. She blew out a breath. "Okay but do you really think us having sex is a good idea?"

"It's a fucking great idea."

He pressed his body closer to hers, and she sighed. She pressed her hands against his chest and pushed him back slightly. "I can't think when you're that close."

"Thinking is overrated. I spend my whole life doing what's best for other people." He leaned back against the opposite counter and stuck his hands in his pockets. "Sometimes it's just nice to do what I want for myself." His gaze trailed down her body like a caress. "And what I want is you."

"But what about after we burn off this attraction?" she asked. "Then what? We're still in this fake relationship and have to see each other. I don't want it to be weird."

"Yeah, cuz it's not fucking weird right now at all," Ryan scoffed. "Seriously Peyton. This whole fake relationship thing sucks for both of us. It's awkward and weird. We should at least get something enjoyable out of it, shouldn't we?"

She laughed. "Nice sales pitch. Everything about being with you sucks, so we should have sex."

"That's not what I said or not what I meant at least." He sighed. "I'm not good at this fake dating thing. Lying to people, it umm... it rubs me wrong, and it's making me a bigger dick than I normally am." He dropped his head back. "I'm ridiculously attracted to you. I don't like how this situation happened, but at least if we're sleeping together, it doesn't feel so much like lying. Sure, we aren't dating, but more like friends with benefits."

"Friends?"

"We're not exactly enemies, we just don't like each other much." He stepped toward her again. "Here's the thing, the fact we don't like each other helps us keep this whole sex part casual. We agreed neither of us is dating anyone else during this shitshow, so why shouldn't we have sex? No reason we need to be celibate just because we've been roped into this thing."

"I guess." Peyton pressed her lips together. "I'm just not a casual sex person, usually."

"This isn't exactly casual. As far as the rest of the world knows, we are in a relationship. I say we get the benefits of that."

"I need that drink."

Peyton picked up the bottle of vodka and winced when she saw her hand trembling as she tried to un-screw the cap. Ryan stepped up behind her and placed his hand over hers to steady the shaking. His warmth surrounded her.

"Relax Peyton. I'm not going to jump you or make you do anything you don't want to do."

"That's the problem, though," she whispered.

"What is?"

"I kind of want you to take the decision out of my hands." His body tensed behind her. Shoot, real smooth. Now he thought she was a freak.

"What do you mean, you want me to take the decision out of your hands?"

Peyton swallowed past the knot in her throat and shrugged.

Ryan turned her around, so she was facing him and pushed her chin up, forcing her to look at him. "No, you need to lay this out for me, Peyton, so I'm not misreading things."

The feminist part of her said shut up, but another part was saying yes, please.

She interlaced her hands together in front of her, then brought them up in front of her mouth. Could she admit this out loud?

She looked up at Ryan. Watching her intently, his eyes filled with fire and passion, but his body stood strongly in front of her, controlled. She didn't particularly like him from what she'd seen so far, but somehow, she trusted him, which was weird. He was so quick to judge her, but he also seemed to have a pretty strong moral compass that guided what he did. For whatever reason, she felt safe with him.

Taking a deep breath, she squared her shoulders and looked at him. "I tend to get in my own head and..." she wrinkled her nose. "Intellectually I know this is a bad idea, and I'll talk it to death, so if there's a hope of this happening, I need you to just grab me and just... you know, convince me without words so that I don't have time to think. Just feel and... figure out the rest after."

"I can definitely do that." With lightning speed, he grabbed the back of her neck. His fingers wove into her hair, twisting slightly as he dug in to hold her in place.

The little zap of pain sent an arrow of arousal down her spine, and she gasped. "Yes."

His mouth crashed down on hers, his tongue confident as he controlled the pressure of the kiss. Peyton's legs trembled beneath her.

CHAPTER SEVEN

Oh my god the man could kiss.

Ryan's hand's cupped her hips, and he hoisted her onto the countertop before stepping between her splayed legs. He firmly pulled her butt toward him, pressing her core against his hard cock, and she bit back a moan. God, if he felt that good through their clothes, she could only imagine how good he would feel buried inside her.

His hands dipped beneath her, changing the angle of her hips as he rocked back and forth. Good lord. She dropped her head back and angled her hips further into him, desperately seeking deeper contact.

His teeth scraped up the side of her neck and goosebumps raced across her skin. "As hot as it would be to fuck you on this kitchen counter. I want to take my time with you, so I'd rather have you spread out on the bed than out here." His hot breath brushed against her ear, and she shivered.

Opening her eyes, she looked into his and trembled. Had any man ever watched her like that before?

Heat and intensity, but something else too. She didn't know what it was, but by god she wanted to find out. "Bed sounds good," she replied, grimacing a little at the breathy way her voice sounded.

A slow cocky grin spread across his face a second before he scooped her off the counter, forcing her to wrap her legs around his waist to hold on. "Where's your bedroom?" he asked.

"First door on the right."

She'd barely gotten the words out before his mouth crashed against hers. Tongues tangling as he thrust into her mouth with his tongue. He paused slightly, pressing her back against the wall. His teeth sank into the side of her neck, and she moaned. Everything was slightly rougher than she was used to and holy cow, did her body seem to like the change. She'd never felt this turned on by a few kisses before in her life.

With his hips holding her in place, he swept her top up and off her body, dropping it on the floor beside her before dipping his head. His tongue traced the swell of her breasts. Peyton arched her back, trying to get closer and closed her eyes as sensation swept through her body.

With an experienced flick of the wrist, her bra quickly followed suit and was tossed to the floor. Ryan sucked her nipple into his mouth. "Oh my god," she moaned as she arched away from the wall. Her hands threaded into his hair to hold him in place. Most guys started out slowly, licking and playing with her nipples. Ryan went right in for the kill, sucking hard. And wow, did she like it.

Ryan spun them away from the wall. His hands dug into her butt, holding her in place as he stalked toward her bedroom. Her heart fluttered. Why was a guy carrying her to bed so flippin' hot?

He pushed her door fully open with his foot. Without letting her go, he followed her down onto the bed. The weight of his body on top of hers made Peyton widen her legs to draw him further down onto her. His hips thrust back and forth against her core. She wanted to feel him naked. Peyton dragged her hand down his body and flicked open the button of his pants.

His hand clasped around hers. "No," he said, stopping her from exploring where she wanted to go.

"What?" she asked. What kind of guy didn't want her to grab his dick?

"You said I was taking the lead here. We go at my pace. I'll tell you when you can touch me."

Arousal zipped down her body. She pulled her hand back. "Okay," she whispered as she waited for what he would do next.

"Good girl." His deep, husky words of approval glided down her body like a caress.

God, why did him saying that turn her on so much? What was wrong with her?

If any other guy had said that to her in any other context, she would have given him a tongue lashing and not in a good way. But Ryan calling her good girl while looking at her like that... Sheesh. It was all she could do not to squirm against him, to ease the ache in her core.

She was embarrassingly turned on already. So much for making him work for it.

A slow, sexy smile curved up the corner of his mouth. He took his lip between his teeth as his gaze raked down her body. "Where should I start?" he murmured.

She had a few ideas. Peyton arched her back and shifted her hips.

"Patience. I'll get there," he said. He traced his finger over the curve of her breast. He undid the button on her pants and slowly unzipped them. Placing kisses against her belly, he eased her pants down her hips. She pushed herself up slightly, trembling as she watched him. As he slid the pants down her legs, he followed the path with his tongue, licking each new swatch of skin as he went.

He tossed her pants to the side and sat back on his knees and stared down at her. "Fuck, you're beautiful."

And she felt it.

Ryan glanced around her room, then eyed the wooden headboard. He scooped her up and moved her further up the bed. "Wrap your hands around the slats and stay there."

Peyton raised her hands above her head and wrapped her palms around the wooden rails.

"Don't make me tie you to them," he said.

"I won't," she whispered.

"Good girl."

At those two little words, once again, moisture pooled in her core. What was happening here? And why did the idea of him tying her up turn her on so much? She hated giving up control. So why was she so eager to do it with this man?

Embarrassed, she dipped her head so he wouldn't be able to see what she was feeling. What must he be thinking of her?

Ryan placed his finger against her chin and tipped her head back up. "Hey, there's nothing to be ashamed of here. You like what you like. You don't ever have to feel bad about that."

Why was he paying such close attention to her he noticed her reaction to his words and how embarrassed she was about it? He was supposed to be focused on getting laid. Not talking about feelings. Oh god, what if he wasn't as into it as she was?

He held her chin in his hand, not allowing her to look away from him. "Besides, it's fucking hot."

"Really?" she asked.

"Fuck yeah." He kneeled beside her. "Peyton, here's the thing. I prefer to be in control in the bedroom. Given who I am, I don't always embrace that side of myself because —" He paused. "—people talk. And I like to keep my private life private. It feels like we're on the same page here."

"We are," she agreed. If he could talk so openly to her about what he liked, she could be brave enough to admit what she liked too. This wasn't a side of her she'd ever explored before but with Ryan, it felt like she could. They both knew the deal. This was a temporary arrangement. They were already willing to lie to keep secrets, so why shouldn't they feel safe to be themselves in the bedroom?

"Good." He grabbed her wrist and placed her right hand back against the slat of the headboard. She hadn't realized she'd brought her arms down while they'd spoken. He took her left hand and did the same. "Keep your hands there."

He trailed his finger slowly down the line of her arm, down the swell of the side of her breast, and she shivered beneath his touch. "I'm going to be paying attention to your body language and your facial expressions, Peyton, but I'm not a mind reader. You like something, tell me, you don't like something, tell me."

"Yeah, right, I'm sure you want to know if you aren't doing something right," she scoffed. What guy wanted to be told that?

"Peyton, I'm not some cocky frat kid who thinks he knows everything. I can handle hearing if you don't like something." He traced his finger around her nipple and she arched her back.

"Believe me, I want to know, because honey, my goal here is to have you so fucking turned on you beg me to fuck you."

"That's not going to happen." She rolled her eyes. So much for not being a cocky frat guy. Guys always thought they were the god's gift in the bedroom. Unfortunately, she had yet to meet one who was. Ryan had certainly been off to a good start, but she doubted he'd live up to the hype.

Ryan's eyebrow arched as he looked at her, then a confident smirk slid across his face. "We'll see." He eyed her hands, wrapped around the wooden slats above her head. "Do I need to tie you or are you gonna keep them there?"

"I'll keep 'em here. Show me what you got, big guy."

Ryan grinned. "Challenge accepted." He hopped off the bed and pulled his shirt over his head and tossed it aside. His stomach muscles rippled with the movement, and her eyes widened. Wow, she'd felt those muscles beneath her hands when she'd touched his chest but seeing them in the flesh was so much different.

He undid his trousers and pushed them down his legs. His fitted boxers molded to his sculpted thighs, and she squirmed, unable to take her eyes off his arousal, pressing firmly against the thin fabric. Holy smokes.

Clad in only his boxer briefs, Ryan kneeled back on the bed. "So where were we?" He picked up her foot and rested her ankle on his shoulder. Gently he kissed above her ankle bone, then slowly ran his tongue up the side of her calf. Her legs fell open further as he placed a kiss against the inside of her knee. His tongue swirled up her inner thigh and stopped at the edge of her panties. Hot breath teased her with the promise of more to come. At this rate, she'd be a panting mess by the time he even took off his boxers.

Ryan hooked his fingers in the edge of her thong. "Right, I remember." He slowly eased her panties down her thighs. "You didn't believe I could make you beg."

"That's not quite what I said," Peyton replied as she shifted on the bed to try to get him to touch her rather than just tormenting her with these teasing licks and breaths that never quite touched where she needed it.

He shifted his body and licked his way across her belly and up to her breast. He teased her nipple with his tongue, swirling it around. Finally, he wrapped his lips around the tight bud and sucked hard, she bowed off the mattress.

"Yes," she hissed. Electricity zipped through her body like a current from her nipple to her clit. Her sensitized skin tingled in anticipation of where he'd touch next.

Ryan's hand trailed down her stomach as he shifted his mouth to her other breast. Peyton wrapped her hands tighter around the rails to force herself not to touch him. She moved her hips, silently encouraging him to move faster, but the jerk just continued his teasing. He kissed up her neck and nipped her ear with his teeth.

"You doing okay? You're awful squirmy."

"Well, if you don't want me to tell you what to do, then you'd better touch me soon."

"Where did you want me to touch you?" he asked. "Here?" He nipped the side of her neck and she shivered. "Or maybe here?" He bent down and sucked her nipple, pressing it against the roof of his mouth. The mixture of pleasure with the slight bite of pain made her back arch off the bed. "Or what about here?" he whispered as he swiped his finger against her clit. "Jesus, you're soaked," he said.

He brought his finger up to his mouth and sucked. "Fuck, you taste even better than I imagined."

"You thought about what I'd taste like?" she asked.

"Fuck yeah." He kissed his way down her stomach, pausing at her belly button. "What you'd feel like coming against my face. How I'd have to hold you down to force you to take more than you thought you could handle. Your pussy coating my beard. Fuck yeah, I imagined it," he growled.

His dirty talk arrowed directly to her core. God, she wanted that more than her next breath. "Show me."

"Ask nicely," he mocked.

Peyton narrowed her eyes as she looked at him. Damn him. That sexy look on his face promised he'd make it worth her while, but why did he have to ask that little bit extra of her? She wasn't sure she could do what he wanted.

"Just do it already."

Ryan blew a breath against her inner thigh, and she shifted to bring him closer. "Ask nicely," he said again. His hot breath teasing her, demanding she do what he told her.

"Come on, Ryan," she whined.

"You want me to fuck your pretty little pussy with my tongue, Peyton. You're going to have to ask."

"Fine," she growled. "Please."

"Please what?" He blew a slow, hot breath directly on her clit, and she let go of the headboard and gripped the back of his head without even thinking.

"Uh, uh, uh." Ryan sat up and put her hand back on the slat of the headboard. "Hands stay here."

"Well, if you would stop teasing me, I wouldn't need to move my hands."

Ryan pressed his mouth against her ear. "Honey, if you'd give in and tell me what you want, I'll make you forget you even have hands."

Peyton swallowed. Wow! A shiver ran down her body, making her clit pulse like it had a heartbeat of its own. "Fine, Ryan, will you please just lick me?"

"Where?" he whispered. His hot breath made her shiver as it hit a delicious nerve ending in her neck.

"You know where," she complained.

"I want to hear you say it?"

"Fine, my clit," she grumbled.

He flicked his finger against her clit. "Your clit?" Moving his finger through her lips, he spread her moisture around before pressing his finger deep inside her. "Or your entire pussy?"

"Both," she moaned as he moved his finger back and forth inside her.

"Come on Peyton, talk dirty to me."

"Just because I don't talk dirty doesn't mean I can't be dirty, Ryan." His cock twitched against her hip and she smiled.

"Is that right? How dirty are we talking?" He bit down on that spot on her neck she loved so much. How had he already figured out so many of her buttons and they'd just gotten started?

The way he kept biting her neck, she knew she'd have a mark tomorrow and she couldn't care less. If anything, she wanted him to do it more.

"If you let me take my hands down, I'd show you."

Ryan pushed back and smiled down at her. "Not a chance. But next time I'll be all over telling you what you can do to me."

At the thought of Ryan directing what she did to him, her nipples pulled tighter. He winked at her. "Seems like we both like that idea." He pressed a kiss against her lips. "I'll go easy on you this time. You don't have to say anything. I'll make a dirty talker out of you yet."

Ryan kissed his way down her stomach, then her hip bone. He spread her lips with his fingers, holding her open for him to look at, and she chewed her bottom lip in anticipation.

The first swipe of his tongue through her folds nearly broke her back as she bowed off the mattress. Holy cow.

He swirled his tongue around her clit, licking and teasing, gently dragging his teeth against the tight bundle of nerves. She wanted to let go of the rails and wrap her hands in his hair and hold him in place. The way he was teasing her was maddening. He hadn't been kidding when he said he'd make her beg him. He sucked her clit firmly into his mouth and she screamed. "Oh, my god."

As Ryan inserted his finger inside her, he continued to lick and suck her clit. "I'm close," she gasped. She gripped the slats hard as she bucked her hips against his face. She curled her leg over his shoulders, holding him in place, pinning him against her body, and he chuckled.

The vibrations of his laugh mixed with the heat of his breath against her body made her clamp her legs tighter around him. He simply laughed more. "Hang on baby, I got you."

He curled his finger inside her and moved it slightly, hitting a spot she'd previously only been able to reach with toys. "Ryan," she groaned.

Peyton's hips moved of their own volition as she climbed higher and higher toward her orgasm. She was so close. Her body was on fire. "Right there, right there, right there," she chanted.

Ryan took her clit between his teeth and the orgasm that had been hovering so close ripped its way through her. Her spine arched off the mattress. She didn't even care that she was making some ungodly moaning sound because it just felt too freakin' good. He kept licking and sucking on her as his finger continued to move inside her.

She was done, she couldn't take anymore. She pressed her foot against his shoulder to push him back. "You can give me another," he growled.

"No, I can't. I'm done."

"I said I'd have you begging me to fuck you. We're not there yet." He inserted another finger inside her, curling them both against her g-spot and rubbing. Peyton instantly shot back to the edge. The intensity of the orgasm building inside her felt too big. A moment of panic shot through her, and she pressed her foot against his shoulder. Ryan stopped what he was doing and looked at her. "We good?"

"I think we should just have sex." What he'd made her feel already was more intense than anything she'd ever felt before. She'd already given up more control than normal. She couldn't give more. It was too much, too intimate.

"Why?"

Yeah, there was zero chance she was telling him he was taking her body into unknown territory, and that scared her.

"You never had multiple orgasms with a guy before?"

"God, boundaries. You let every little thought in your mind fly, don't you?" she grumbled. Why did he have to read her so well?

"Trust me, Peyton, I'm not going to let anything happen to you. I got you. It's okay to let go."

She stared at him as he held eye contact with her. She did trust him. Probably shouldn't but she did. There was no judgment on Ryan's face. He honestly looked like he just wanted her to enjoy herself. No other agenda, which was weird.

What did she have to lose? She'd always been pro-girl-get-some for everyone else, so why not her? Why shouldn't she make the most of a guy who was willing to give her multiple o's?

She took her foot off his shoulder and opened her legs again. The smile that spread across Ryan's face made Peyton's stomach flip. Crap, this was sex. She wasn't supposed to like him, so what the heck was that about?

"There's my girl." He pressed a kiss to her ankle, where it rested on his shoulder. "Mmm, I haven't had nearly enough of this pussy."

Peyton eased her grip on the headboard. As Ryan's tongue swept across her clit, she tightened her hands again. She'd expected him to have to work so much harder to get her there now that they'd paused, but shockingly, she was already close.

He hooked his hands under her butt and brought her to his face, changing the angle. His beard brushed against her skin, making her moan. This man had a magic tongue. Holy cow.

Her orgasm built. Peyton adjusted her hips, then clamped her thighs tightly on his ears. Oh god, she was so close. She needed something to send her over the edge. Unfortunately, she wasn't sure what. She squirmed against the mattress, her grip on the headboard so tight she was sure she'd have permanent ridges in her palms.

Ryan reached up and pinched her nipple at the same time he sucked hard on her clit and she exploded.

Peyton's grip on the rails lightened and she simply dropped her arms weightlessly between the slats of the headboard. Boneless, she looked down to see Ryan smiling at her from between her legs. The cocky grin

shouldn't have looked so freakin' sexy, but it did, especially with her moisture glistening off his beard.

God, she wanted him inside her right now. "Get up
here."

He wiped his hand over his beard, wiping her juices
off his face. As he looked at her, he held her stare, then
flattened his tongue and swiped up all of her moisture
from his hand.

He shoved his boxers down and stroked his cock with
his wet hand, once, twice, never breaking eye contact
with her.

Holy hell, that was hot.

"I want you inside me *now*, Ryan."

He stood up and kicked off his boxers, then grabbed
his wallet from his pocket and pulled out a condom.
Standing proudly erect with a condom in hand, he
stepped toward the head of the bed. He held out the
condom. "Put it on me," he ordered.

Peyton sat up and eased to the side of the bed. Taking
the condom, she tore open the wrapper. She placed the
little ring against the head of his cock and locked eyes
with Ryan.

"With your mouth," he told her.

Wow, okay, that was also really flipping hot.

Everything about the look on his face was so com-
manding, so in control. A slight bulge of the muscle in his
jaw the only indication that he wasn't quite as calm as he
was giving off. The urge to see him break even slightly
was strong.

"While lying down or on my knees?" She cocked her
head to the side and bit her bottom lip like she was
imagining all the possibilities.

"Oh, definitely on your knees." Ryan's nostrils flared as she got off the bed and dropped to her knees beside him. The condom sat precariously resting on the tip of his penis. Peyton looked up at him, batting her eyes, and smirked.

"Fuck," he growled. His hand roughly wove into her hair as he wrapped the long strands around his fist. Her scalp tingled, and she winced slightly at the same time she clamped her legs together to ease the instant arousal the controlling pain brought.

Peyton kept her eyes on Ryan's face as she ran her tongue along his cock from root to tip. He groaned. "Just fucking do it."

She smirked. Definitely not as in control as he pretended. She wrapped her mouth around the tip of his cock, using her lips to keep control of the condom as she eased it down onto him. Ryan's hands gripped her hair tighter.

"Jesus," he grunted as she took him deeply into her throat to fully seat the condom.

She glided back up, then back down once.

"Enough," he growled. "Stand up."

Peyton did as she was told, wiping the corner of her lip with her finger

Ryan grabbed her pillows and set them on the edge of the mattress. Peyton eyed the pillows skeptically. What was he doing?

"Lie down on your stomach," he told her. She eyed the pile of pillows again, then lay down on top of them. The mountain of pillows had her feet dangling down the bed, making it so she couldn't touch the floor. Leaving her feeling vulnerable, exposed, and really freaking turned on.

Ryan ran his hand down the curve of her butt. The pillows elevated her to a height that was perfectly lined up with his waist.

He placed himself at her entrance and eased the tip inside. She tried to press back against him but couldn't from her place pinned to the mattress.

He swatted her on the butt.

"Ow," she squealed.

"Don't be greedy."

"I wasn't."

"Sure felt like it to me. I'll tell you when you can have my cock."

She wiggled her hips back and forth to try to entice him more. He swatted her butt again. She'd never been spanked before and unfortunately, it didn't do much for her. Should she tell him? She glanced back over her shoulder. Screw it. He'd said he wanted to know what she liked and could handle it. "I don't really like being spanked.".

"No?" he asked. He pulled out. And stepped back slightly, then before she knew what he was doing he spanked her clit.

"Holy fuck," she moaned. Fire shot from her clit through her body, pulsing and burning in the most delicious way.

"There's my dirty girl," he chuckled.

So much for her no swearing rule. But oh my god, why did that feel like that?

"I'm guessing you don't mind me spanking your pussy." He didn't so much ask as tell her she liked it and he wasn't wrong.

"Apparently not," she agreed. "Who knew?" She glanced over her shoulder at him. "How'd you know I'd like that?"

"You certainly seemed to enjoy when I was a little rougher with your clit, so I figured it might be your thing."

"Good to know," she agreed. She pushed back toward him as best as she could. "Can you please just go already?"

He swatted her pussy again, and she moaned loudly.

"So greedy, Peyton."

She felt the blush crawl up her face just before he said, "I fucking love it." And any embarrassment she'd been feeling disappeared.

"Then don't keep me waiting."

"A little longer won't hurt ya." He ran his tongue up her spine, and she shivered. Lord, if she could have jumped on his cock right then and there she would have. She wanted him inside her.

"Ryan, *please*."

He pressed himself to her entrance, and in one deep thrust, he seated himself fully. "That's what I was waiting for."

Crap, she'd practically begged him. But as he moved his hips, she honestly didn't care. Oh, my lord. She tried to move back, but couldn't gain traction with her feet off the floor.

Ryan reached down and moved her leg so her knee was on the bed, allowing her to push back against him the way she wanted. When he thrust deep, she moaned as he hit the spot she needed.

"Oh my god, right there," she told him.

He thrust into her. Peyton's nipples tightened as they rubbed back and forth against the mattress while he pounded into her. Ryan reached around and rubbed her clit, and Peyton's orgasm built. His breathing changed behind her as he thrust harder and harder into her. She could feel how close he was. She just hoped he could hold off a little longer until she came again. Ryan pinched her clit hard, and she screamed out her release, taking him along with her.

He collapsed against her back. "Holy fuck," he muttered.

After several seconds, he finally stood up and dropped the condom into the garbage can beside the bed. Peyton never moved.

He scooped her up and set her fully on the mattress. Picking up the pile of pillows they'd used, he held them in his hand as he looked at her. "You up for me sticking around for round two, or would you rather I got out of here?"

She smiled drunkenly. "The answer is always going to be round two."

Ryan grinned and nodded his head. "That's what I like to hear."

He settled the pillows and dropped into the empty space beside her. Sticking out his arm, he pulled her into his chest.

"Wow, great sex and a cuddle. You might just be the best fake boyfriend ever," Peyton teased as she snuggled up against his muscular chest.

"Might be? Fuck that. There's no question I'm the best fake boyfriend ever."

Peyton snorted. "My god, not everything is a competition."

"Who are you kidding? Everything in life is a competition."

Peyton glanced up at Ryan, his blue eyes looking back at her. Did he really believe that? If so, that was kind of sad. There was more to life than fighting to be the best all the time.

"What do you do for fun?" she asked.

"Jesus, woman, I just showed you some of my best work, and you have to ask?"

Peyton snickered. "Right, sorry. I meant besides the obvious."

"During the season, honestly, not much. I'm too busy." He yawned so big his jaw cracked loudly. "Sorry."

"No problem." She pushed off him. "I'm going to grab a glass of water. You want one?"

"Sure, that'd be great."

Peyton grabbed Ryan's button-up shirt off the floor and slid it on.

"Looks good on you."

She glanced back at him lying in her bed, and her stomach flipped again. She definitely needed a little space. It was just great sex. Okay, mind bending sex, but still just sex. Nothing else.

She quickly went to the bathroom, then padded into the kitchen and poured two glasses of water.

When she walked back into her bedroom minutes later, Ryan was asleep in the bed. She breathed a sigh of relief, probably for the best. The last thing she needed was to get to know him better and find out her first impressions had been completely wrong. Nope. Not doing that.

CHAPTER EIGHT

Peyton glanced down at her ticket, then slowly made her way down the stairs to her seat. She eyed the empty seat and the woman beside it. Taking a deep breath to fortify herself, she slid into the vacant seat.

"Hi Kendall." She eyed Ryan's sister, clad in her Saunders jersey and Hawks cap. Looking down at herself, she suddenly felt decidedly under-dressed. Should she have worn a Graves jersey for effect? Isn't that what girlfriends did? Even fake ones?

"Hey Peyton, how you doing?"

"No complaints. Thanks for allowing me to sit with you." Peyton scanned the surrounding area. A group of men middle-aged men lined the row in front of them. A family sat beside Kendall. "I would have thought you'd sit with the other wives and girlfriends."

"Nah, too much drama and besides, I like to sit here, so I'm closer to Pete."

"Right, close to shortstop." Peyton glanced down to the field. "How come you don't sit in the first row, then?"

Kendall wrinkled her nose. "Too many asses in your face down there. Everyone lines up along the railing before the game and during the stretch, trying to get closer to the players. I like to be up a few rows so Pete can see me when he comes on the field."

Peyton looked down at the railing lined with fans. "I see what you mean."

The crowd roared as the players began taking the field for warmup. Kendall jumped up so she was standing. The infield players took their positions, and Pete looked up into the stands. Kendall blew a kiss down to him, and the man's face lit up like he'd won the lottery.

Peyton's heart did a little flip in her chest. What would it be like to be loved like that? To know in a crowd of people that someone was looking for you and only you and the moment they found you, it was like they had everything they'd ever wanted.

Kendall continued standing, and Peyton glanced around. The odd person was standing, but overall, everyone else was in their seats.

Peyton spotted Ryan walking across the field and taking his place on the mound. And just like Pete had done, he scanned the crowd along the third baseline. He smiled and tipped his hat. Kendall dropped into the seat beside her, and Ryan continued to look their way.

She sucked in a breath when it felt like he was looking right at her. But unlike when Pete saw Kendall, Ryan gave no outward indication that seeing her influenced him at all. Her chest tightened painfully. It shouldn't hurt that he didn't particularly care she was there but it did.

What was wrong with her? Of course, he didn't care. She didn't care either.

But she kind of did a little.

Had Kendall and Pete not had this lightning bolt kind of moment she wouldn't have even known that kind of thing existed, but now that she'd been hit by the blowback of their look she knew, and had to admit she kind of wanted that for herself. Maybe not with Ryan, but with someone.

Kendall glanced over at her. "Sorry, just a little pre-game routine I have with both of them."

"No problem, it's sweet."

Kendall laughed. "For my brother, it's not about being sweet, it's all about superstition. When he moved away to billet, he did it at the first game we attended and had the best game of his life. The next time I saw him play while we were there, we were fighting, so he didn't look at me and they lost, so ever since then it's been this whole thing."

Peyton didn't respond. She simply smiled at the other woman. But god, that little superstition kind of made it even cuter.

The person selling beer walked past and Kendall let out an ear-piercing whistle. The man turned around with the shelf of beer resting on his stomach and scanned the crowd.

"You want one?" Kendall asked.

"Absolutely." Alcohol was a necessity to get through this day. What had she been thinking, agreeing to hang out with Ryan's sister? She barely knew the guy.

Okay, so they'd had sex, but they'd barely spoken since. It had been completely physical, or at least that's what she was telling herself. And they certainly weren't friends. Gah, she didn't have a clue how she was supposed to act in this situation.

Had he told his sister that they were fake dating, or did she think this was real? Why hadn't she thought to ask him about the situation before agreeing to this?

Kendall held up two fingers and two beers were passed down the line. Peyton reached for her wallet and Kendall shook her off. "I got the first one."

"First one, meaning there will be more?"

"Well, yeah, it's a ball game." Kendall scoffed like it wasn't even a question that multiple beer would be consumed.

"Two's gonna be my limit since I'm driving," Peyton replied.

"Sounds good, or Ry can drive you home after the game." Kendall looked over at her, watching and waiting for a reaction.

"Umm, yeah, no, I'll be driving myself home."

Kendall continued to look at her, not saying a word, and Peyton shifted in her seat. What else was she supposed to say? "I mean, who can afford to pay for overnight parking?"

The most unladylike snort Peyton had ever heard rocked Kendall and she covered her mouth. "Oh my god, parking is seriously your lame-o excuse?" Kendall shook her head. "My god woman, you really need to work on your lies if you're going to have a hope in hell of pulling this whole thing off."

Crap. "That bad, huh?"

"It wasn't good." Kendall laughed. "We need some A-game shit here, girl. I expect better next time."

Who knew Ryan's sister was so cool? Go figure, because he sure seemed to have a stick up his butt most of the time she was around him. Except... She shook her head. Nope, she wasn't going to think about how hot he was in the bedroom. "I'll see what I can do."

The announcer broke over the PA. "Ladies and Gentlemen will you please stand for the national anthem."

Peyton stood up beside Kendall as the music started.

When the anthem was finished, they took their seats. The announcer told the crowd that the first pitch would be thrown out by Tommy MacDowell. Pictures began flashing on the jumbotron of Tommy at various stages of his cancer journey and ending with a big Make a Wish banner. As the ten-year-old boy was wheeled out on the mound, the crowd cheered.

Ryan crouched down and talked to Tommy before handing him the ball. The boy eyed the catcher and even from where she sat, Peyton could see how nervous the kid was. Ryan bent down and said something that made a smile split across Tommy's face. Ryan nodded at him. Then Tommy wound up and threw the ball. It made it about halfway to the plate. The boy's face sunk. Ryan leaned down and spoke to him and he smiled. Then the two wheeled up to the ball, Ryan picked it up and handed it to him, then they continued up to home plate. As they got onto the dirt in front of home plate, Tommy threw the ball. Then, before the crowd could even register what was happening, Ryan took off like a shot, pushing Tommy's wheelchair toward first base. The boy threw his head back, laughing as they rounded second.

Pete ran to coach third, waving Ryan home as they ran toward the base. Kendall and Peyton jumped up along with all the other fans, cheering their encouragement. The entire Hawks team cleared the bench and ran toward home plate. As Ryan crossed home plate, the stadium erupted. The team swarmed around Ryan and Tommy. The jumbotron zoomed in on Tommy's face, and the only way to describe it was sheer joy. Gonzo held up the home-run blazer, and Tommy threw his hands up in the air in celebration.

With the jacket wrapped around Tommy's shoulders, Ryan pushed the boy's chair down the line for high-fives from the team. The Texas bench cleared and made their way toward home plate to offer their high-fives as well.

Ryan stopped the chair beside what Peyton imagined were the boy's parents as the couple stood with tears streaming down their faces. The woman wrapped Ryan in a hug, holding him like she didn't want to let go.

Peyton's chest tightened. Judging by the organizers and the players' reactions, that had been completely spontaneous. How could the jerk she'd encountered so far be the kind of guy who would do something like for a kid? He'd delayed the game and probably would get some heat for going off-script, but he didn't care in the least. What a gift for that boy and his family.

As the organizers wrapped up the first pitch ceremony, Peyton sat down in her seat at the same time Kendall dropped into hers. Kendall wiped tears from her cheeks.

"That was pretty amazing," Peyton said.

Kendall wiped her nose and sniffed. "That kid's going to be a celebrity at school tomorrow when this shows up on all the highlight reels."

"No kidding." Peyton looked down at the field and watched as Ryan walked back toward the mound. She really hoped that wasn't who Ryan really was because that kind of man would be hard to resist. Sex was one thing. Getting emotionally involved was something else.

Peyton picked up her beer and took a sip as she tried to get her emotions under check. It didn't matter what kind of man he was. This was fake, and she had no intentions of falling for a professional athlete. Now that she'd done her research and read the stories, she knew what that kind of relationship would entail. Heck, been there done that and had the guilt to prove it. There was no way a man that looked like Ryan wouldn't have women throwing themselves all over him.

"That little move just got Graves more pussy than he'll be able to handle," the guy in front of them said to his friend.

"No shit," his buddy replied.

Kendall shifted in her chair and brought her foot up and shoved it into the shoulder of the two men in front of her, jolting them both in their seats.

"What the fuck?" They both spun in their chairs, looking like they were ready to fight.

"Oops, sorry, my leg slipped. Long legs." Kendall pointed down at her thigh. "Hard to get comfy."

The men looked at Kendall's bent legs, then up to her face, where she smiled contritely. Seemingly satisfied it had been an accident, guy number one nodded, then turned back around.

"No problem," replied guy number two.

Peyton glanced over at Kendall, who rolled her eyes. "The last thing on my brother's mind would be getting laid when he does something like that. God, men are so stupid."

"I'm sure it will get lots of women interested," Peyton said.

"Did it make you interested?"

"What?" Peyton blinked over at her.

"You heard me?"

"That's not our agreement," Peyton replied. It really didn't matter if that little run around the bases had been like a shot to her ovaries. Their relationship was fake. He was sexy as sin in the bedroom and a jerk out of it. Well, sometimes he was a jerk. Sometimes he was...

"That's not what I asked you." Kendall pinned her with a stare.

Peyton took another sip of her beer and winced when she realized Kendall was still watching her, waiting for an answer.

The Texas batter walked up to the plate. "Oh good, the game is starting," Peyton said.

"Chicken," Kendall muttered.

Well, she wasn't wrong.

As the game wrapped up with a 6-4 win for the Hawks, Kendall remained seated while the surrounding fans got up from their seats. Peyton stood up.

"Where do you think you're going?" Kendall asked.

"Um, home."

"Not a chance, honey. You're coming downstairs with me. This is a 'be seen' activity. Can't 'be seen' if you don't wait for them to get out of the dressing room." Kendall looked up at her from her seat. "Besides, don't you want to lay claim to your guy so all those women who went gooey over that display don't try to swoop in?"

Peyton's stomach knotted at the idea of a bunch of women throwing themselves at Ryan. "I'm not really a lay your claim kind of girl."

Kendall snorted. "Well, you better become one, fast.

"Is that what you had to do with Pete?"

"Not really no, he shuts things down mighty quick when he gets hit on, but sometimes with some fans it takes a woman's touch to get the point across."

"A woman's touch?"

"Yeah, you know, more delicate" Kendall laced her fingers together and stretched her hands out in front of her like she was cracking her knuckles in preparation for a fight.

Peyton snickered at Kendall's snarling face. There was nothing delicate about that look. "Got it."

Kendall didn't strike Peyton as the kind of woman who would tolerate her partner cheating on her. But then maybe, given that her brother was on the team, that wasn't an issue for her. "With their schedule and how often they're away and the fans, do you ever worry about Pete cheating on you?"

"God, no. I'd rip his nuts off." Kendall shook her head. "But honestly, Pete isn't that kind of guy. It's not something I worry about."

"Hmm."

"He's not," Kendall growled. "Look Peyton, not all guys are like Andy. Sure, there are some assholes on the team, but they aren't all like that. Pete isn't, and my brother sure as hell isn't."

"How do you know?" She hated the insecurity in her own voice, and why did she care? This wasn't real, so it didn't matter anyway.

"Some things you just know. Besides why would you be with someone you can't trust?"

"Well, it doesn't matter anyway because Ryan and I aren't anything."

"You sure about that?" Kendall asked.

"Absolutely."

Kendall pushed up out of her seat. "Well, alright then, let's go find out."

Peyton stood up and followed Kendall through the stadium. She flashed some sort of ID to the security guard to let them through the gate marked private. Fans surrounded the fence line, waiting for a chance to get an autograph from their favorite players.

After several minutes, players began exiting the change room. Peyton's heart pounded in her chest. What was that about? She was acting like a giddy fan. In an effort to look nonchalant, she shoved her hands in the pockets of her jeans and watched the byplay of fans vying for players' attention as they screamed through the gate.

Kendall pushed off from the wall the second she saw Pete, leaving Peyton alone. The man that had been walking beside Pete walked toward her. "Hi there," he said as he stopped in front of her.

"Hi?" She looked at him in confusion. Did she know him?

"Fuck off, Bryce." At the sound of the deep masculine voice, the man in front of her turned.

"Seriously, Graves?"

"Seriously. So fuck off," Ryan said again.

Peyton chewed her bottom lip as she looked at Ryan. Why did he have to look so good? And why was he looking at her like that? Should they hug? Kiss? God, she was a mess.

Ryan walked up to her and cupped the back of her head and pulled her toward him. She briefly heard him say, "Just go with it." A moment before his mouth hit hers.

She sucked in a breath. Wow!

Her lips tingled as he pulled away. The kiss that should have been nothing. It was just a light peck, so why was she feeling so rattled? And why were her freakin' nipples so tight?

When she looked up, Ryan was staring down at her with a slight smirk on his face. Arrogant jerk. Annoyed that the kiss had seemingly no effect on him, she scowled.

"You ready?" he asked.

"For what?"

The arrogant smile on his face grew. He draped his arm around her shoulder like he'd done it a million times. The absent gesture staking a claim for everyone to see. He was a lot better at this game than she was.

As they walked by the women lining the fence, she winced when she saw the look on their faces. Jealousy, malice, judgment. Okay, that she could do without. Where did they get off? What was wrong with people?

Outside, Ryan glanced around. "Where are you parked?"

"Oh, you don't have to do all this." She waved her hand around absently.

"All what?"

"The whole doting boyfriend thing," she replied. This was so awkward. Maybe they should have discussed post-sex-fake-relationship protocol. Did he think they'd have sex every time they saw each other? Did she want to? Kind of, but did he? She bit down a growl of frustration. This was ridiculous.

Ryan scanned the parking lot, his gaze lingering on a group of people watching them. "Uh yeah I kind of do."

"I parked at work and walked over."

Ryan's eyes widened. "Why wouldn't you park closer?"

"It's close. It's free." Peyton shrugged. "Daytime game, why not?"

"Okay, well, at least let me drive you to your car."

"Honestly, Ryan, it's unnecessary."

"I don't mind." He looked back at the group of bystanders who now had their phones out and aimed at them. "Besides, it probably looks better if people see us leave together."

"Sure, thanks."

"No problem. I'm just over here." He gestured toward a large black SUV. Ryan shifted his bag up on his shoulder as they walked toward his car. "So about kissing you."

She'd wondered if he was going to address that elephant in the room. "Mmm hmm."

"Just lots of prying eyes. I tried to make it as quick and painless as possible."

"No biggie, I should have expected it." What she hadn't been expecting was how that brief touch of his lips had made her feel. How she'd wanted him to sweep his tongue in her mouth and take a deeper kiss. The second his mouth had touched hers, she'd instantly been transported back to the night they'd had sex. Which was weird considering how chaste the peck had been. Why he affected her this way, she had no idea. She watched him as he opened the hatch of his vehicle and threw his bag in the trunk. His muscles clenched and rippled beneath the fabric. Okay, so perhaps she had some idea why she'd reacted that way. Holy smokes.

She slid into the passenger seat. Dang, the leather was soft. There were definitely some perks to a luxury SUV. She ran her hand over the leather seat. Sure was a lot nicer than her fabric seat covers.

Ryan turned on the vehicle and backed out of the stall. "Thanks for coming today."

"I'm glad I did. That was really sweet what you did for that little boy."

He shrugged like it was no big deal. "He was pretty bummed he couldn't throw it over the plate. When I visited him in the hospital, we'd talked about how big the stadium was and how cool it was to hit a home run and have fans cheering for you." A smile quirked up from the corner of his lips. "I figured the pitch wasn't what he wanted, but I could at least give him something that was close to the feeling of hitting a home run."

"I'm sure it meant the world to him."

He flicked a glance over at her. "I think wearing the jacket was a bigger thrill. I felt a little bad that we didn't dump the jug over his head. He kept looking over his shoulders, hoping someone would pour it over him." He laughed. "Somehow, I don't think his mom would have felt the same. That shit is cold."

Peyton giggled. "Hard to say. She'd probably deal with pretty much anything if it made her son smile like he did today."

Ryan's smile grew. "Yeah, it was pretty awesome."

He pulled the car into the parking lot of Kidsplay and stopped beside her car, since it was the only one in the lot.

"Thanks for the ride." Peyton looked over at him. Why did this feel so awkward?

"Yep." He tapped the steering wheel absently with his thumb. "We're heading out tomorrow for the next road series."

"Good luck." Okay, this was ridiculous. It wasn't like this was a date, so why was she acting like it had been? How pathetic. She pushed open the passenger door. "Any idea when you might need another fake date?"

His face scrunched up. "Hopefully not anytime soon."

Peyton's head snapped back. Ouch. That was kind of brutal.

"Fuck." He grimaced. "That didn't come out how I'd intended. I just meant, well, you know what I meant, you're stuck fake dating me too."

She stepped out of the car. "Well, keep me posted."

"Shit," Ryan muttered. "This is stupid. Do you want to grab some food or something?"

"Umm..." She chewed her bottom lip. Was that a good idea?

"Jesus, Peyton, it's a fucking meal, not an engagement. This whole thing is so awkward." He sighed. "Maybe if we hung out a bit and got to know each other it wouldn't feel so weird every time we saw each other."

"That's the problem though. It doesn't always feel weird."

His eyes heated as he looked at her. "True. The sex was unreal. That's been the only good thing about this ridiculous arrangement."

"Is that why you want to get something to eat? You're hoping to have sex again?"

He shrugged. "I definitely wouldn't be opposed to having sex with you any chance I could get, but no that's not why I asked you to eat." His muscular forearm flexed as he shifted his weight in his seat. "Coming out of the change room today and seeing you there. I didn't have the first clue how I was supposed to act. Kiss you, don't kiss you. I don't question myself when it comes to women." He rolled his eyes. "I realize I sound like a dick saying that, but it's true. As amazing as the whole sex thing was, it kind of fucked up my thought process when I saw you. Maybe if we eat and get to know each other away from prying eyes and obligations things will be less weird."

"Less weird sounds good."

"Cool."

"There's a good Italian place just down the block from my apartment. L'Isola Bella."

"Sounds good. I'll meet you there," he told her.

She shut the car door and walked toward her car. Clicking the lock, she opened the door and slid inside. She glanced at Ryan's car as it sat idling in the parking stall beside her. When she fired her car to life, he pulled away. Had he been waiting to make sure her car started safely? No, that was stupid. He wasn't that sweet of a guy. He probably had just been checking his phone or something. Ryan was right. They were both overthinking everything way too much.

CHAPTER NINE

Ryan walked up to the bistro in Little Italy Peyton had suggested. A handful of tables covered in red checkered tablecloths made up the outdoor seating area. A large awning extended over the sidewalk, ensuring guests were protected from the California sun. Was Peyton an inside or outside kind of girl? Fucking ridiculous. This was exactly why they needed to get to know each other. When he'd first agreed to this thing, he hadn't given two shits about what she liked. His goal was to get in and out of these dates as painlessly as possible. Sex had kind of gummed up the works.

His body was instantly alert as he watched Peyton walk across the parking lot toward him. He couldn't take his eyes off her. Ignoring the chemistry between them hadn't been an option. Getting to fuck Peyton was the only good thing about this whole messed up arrangement.

If he had his way, they'd be having plenty more of it too. Unfortunately, at the moment the only thing on his mind was fucking her, which wasn't a problem in and of itself, but it sure as fuck made things awkward at social events when he didn't know the first thing about the woman. Including something as simple as whether she liked to sit inside or out. That was something a supposedly doting boyfriend would know.

"Hey," he said when she walked up beside him.

"How come you didn't grab a table?"

"I didn't know if you wanted inside or out."

Peyton cocked her head to the side and studied him. "It didn't occur to me you'd care which I preferred," she replied.

"Go figure." He shrugged. "So, which is it?"

"Out would be great. They usually keep the air conditioning cranked inside, so you practically need a sweater to sit indoors."

"Out it is." He pulled open the front door of the restaurant and walked up to the hostess stand. "Two, outside please."

Seated at the table in the middle of the outdoor seating area, Ryan picked up his menu. "What's good here?"

"I usually get pasta."

He glanced over at the only other occupied table outside and wrinkled his nose as he looked at the plate of pasta. There was no way that would fill him up. After a game, he was ravenous and needed protein. Lots and lots of protein. "You into appies?" he asked.

"Like to share?" she asked.

"Yeah. Why are you looking at me like that's a weird thing to ask?"

"I don't know. I didn't think we were really there."

"Where? Sharing food?" What the hell was she on about?

"Yeah, I mean that's kind of..." she broke off.

"Jesus, Peyton, I've had my dick in your mouth. I'd say we are past the point of whether or not we can share food."

She scowled at him. "You don't have to be crass."

Was she for real? She continued to look at him expectantly. Apparently so. "Sorry. Good to know, you only like a crass mouth in the bedroom."

A rough kick landed square on his shin, and he winced. "Fuck, why'd you kick me?"

"Because you're being a jerk again."

Ryan pinched the bridge of his nose. This had been a bad idea. What happened to the cool chick he'd met at the youth center? Or the woman he'd fucked last weekend? She was back to being the snooty woman who dated Andy. "Sorry," he muttered. They just needed to get through this dinner. Learn a little about each other so they could pass as dating and get out of here.

"I'm sorry," Peyton said. "I'm being as big a jerk as you are."

Ryan bit back a smile at her refusal to swear. "What do you say we start again? I'm ordering an appetizer. You want in on that?"

A shy smile kicked up the corner of her mouth. "Depends on what you're getting."

"Oh, she's being picky now," he teased, enjoying the way Peyton wrinkled her nose at him in a mock scowl.

The server stopped at their table. "Can I get you some drinks or appetizers to start?"

"White wine," Peyton said.

"What do you have on tap?"

The server ran through the list of beers. "Can I get the pale ale, and can we also get some bruschetta and like a Caesar salad to start?"

"Actually, can we do the house salad instead?" Peyton asked. She looked over at him. "Trust me, it's bomb."

"Okay, house salad it is. Thanks."

Ryan leaned back in his chair and kicked his legs off to the side so he could stretch out his 6-foot-3 frame without giving Peyton the boots under the table. "So how long have you run Kidsplay?"

"I've been working there about five years, running it for two."

"You seem pretty young to be in charge of a place like that."

Peyton smiled at the server as she set their drinks on the table. "I am, but I've worked really hard to prove myself. The managers of most of the other agencies are significantly older than I am, and they don't always believe someone my age would know what they are doing."

"But you've proved them wrong."

Peyton's chest puffed up with confidence. "I have. I'm not going to lie. Earning the contract with the Hawks is a big win for me. I have some really great ideas for the program, and I'm thrilled that the team agreed with my vision."

Ryan's shoulders stiffened. "Did Andy have much to do with that decision?"

Peyton sighed. "Some, I guess, yeah." She placed her hands on the table. "Look let's just clear the air here. Yes, I met Simon because of my job, and yes, to a degree, I'm sure he had a hand in us getting the contract, but not as much as you think. When he talked to me, he really liked the program at the San Diego Youth Center. I may have used that to my advantage in my pitch because I was able to reference all the things he said about why he was leaning that way to my advantage to point out why our team was a better choice. Maybe that was shady of me but—" She shrugged. "My program means a lot to me, and I'm not above using any advantage I can get, but truthfully I did the same thing with the information Kirsty told me, so I didn't see it as doing anything wrong. Although I probably should have waited to date Simon, Andy, whatever he goes by." She flicked her wrist absently. "But I didn't date him because I wanted to lock in the contract. That's not the kind of advantage I'd want. I wouldn't be able to live with myself. Sheesh, I don't even swear around the kids—I'm sure as sugar not going to have sex with someone to lock a contract for them."

He bit back a smile at her language. "Sure as sugar?"

"Shut up." She lightly kicked him on the leg again. Except this time, it felt flirtatious rather than aggressive.

"So why did you date him?"

"Honestly, now that I've seen the real him, I have no idea. If I'd had any idea what a jerk he was, I never would have given him the time of day."

"You seem like someone who cuts through the bullshit pretty easily. I'm surprised you couldn't see his from a mile away."

Peyton picked up her drink and took a sip. "Me too. I'm not sure where my head was at. I just wanted to believe he was a good guy. He spouted all this stuff about the importance of youth in sports and keeping kids out of trouble. It sounded like he could relate to the needs of the program, and I guess I just saw what I wanted to see."

"You didn't seem to have that same problem when it came to me." He raised his eyebrows as he remembered their first encounter where she'd demanded he stop the car on the side of the road.

"Hmm, but the difference is you weren't trying to play me. There was no doubt in my mind what you thought of me."

He winced. "Sorry about that. In hindsight, I could have been less of a dick."

Peyton laughed. "It's all good. Unintentionally dating a married man was not my finest hour."

"Glad to hear it." He took a sip of his beer, letting the malty hops linger in his mouth for a moment before he swallowed it down.

The server set down their appetizers on the middle of the table, and he eyed the salad Peyton had ordered. It looked damn good with the olives, huge croutons, ricotta, and some kind of pickled pepper.

"Did you want to divide this up onto plates?" she asked.

"Jesus, woman, just dig into the damn thing." He stuck his fork into the salad and stabbed some lettuce and onion and took a bite. "It's good." He wiggled his fork toward her to indicate she should eat.

Peyton rolled her eyes, then dug her fork into the salad as well. They ate in companionable silence for several minutes before he spoke. "So, I never asked, how are things with Andy when he comes by the center?"

"Mmm, they're fine now. He um, he wasn't great at being told it was over, so we had a few bumps dealing with that. Now he's just pouting." She snickered. "He basically took his ball and left."

"What do you mean?"

"He told Kirsty he didn't want to volunteer at the center."

"Seriously? Like at all?"

"Nope. Apparently, he's too busy with his other projects." Peyton picked up her glass of wine and swirled the liquid around the glass. "Honestly, I can't say that I'm too upset about it. If he doesn't volunteer, that means Carmella won't either, which is good. I was not looking forward to having to see her and lie, and it's not like I could admit what happened." She shuddered. "It would have been a nightmare. No, this is definitely better. For once, the fact he's a spoiled idiot came in handy."

"You're not upset the kids won't get to know him?"

"Nah, not really. When I envision the partnership, I want the kids to learn that people with money and fame can still be kind and generous. Now that I know Andy, I realize that's not who he is, so I'd rather we didn't have a bunch of fake people mentoring the kids. Maybe I'm kidding myself about how this will all play out, but that's the dream." She smiled over at him. "I've never seen the kids as animated as they were with you. That's what I want. Athletes who use their fame to do something good. To really show the kids how to be the kind of humans they should be."

"Not asking for much, are ya?"

Peyton shrugged. "I don't think so. You guys have all this power and influence just by existing, which is kind of wild and you could do so much good with it. I'm simply trying to cash in on that for my kids."

"But no pressure," Ryan teased. As she looked at him, he understood the weight of what this program really meant. She was right. It had the potential to be amazing if the guys got on board and really bought in. He loved the idea of impacting these kids in a positive way. "Well, I guess it's a good thing your fake boyfriend is so cool."

Peyton snorted. "Good thing."

"So, I'm curious how come you didn't sleep with Andy after a month, but you had sex with me the first night."

The server let out a rough cough to announce themselves, and he winced. Shit, not the best timing to ask that.

The server gave him an apologetic smile and placed their meals down on the table. After several minutes of companionable silence, he glanced around to make sure they wouldn't be interrupted again then asked, "You gonna answer the question?"

Peyton set down her fork. "I don't know. It's not just one thing." She shifted in her seat. "With you I knew it was just sex—it didn't mean anything. With Andy, I kind of thought we were potentially building something."

"Ouch, I can't believe you were just using me for my body." He rubbed his chest like it hurt. "I feel so cheap."

"Shut up."

He snickered. "You said there was more than one reason. What else?"

Peyton's cheeks grew red, and she picked up her fork and absently picked at her food.

"Come on spill it, Sharp. What else?" Why was she acting shy all of a sudden?

"Because you're hot okay?"

He barked out a laugh. "Wow, you don't have to sound so annoyed about that."

"I'm not annoyed it's just...I've never had this kind of chemistry with someone before."

He couldn't help himself when he puffed up his chest. "You just couldn't resist my sexy bod, hey?"

She chucked her napkin at him, hitting him in the chest with the piece of linen.

He picked up the napkin and set it back on the table. "I'm just bugging you, Peyton."

"You're bugging me alright," she muttered, making him laugh again.

He shook his head. "I'm offended that I'm just a piece of meat to you. Good enough to fuck, but not good enough to date." He almost pulled it off, but he cracked a smile at the very end.

"It's not that I think you're not good enough it's just..." She paused. "I hadn't dated anyone in almost three years when I started seeing Simon and look where that got me."

"Whoa, why haven't you dated anyone in three years?"

"Well, like you said, running a non-profit program at my age doesn't come without hard work, so something had to give, and that seemed to be my social life. With Simon's schedule, he was away so much it made dating seem like a possibility, but I don't know." She sighed. "I'm out of practice, and I wasn't entirely sure what my feelings were about him. At first, I didn't want to rush things, and he was really sweet and seemed fine with that. I'm not too proud to admit my ego liked being pursued by him and knowing he liked me enough to wait."

"Any guy you're dating should like you enough to wait until you're ready Peyton, that shouldn't be unusual."

"Well, unfortunately, in my experience it is." She pursed her lips. "Then when we almost had sex and got interrupted, he was a jerk, reminding me more of the guys I used to date and suddenly I remembered all the reasons I hadn't been dating. Then at the party, I really found out who he was and I'm not all that interested in trusting anyone like that again."

"I can see that, but not every guy is like Andy. You trusted me the other night."

Peyton blushed and dipped her head slightly. "That's different. That was sex, not a relationship."

"I don't know. I think the fact you don't want to date me, but you do want to fuck me is a good thing." He set his own napkin on the table and leaned back in his chair. "Hear me out. You're not ready for a relationship and I sure as hell don't want one. According to you, all I have going for me is my bedroom skills. Maybe you should take advantage of those while you have the chance, work your way up to trusting someone with more than just sex."

"Oh I should? Should I?" Peyton smirked. "And what did you have in mind exactly?"

"Like you said. The Hawks' schedule is crazy, but so is yours. I don't have that many things I need a date for in the next few months, but I can absolutely see the benefit to us meeting up regularly to enjoy this chemistry, as you put it."

"So what? Instead of being a fake couple, we'd be sex buddies?"

"Exactly, sex buddies who also fake date when necessary. You learn to trust a little and I'm more than willing offer up my body for the cause." He raised his eyebrows and smiled.

"How gracious of you." Peyton rolled her eyes. She sat forward, resting her elbow on the table. "Don't you think that would complicate things even more than we already have?"

"Why would it? Do you plan on falling in love with me?" He smirked.

Peyton snorted. She actually fucking snorted, like the idea was ludicrous.

"Uh, no, definitely not."

He winced a little. A simple no would have sufficed. Shaking it off, he sat up straight. "So, what do you say? When I'm in town between games, we hook up and blow off some steam?"

Peyton chewed on her bottom lip and watched him for several seconds. She picked up her glass of wine and took a drink then set it down and still didn't say a peep. What the fuck? Was it really that hard of a decision?

Finally, a sexy smiled curled up her mouth and her eyes heated. "I definitely think we should blow off some steam. Lots and lots of steam."

"Check please," he called and held up his hand.

Peyton lay sprawled across Ryan's chest, absently tracing her fingers along the ridges of his abdominal muscles as they flexed each time she dragged her nails lightly over his skin. Who knew he was so ticklish?

The past six weeks or so had been amazing. Fake boyfriend or not, she'd never been in any kind of relationship that was anywhere close to as amazing as what they had. Sure, they didn't go out all that often and maybe they spent an obscene amount of time in bed, but who could blame them when the sex was this flippin' good?

In the beginning, he'd barely stuck around after having sex, but for the past month or so whenever he came over, he stayed. It almost felt like an actual relationship. Not that they'd ever talked about altering their original agreement. But honestly, did they need to when it felt like this?

Ryan's fingers combed through her hair, and she closed her eyes. Now she understood why cats purred. It felt so good.

"How's it going with Kirsty? You guys plotting all the ways you can make the team participate?" he asked.

"It's coming together. I think if your teammates jump on board like Kirsty thinks they will, it's going to be amazing."

"They will."

She pushed herself up on his chest so she could look at his face. "How do you know?"

"Come on, Peyton, you know how cool your program is. Once the guys get over there and start getting to know some of those kids, they'll be all in." He continued to comb his fingers through her hair. "Besides, if they don't, I'll kick their ass," he said with a wink.

"Do you think it will come to that?" She really wanted this program to be a success. Now that the kids and the neighborhood knew about the program, she'd been fielding questions left, right and center. She couldn't stand the idea of letting the kids down.

"Nah, I mean I'm not going to lie. Not all the guys on the team are as cool as me." He waggled his eyebrows at her. "So, I don't think they'll have the same in as I do, but you work with what you've got."

Ryan really enjoyed spending time with the teens, which surprised her since they were hard and rough and not always pleasant to outsiders. But somehow her toughest kids seemed to gravitate toward him. And for a couple of them, Ryan was the first positive experience with a man in a position of authority. Already he'd made a difference and the program hadn't even begun. And that was only with one person. She could only imagine how amazing it would be with the entire team.

"Smitty was asking me if you planned to do some camps. He's all over dominating the tee ball league."

"Oh yeah? He feels that's where he'll really shine?"

"Apparently."

"I'm glad you guys were talking about the program and getting excited."

"I wouldn't say that. They were being nosey and asking about us, so the program came up."

She bit back her smile. It had to be a good sign that he was talking to his friends about her. "You were talking about me to your friends. What'd you say?"

"You mean besides how insatiable you are in bed?"

She pushed up and glared at him. "You did not say that."

Seriously, he better not have.

"No, but I told them what a great rack you have."

Peyton's eyes widened. "Oh my god, you didn't."

Ryan chuckled. "You're so easy. Of course I didn't." He gave her a light shove, so she was laying back down on his chest. "I told them you were cool, then I talked about your program, and they're looking forward to helping out."

He began rubbing his fingers into her scalp, and she couldn't help the moan that slid out of her. "You like that?" he asked, pressing his fingers into her scalp like they did at the hairdresser.

"Mmm, that feels amazing. If you ever lose your job on the field, I know a salon that will hire you in a heartbeat."

"Good to know I can put scalp massages on my list of marketable skills," he chuckled.

His thumb dug into the base of her skull, and she let out a long, deep moan. "Yes, right there. But harder."

"Damn, I didn't know the way to get you to talk like that was a little massage action."

She smacked him on the chest. "Shut up."

"Hey, I'm not complaining. I think it's hot. I'm just not sure how much longer I'll last if you keep making those noises."

She trailed her hand down his stomach. She'd barely gotten her hand under the sheet when he grabbed her thigh and pulled it over his hip, shifting her body so she was straddling him.

His fingers dug into her hips as he urged her to move forward. "Fuck it, I'll make you moan a different way," he growled. "Now get up here."

CHAPTER TEN

This entire week sucked. After spending most of last night in the emergency room and the better part of today at the hospital with one of her kids, Peyton's body was done. She pulled her car into the parking lot and glanced up at the sign for Ananda Yoga & Wellness Center. Her best friend couldn't have chosen a better name for her wellness center because bliss was exactly what she felt every time she was here. A session with Rayne was exactly what she needed after a day like today. Clear out the garbage and let the day go as best as she could.

She stepped to the side and held the door to let a group of women with babies exit the center. The mom's all looked relaxed and energized. Peyton couldn't help but smile at each of them as they passed. She loved that Rayne had incorporated mommy and me yoga classes into the studio. It was such a great idea, and judging by the number of women leaving, a very popular class.

When she walked in, she immediately saw Rayne and Shyla behind the counter. "Hey girl, you made it. On time and everything," Rayne teased.

"I did. It was touch and go there for a bit, but I'm here," Peyton replied.

"It's good to see you, Peyton. You haven't been here in forever," Shyla said.

"I know. I keep meaning to come to some classes, but life happens." She sighed. "What can you do?"

"Put it in your calendar? That might help," Shyla teased.

"Maybe."

"Maybe," Rayne scoffed. "That thing is like your bible. If it's in your calendar, it's happening."

"Okay, yeah." Peyton laughed. "No, that's totally true."

"Alright, girl, come on back. I've got the treatment room all set up." Rayne gestured toward the hallway that led to the various rooms in the center.

Peyton followed Rayne into the room. Soft, soothing music filled the air, and it smelled amazing.

"What is in that?" Peyton pointed at the diffuser puffing in the corner.

"It's a relaxation blend that I make."

"You make it?" Peyton asked. "Wow, that's amazing, Rayne. Do you sell it?"

"Of course I do." Rayne waggled her eyebrows. "Gotta cash in where I can."

"Yeah, that's you, greedy, greedy, greedy."

"I choose to see if as accepting abundance in all areas of my life," Rayne said. "I have several unique blends that I make, and people kept asking me if they could buy them to take home after their treatments, so I figured I probably should start selling them."

"That's amazing. I didn't know you knew how to do all that." Peyton looked around the room. "Every time

I come here, I'm more and more amazed by everything you do." She wrapped her arms around her childhood friend. "You've really built something to be proud of here, Rayne."

"Who knew that weird little ADHD kid who couldn't pay attention would become this blissed out goddess you see in front of you," Rayne joked.

"Don't laugh. You are a freaking goddess." She squeezed Rayne tighter. "When I feel like garbage, I always know that I can come to you, and I will leave feeling better."

"Thanks, honey." Rayne squeezed her back. "With that said, let's get you cleared. I could see how bogged down your aura was when you walked in. And your energy is feeling really—" She moved her fingers together and rubbed the tips back and forth, then flicked her wrists like she was sweeping it away. "I don't know, heavy, sludgy maybe. Not like you. But that makes sense, given the past few days."

"Sludgy, that's comforting," Peyton mumbled.

"Sorry, I don't always have the best words to describe what it feels like to me. But don't worry. I'll get you sorted out." Rayne walked over to the table and picked up a remote, then the music changed.

Peyton raised her eyebrow at Rayne as a woman's angelic chant began streaming through the speaker.

"Trust me," Rayne said. "It's for sound therapy. I'm going to hit you with everything today. We'll do some reiki and energy clearing, then we'll do some yoga and meditation together at the end. By the time you leave, you'll feel like a new woman."

"I always do." Peyton walked over to the massage table and lowered herself down.

Rayne adjusted the bolsters underneath her knees. "Are you warm enough?"

"I'm good."

"Okay." Rayne closed her eyes, brought her hands out in front of her, and raised them up to her throat as she took a deep breath and exhaled. "Ready?"

"So ready." The music built and Peyton felt a wave of calm rush through her as she closed her eyes and surrendered to the treatment.

Peyton looked around the small yoga studio. How could she feel so completely different in two hours? Amazing. She could completely understand why her friend had chosen this career path. Rayne truly had a gift.

"You're right, I need to regularly attend classes. Let me grab my phone and put it in my calendar because we both know if I don't do that it's not happening."

Peyton grabbed her bag and sat back down on her yoga mat across from Rayne. She dug through her clothes, finally finding her phone at the bottom of the bag.

"Please don't be work," she muttered as she looked at her phone and the missed message showing on the screen.

"You know, you could just not answer it. You aren't on call 24/7. The only person who expects you to be everything to everyone is you." Rayne untangled her legs from her lotus position and stood up in one graceful move. How anyone could just comfortably sit in lotus for hours on end was a mystery, but somehow Rayne made it look so effortless.

"I know, but just in case it's about today, I should check."

Rayne smiled. "Of course you should."

"Thanks for understanding." Peyton took a breath to mentally prepare herself for the possibility of dealing with work, then dialed into her voicemail.

Her heart stuttered when she heard Ryan's voice. What was that about? Why did her stomach catch like that? Maybe having sex with him hadn't been such a great idea. Ryan's voice slid across the phone line.

"Hey, a few of us are going out for a beer after the game, and I thought you might want to meet up with us at Rays. Kendall will be there, and she's hoping you'd come." He paused, and she waited to hear what else he would say. "Yeah, so come. Rays. We'll be there for a while."

Did he want her there? God, why did she care? They were fake dating and okay, now sleeping together, but it wasn't real.

"Agh," she growled and dropped her head into her hands.

"What? Work?" Rayne asked as she handed Peyton a glass of water before sitting back down on the floor across from her.

"No, Ryan called and asked me to meet them for a beer after the game."

"Okay? So why the face?"

"I don't know. Because everything changed, now," she whined. "God, why am being one of those girls? We're having sex, freakin' fantastic sex but sex. It doesn't have to mean anything. Gah, we don't even like each other."

"Don't you?"

"I don't know. Sometimes he seems like he's a good guy, then other times he's so cocky and judgy." She chewed her bottom lip as she pictured him playing catch with Markus. "No, not judgy. He's amazing with the kids and doesn't judge them at all. He's really sweet and patient with them." She sighed. "But with me? Definitely not."

Rayne cocked her head to the side as she pinned Peyton with a stare. "I thought so," Rayne said with a knowing smile.

"What?"

"You really like him."

"No, I don't."

"Honey, your aura and your energy say otherwise," Rayne said.

"Don't be sneak attacking me with that woo woo stuff." Peyton pointed a finger at her friend. "My energy and aura are all blissed out from that treatment and then the yoga and meditation." Peyton rolled her eyes at her friend. "My energy would love just about anything right now, so it's not to be trusted."

"Love?" Rayne smirked. "I didn't say anything about love. I said you liked him." Rayne rubbed her hands together with glee. "We are definitely meeting them for beer. I have to meet this guy who has you all tied up in knots."

"He doesn't have me tied up in knots," Peyton grumbled. "My body is just a bit confused because of the sex."

"Ananda, baby," Rayne said.

"Bliss this." Peyton stuck up her middle finger.

"Ouch, harsh." Rayne jumped up. "Either way, we are going for beers so I can get a better look."

"Fine," Peyton agreed. "But no reading auras or any of that other stuff."

"I'll try my best, but sometimes things just push through."

"Mmm hmm." Peyton shook her head. "Block it or keep it to yourself because I don't want to know."

"Okay. I won't say anything woo woo. I promise." Rayne made an X across her heart. "This is going to be fun."

"Oh god," Peyton groaned. "Let's get this over with."

Ryan flicked his wrist to look at his watch for the umpteenth time.

"Dude, chill. What is up with you tonight?" Pete asked.

"What? Nothing's up with me." He glanced at his sister and three teammates around the table and winced when Gonzo raised his eyebrow.

"Then how come you keep looking at your watch? You got someplace you need to be?" Smitty teased.

God, even Smitty noticed how preoccupied he was. Shit, he must look pre-occupied. "No, I'm just wondering how long I have to stick around with you bums before I can make a break for it." Ryan picked up his beer, ignoring the look he was sure his best friend Pete was giving him.

What he was really wondering was how long he should wait to see if Peyton was actually going to show up or not. He couldn't stop thinking about the last time he'd seen her. When they'd agreed to fake date, the idea of having sex with her hadn't even entered his mind.

Okay, Peyton was gorgeous. Of course, it had entered his mind, but he hadn't really considered it was an option since she hated him. But damn, the sex between them was unreal.

Unfortunately, now he didn't know what the fuck it meant. He still thought she was unbending and snippy, but when she let go... Fuck, he'd never seen anything hotter in his life.

"Well, well, well, look what the cat dragged in." Smitty nudged Ryan's arm.

Following the direction of Smitty's stare, he looked toward the front door. Peyton stood by the hostess table scanning the restaurant. He could tell the exact moment she'd spotted him because her entire body language changed. Even from here he could see the little hitch in her breath a second before she squared her shoulders, flashed him a wave, then turned and said something to the brunette beside her.

The little hitch was interesting. Her need to steel herself before she acknowledged him was also interesting. He just wasn't sure if it was good or bad.

Peyton's hips swayed as she walked across the restaurant. Her ripped jeans hung loosely on her hips, leaving a tiny swatch of skin visible between the waistband and her cropped t-shirt. That teasing glimpse of skin was sexier than anything revealing would have been. Especially now that he'd seen her naked, and he knew exactly what lay beneath her clothes.

"I see how it is," Smitty mumbled.

"What?" Ryan tore his eyes from Peyton and looked at his friend.

"Is this thing real now?"

"Umm..." Ryan licked his lips. How the fuck was he supposed to answer that? Thankfully, Peyton made it to their table, saving him from having to give any kind of response.

"Glad you could make it." Ryan smiled at Peyton as he shoved Smitty further into the booth to make room for Peyton and her friend to slide into the end.

Ryan leaned around Peyton. "Hi, I'm Ryan." He stuck out his palm to shake the other woman's hand.

"Of course you are," the woman replied with a smirk. Peyton elbowed her friend in the side and the woman coughed out a laugh before turning back to Ryan. "I'm Rayne."

"Nice to meet you." Ryan gestured to his buddies around the table. "This is Smitty, Gonzo, my sister Kendall, and Pete."

"Pleasure." Rayne studied him for several moments, then smiled like she was pleased with what she'd seen, and for whatever reason he relaxed. He shouldn't care that he'd somehow passed some mysterious first impression test from Peyton's best friend but he did.

Peyton smacked her hands together. "We need drinks." She looked around the table. Her gaze lingered on his glass of beer.

Ryan bit back a grin. She was nervous, trying to hide it for sure, but definitely nervous. She kept flashing him little sideways glances as she sat beside him. Rayne slid around on the seat to try to get the server's attention. The movement pushed Peyton closer to him on the bench. When her thigh pressed against his, she jumped, then gave a little giggle as she shifted in her seat. With him on one side and Rayne pushing against the other, she wasn't able to move at all. Sure, he could have shifted over to give her space, but he didn't want to.

Peyton turned her head to look at him. Her gaze latched onto his mouth, and she licked her lips. Jesus. He bit back a groan. It took everything in him not to take her lip between his teeth and pull her toward him.

Breaking eye contact, she tried to shift again on the seat. He clamped his hand on her thigh to hold her in place. "Stay," he ordered.

He'd expected her to argue purely because of the tone he'd used. Instead, her eyes darkened slightly, and she nodded in agreement.

Damn. He could not get a handle on who Peyton really was. The feisty woman who'd yelled at him the first time they met, the submissive woman in the bedroom or the barracuda that Andy kept trying to intimate that she was. She was like a puzzle whose pieces didn't quite fit properly, and he couldn't decide if he wanted to rip it up or brute force it together. Somehow this woman had gotten in his head, invading his thoughts and he never let that happen.

"So, how was your game?" Peyton angled herself to look at him. "Did you win?"

"Yeah, it was close, but we pulled it out." Ryan rolled his shoulders. Even though he hadn't played tonight his shoulders were tense. Sitting, watching, wishing he was in the game was always hard even when they pulled out the win.

"Who pitched tonight?" Peyton asked.

He rolled his shoulders again. "Johnny."

Peyton wrinkled her nose at the mention of his teammate.

"I thought you were the pitcher," Rayne cut in.

Clearly, the woman was not a baseball fan. "I'm just one of many pitchers on the team."

Rayne's forehead wrinkled in confusion. "Hang on, you don't play all the time?"

"Nah, he's soft, has to rest his delicate little arms so he only plays part-time," Gonzo teased.

"Really? You only play like half the time?" Rayne's forehead wrinkled as she looked at him.

"Yeah, about that, give or take."

Smitty snorted beside him. "What?" Ryan sat up straighter in the booth as he looked at the other man.

"I don't know. Hearing it like that, I feel like I'm underpaid, or maybe you're overpaid. I'm not sure which," Smitty said.

Rayne's brow knit with confusion. "I thought you were like this big shot pitcher. Wouldn't your team want you to pitch more often if you're that good?"

"I'm no good to anybody if I'm hurt." Ryan picked up his beer and took a sip. Shit, he knew it was a safety thing, but hearing her question it like that with his friends teasing him, he almost felt like he needed to defend himself.

Peyton shifted as she turned to face her best friend. "Ryan's fastball is ridiculous. It's over 100 miles an hour. You can't do that all the time, or you'll wreck your arm. The league has done all kinds of research on how many pitches they think are safe to throw in a game and no-body pitches full-time."

Gonzo's bottom lip jutted out slightly as he pursed his lips, his head bobbing up and down in approval. "Wow, your girl has done her research."

Peyton wrinkled her nose at him. "I knew this before I met Ryan. Thank you very much."

Rayne gaped at him with wide eyes. Her mouth hanging partway open. "You can seriously throw the ball faster than 100 miles an hour? How is that possible?"

Ryan shrugged.

"How do you know how fast you throw?" Rayne continued.

"They clock each pitch." He still remembered how nervous he'd been the first time someone told him they wanted to clock his fastball. Ryan had seen the gun and completely choked. Now it wasn't something he even gave any thought to. It was as much a part of the game as reporting a batting average.

"Wow, that's impressive. I didn't know that was possible." Rayne shifted in her seat to face the rest of the table. "So, what positions do you all play?"

"I play shortstop." Pete flicked his thumb, pointing beside him. "Gonzo is third and Smitty is center field."

"But you guys play every game, right?" Rayne asked.

Gonzo nodded. "For the most part, we get to rest the odd game."

"That's so cool. I've never met anyone who played a professional sport before," Rayne told them.

Picking up her drink, Kendall held the glass in her hand, speaking before she even brought it to her mouth. "What is it you do, Rayne?"

"I run a wellness center."

Kendall sipped her drink and set it back down on the table. "Like a medical center."

Rayne snickered. "No, no. I teach yoga and do energy healing."

"Energy healing? What's that?" Before Rayne had said it, Ryan hadn't even known that was a real thing.

"Reiki, breathwork, chakras, that kind of thing." Rayne paused and looked around the table. "It's a bit woo woo for most people."

"I don't know what any of that means." Ryan stared at Rayne. She may as well of been talking a different language because he didn't have the faintest idea what she was talking about. What the fuck were chakras?

Rayne laughed. "Not many people do. Mostly I help people clear energy and emotion through their body, so everything works smoother."

Peyton leaned over and rested her head on Rayne's shoulder. "She did a treatment on me tonight, and it was amazing. I was blissed out when she was done."

"Blissed out, huh?" Ryan's dick twitched at the satisfied way Peyton described how relaxed she felt. Her voice had gone all soft and husky. *Fuck, she was sexy.*

Peyton lifted her head from Rayne's shoulder and shifted closer to him. "Yep, blissed out. You should have been there."

"I'm sorry I missed it." He'd seen what she looked like post orgasm. Did whatever it was Rayne did make her face look the same? Damn, he really wished he'd seen her post woo woo whatever.

"Sign me up," Gonzo said.

Rayne pushed her hair off the side of her face. The bangles on her arm clinked together as she moved.. "I know it sounds a bit strange, but it really works."

"Oh no, I'm totally down for anything that Peyton says makes her feel blissed out. Plus, you do yoga, so that means you're like super bendy, right?" Gonzo waggled his eyebrows and grinned.

"No," Ryan growled at him.

"What?" Gonzo raised his palms in question. The picture of innocence as he blinked at Ryan.

"Just, no." Ryan stared down his teammate. Gonzo was not hitting on Peyton's best friend. He was still trying to figure out what the hell was going on with them. The last thing he needed was Gonzo hooking up with Peyton's friend and things getting awkward when they went their separate ways.

"How many drinks have you had?" Ryan asked Gonzo.

"I don't know a couple. Why?"

"Bendy, Jesus," Ryan muttered. "You're switching to water."

Gonzo chuckled. "Message received, Ry. I hear ya."

He felt Peyton stiffen beside him. Following her gaze, he spotted Andy and Johnny in the corner playing pool with a group of women fawning all over them. Honestly, could he really blame Peyton for not knowing the guy was married? Both he and Johnny certainly acted single.

"He's unbelievable." Peyton shook her head as she stared towards the back of the bar.

"Who?" Rayne's attention snapped back toward Peyton.

"Simon."

Rayne pivoted in her seat. "He's here? Which one is he?"

"The dark-haired guy playing pool with the blonde wrapped around him," Peyton replied.

Rayne's face scrunched up like she'd sucked a bucket of lemons. "Ew."

Kendall snorted loudly. "Looks like you're an upgrade, bro."

Rayne spun back toward him. "Oh my gosh, you are an upgrade for so many reasons. The fact you're actually single is just one of them." She turned to Peyton. "Seriously, Pey, really?"

"Obviously now I can see how skeezy he is, but he seemed nice at the time."

"Yep, Andy's a real gem," Pete said, eliciting a laugh from Gonzo and Smitty.

"His aura is all mucky and gross." Rayne stared at Peyton. "You really couldn't feel that after all the times I've made you go to events with me?"

Peyton squirmed on the seat beside him as everyone watched her, waiting for a response. Ryan shifted so their fingers touched against the bench and her hand twitched, moving closer to his.

He looked over at Andy. Sure, the guy was a dick, but as far as he could see there was nothing visibly gross or whatever Rayne had said about him. Could Peyton see that kind of thing too? Rayne seemed surprised she hadn't noticed it, but if she could why didn't she avoid Andy?

"Okay, so this aura thing, how's that work? What's mine look like?" Ryan wasn't sure what it was supposed to look like, but how she described Andy's didn't sound good.

Rayne turned to Peyton. "Is it okay if I do this?"

"What?" Peyton's brow wrinkled in confusion. "Of course. He asked. He obviously wants to know."

"Why wouldn't it be okay?" Smitty asked.

"Long story." Rayne waved her hand effectively brushing off the question. She turned to Ryan. The corners of her eyes crinkled slightly as her expression softened. "Yours looks good. You definitely have a guarded energy, but your aura is warm and clear. Can I take your hand?"

"Uh, yeah sure." Ryan slid his hand across the table.

Rayne picked up his hand and closed her eyes. After several moments, she opened them. She looked at Peyton, smiled and nodded as if some silent communication passed between the two women. Ryan shifted uncomfortably. He wasn't even sure if he believed in all this crap, and suddenly he was nervous about what she might say she'd felt.

"So, what's your read on our boy here?" Pete rubbed his hands together. "Is he good?"

"I'd say you are hardworking, determined. Probably a bit of a perfectionist." Rayne studied him. "Loyal and warm, but don't trust people easily."

Ryan shifted in the seat, looking for an exit. *Jesus.*

"Holy shit." Pete's mouth dropped open. "You got all that from his aura, or whatever?"

"His aura, his energy." Rayne fiddled with her beaded bracelet. The little rocks clicked together as she spun it on her wrist. "It's not an exact science or anything, more of a feeling."

"It's pretty bang on," Pete said. "I've never heard of this stuff before but damn."

"Do you have like a card or something? Because I am totally coming to see you," Kendall leaned forward, clasping her hands on top of the table. "That's amazing."

"Just wait until you have a treatment." Peyton's shoulders drew up and she closed her eyes like she was getting all cozy. "Mmm."

Rayne blushed, then shyly reached into her purse and handed Kendall a card.

"Well, well, what do we have here?" Andy's voice interrupted.

Peyton tensed beside him. Ryan wanted to wrap his arm around her and pull her closer to him to get her as far away from Andy as possible, but he didn't. Couldn't. She wasn't really his to protect, and from what he'd learned about Peyton in the past few weeks, she was strong enough to stand on her own two feet. He didn't know anything about auras, but mucky and gross was a good way to describe the other man.

"It's nice to see you, Peyton." Andy tried to push himself closer to her by leaning in front of Rayne.

Rayne puffed up her body. "Sorry, can you move back a bit? You're blocking my drink."

Andy glared at her but didn't move. Rayne placed her hand near Andy's shoulder and flicked her hand like he was an annoying gnat or something. "Seriously dude, boundaries. A little space please."

Ryan bit back a laugh. Rayne might look all ethereal and shy, but the woman had some balls he'd give her that.

Andy scowled at Rayne as he stood up, then honed in on Peyton again. "What are you doing here?"

"Having a drink?" Peyton replied.

"I see that but, why are you here?"

Oh, fuck this shit. Ryan cupped the back of Peyton's neck. "Because I asked her"

When Peyton leaned into him, resting her weight against him, he breathed a sigh of relief. When he'd touched her, he hadn't known whether she'd welcome the support or elbow him in the gut.

Anger radiated off Andy as he glared at him. Well, screw him. He was the one who'd cheated on his wife and needed rescuing. It's not like he had anyone but himself to blame for this situation.

The blonde from the pool table walked up and saddled up beside Andy. "Simon." She pressed her breasts against Andy's arm.

"Yeah." Andy absently flicked a glance at the blonde before glaring back at Ryan. And just to rub a little salt in the wound and because he could, Ryan teased her earring with his fingers as he continued to cup the back of her neck. Peyton shivered beneath his touch, and from the way Andy's nostrils flared he'd seen the way her body reacted.

"When are you coming back? It's lonely over there without you," the blonde whined.

"I'll be right there, babe," Andy told her. "I'm just chatting with my teammates."

The blonde straightened up and stared around the table.

"Jesus," Smitty muttered quietly beside him. It was like seeing a predator who'd caught a scent. *How the hell did Andy go from Peyton to that?*

"Oh my god, you're Ryan Graves," the blonde gushed. "I just love you."

Shoving away from the table, Andy pushed so hard the drinks shook on the surface. "I'm done here."

Ryan could practically feel the animosity coming off Andy in waves. Maybe he knew what Rayne was talking about after all.

"Just a second," blondie said. She flicked a glance at Andy before focusing back on Ryan. Blondie leaned forward, putting her ample rack on full display for the table. "You're so much cuter in person."

"Thanks, but as you can see, I'm with someone." He wrapped his arm fully over Peyton's shoulder.

"That's okay. I don't mind." The blonde chewed on her bottom lip in a practiced move as she continued to stare at him.

"Really?" Peyton growled at the woman.

"Let's go," Andy snarled as he grabbed the blonde's arm.

She teetered on her feet and giggled when she stumbled into Andy. She looked up at Andy and licked her lips. "Alright, Simon, what do you say we get out of here?"

Andy looked at Peyton, then back at the blonde. "Sounds good." He turned, taking the blonde with him and held up his hand in a wave. "Later chumps," he called back to their table.

"He's such a douche," Smitty said as Andy and the blonde walked away.

Rayne wrinkled her nose in disgust. "I'll just say it again, Peyton. Ew."

"Yeah, I have no excuse. He's umm... yeah, ew." Peyton shook her head. "I have no words. All I can say in my defense is he was apparently on his best behavior when I met him because believe me, I would never have given him a second look if that had been the person I met."

"Unfortunately, that asshole is the only one we've ever seen," Gonzo said. "Not to be dick, but you don't seem like the normal girls he goes for. So, I'm gonna have to give you the benefit of the doubt that he had to be different with you because otherwise it doesn't really make a hell of a lot of sense."

"Agreed." Kendall scrunched up her face. "He's gross and you're great. Good riddance."

"And on that note, I'm going to take off." Rayne reached behind her and unhooked her purse strap from the back of the chair. "I have an early class tomorrow and a full day, so I need to get some sleep." She turned to Peyton. "You coming with me or—?" She looked at Ryan over Peyton's shoulder.

Peyton glanced at him, then turned back to her friend. Ryan held his breath while he waited for her to answer. He really fucking wanted her to stay but wasn't sure where she was at with things. They hadn't ever discussed nights like this. There was a big difference between hooking up at her place and going home with him after getting to know his friends. "I'll catch a ride with Ryan."

He breathed a sigh of relief and squeezed her knee in agreement.

Peyton leaned over and hugged her friend. "Call me tomorrow?"

"Will do," Rayne replied. She stood up and looked around the table. "It was really great meeting you all."

"You too," Ryan said. Shit, now that he knew Peyton had stayed with him, he really wanted to get out of here and take her back to his place. How long did they actually have to stay?

CHAPTER ELEVEN

After about twenty minutes, Ryan had had enough. Sitting beside Peyton was driving him crazy. He set his hand on her knee and gave her a little squeeze. She turned and looked at him. "You ready to get out of here?" he asked.

"Yeah, if you don't mind. It was a long day."

"No problem." He turned to the rest of the table. "We're out. I'll see you guys tomorrow at the airport. Ken, good luck on the new campaign." He nudged Peyton to slide off the bench.

She exited the booth, then smiled at the group. "Enjoy the rest of your evening. Good luck at the next game."

"Night, Peyton," they all called.

He placed his hand on her lower back and guided her out of the pub and onto the street. "My car is just down here." He pointed to the lot down the block where he'd left it.

Stopping at his car, Ryan caged Peyton against the passenger door. He leaned in and kissed her. What was supposed to be a light peck quickly turned into something more carnal. When he pulled away, they were both breathing heavily. Ryan rested his forehead against hers. "I've been wanting to do that all night."

A soft smile curved up the corner of her full lips. "What happened to casual?"

"This is definitely casual. My brain is only focused on fucking you and nothing else, trust me."

Peyton's deep, throaty chuckle pierced the night air. "Got ya. Casual monkey sex versus like planning a date or something awful like that."

"Exactly." He rested his elbow on the open car door beside her head. "So, you gonna come back to my place with me this time, or would you prefer we go to yours?"

"Kind of presumptuous of you to assume you're getting sex, don't you think?" she teased.

"What can I say? I'm an optimist." He waggled his eyebrows. "I have great visualization skills and imagine the outcome I want."

Peyton snorted out a laugh. "Oh well, god forbid your ability to visualize the outcome should fall short. Maybe you should tell me which location you're gunning for."

"I was thinking it'd be cool to have you at my place. I could drop you off on my way to the airport in the morning. If that works for you."

"Wow, staying over that's different." Her eyebrows raised, then softened as she teased him.

"Don't read anything into it, Peyton. It's purely logistics."

"Logistics?"

"Mmm hmm." He leaned in and ran his tongue up the side of her neck. Enjoying the way her body trembled against him, he placed his mouth against her ear. "I plan to fuck you raw, and we'll both be too tired to move." The moan that escaped her lips instantly made him hard. "Purely logistics. I like to sleep in my own bed. This way I get to fuck you, roll over and go to sleep. Maximum pleasure, maximum rest. It's win-win," he told her.

She snorted out a laugh. "Alright, Romeo." Peyton stood on her tiptoes, pressed a quick kiss against his lips, then ducked under his arm and slid onto the seat. "Let's go."

Ryan rounded the car and hopped into the driver's seat. He pressed the button to turn the car on and the engine roared to life. Peyton's blonde hair shone from the glow of the streetlights. "So, your day kind of sucked, I gather?"

Peyton blinked at him. "Wow, that was not the direction I expected this conversation to go."

"No?"

"Not at all. I was expecting either sex talk or no talk."

"Is that what you'd prefer?" he asked.

"Honestly?" she looked at him consideringly. "Not really. But I don't want to cross into the friend zone here."

"Ah fuck it, boundaries are for pussies. We both know what this is. It's not like us having conversations is going to make me forget that neither of us honestly wants to date the other."

"That's true." Peyton slid deeper into her seat. "You mind if I turn the seat warmer on?"

"Knock yourself out," Ryan told her. Why someone would want a heated ass in the middle of summer was beyond him, but whatever worked for her. "So, what happened today that made you need to do your energy thing with Rayne?"

Peyton shifted and leaned her body partly against the door, so she was facing him. That was one thing he'd noticed about her, and he had to admit he really liked. When Peyton was talking to someone, she was one hundred percent engaged. Her focus was always on the person and nothing else, her phone was never out, she looked at you. In his experience, it was pretty unusual.

"Last night I ended up getting called to go down to the hospital for one of my kids."

"Shit, is everything okay?"

"Not really no. The police couldn't reach her mom, so she gave them my name as an emergency contact."

"Is that something that happens a lot?" Ryan asked.

"Not really, no, but it happens. The kids that come to our program trust us. They know we'll be there so—"

"Going down to the hospital in the middle of the night seems above and beyond."

"Well, like you said, boundaries are for pussies," she said.

"Whoa, shit, did you just say pussy?"

"Shut up." She laughed and smacked his arm. "Anyway, I'm glad I went. No one should be alone after something like that."

"What happened if you don't mind my asking?"

Peyton sat silent for a few breaths, and Ryan wondered if she was going to answer. Finally, she spoke. "She was sexually assaulted."

"Jesus," he muttered.

"Yeah, it was pretty brutal." She paused. "She'd gone to this party after the big rivalry basketball game at her school and, umm... a few of the guys on the opposing team decided that's how they wanted to celebrate."

"Are you fucking kidding me?"

"I wish I was."

"Wait, you said the opposing team? Why was she partying with them?"

"From what I gather, the guys on the other team were cute and asked her and a few of her friends to come to a party. The girls had never been to a party on that side of town, so..." She sighed. "I don't know. Apparently, a girl from the wrong side of the tracks was disposable to them and a whole lot less valuable than they are and that somehow justified them treating her worse than garbage."

"Fuck." Ryan stopped at the light and looked over at Peyton. "That's fucked up, Peyton. I'm really sorry."

"Me too."

How could a group of teenage boys do something like that? Shouldn't at least one of them have tried to stop it? What the fuck was wrong with these kids? "What are the police going to do?"

"Too soon to tell how it will all play out, but we all know money talks. She doesn't have any and they do." Peyton flicked off the seat warmer. "Sorry, this is kind of a depressing conversation. Are you sure you want to hear this?"

"You don't have anything to be sorry for." When the light turned green, he continued toward his house. He was glad he needed to focus on driving. It forced him to detach slightly from the conversation. He couldn't imagine what that must be like for Peyton to sit through that and support someone. "Is she going to be okay?"

"I think so, yeah." Peyton shifted on her seat. The sound of her body moving against the leather seemed so loud in the heavy atmosphere in the car. "She had to have surgery last night, and then this morning we did the statement to the police. So, I spent the day at the hospital. Police still hadn't reached her mom when I left, but she'll be in the hospital for a few days. I'll go check on her tomorrow afternoon."

"Holy shit, I had no idea you had to deal with that kind of thing in your job."

"Who'd of thunk, huh? Sadly, my social work degree gets put to very good use running the program. Thankfully, I don't deal with this kind of thing too often, but it happens."

"Are you sure you want to come back to my place? I'd completely understand if you didn't."

Peyton reached out and squeezed his thigh. "I wouldn't be here if I didn't want to be, Ryan. As awful as this situation was, it isn't my trauma, and I can't let it be or I'd be useless at my job."

"I guess. I just don't know how you do it." How could she see such a horrific side of life and not get sucked into a black hole when she realized how much she couldn't change?

"Some days it's definitely easier than others." She reached over and squeezed his thigh.

"I can't even imagine." He glanced over at her. The more he learned about Peyton, the more he realized his original impression of her had been so far from reality.

He pulled his car up to his driveway and tapped the screen on the dash to open the gate.

"Wow, fancy," Peyton said as they waited for the gate to open fully so he could head up the driveway.

"It's just a gate, Peyton. It's no big deal."

"Only someone who owns a house with a gate would say that." She leaned forward in her seat and stared down the driveway with wide eyes. "Holy cow, you live here by yourself?"

He chuckled. "Who else would live here?"

"I don't know. It's just..." She paused. "It's huge."

He pulled the car up in front of the house, not bothering with putting it in the garage because he'd be using it again in the early morning hours to head to the airport.

By the time he walked around the front of the vehicle, Peyton was already walking toward him.

He placed his hand on her back and guided her up to the front entrance. Opening the front door, he quickly deactivated the alarm. Peyton paused on the threshold of the foyer. Her blue eyes widened like saucers as her gaze darted around the entranceway, taking it all in.

"Wow." The awe in Peyton's voice made him smile. That was what he'd always wanted. Growing up, he'd pictured having a beautiful, big house, with an amazing view and a gate. As a kid, a house with a gate was the ultimate sign someone had made it. He'd only seen houses with gates on TV and movies, and somehow it became the status symbol that meant he'd achieved his dreams. Every time he opened that gate, it reminded him his hard work had paid off. Sure, the house that came along with it was bigger than any one person needed, but he

hoped someday to have a family to fill it. In the mean-
time, he had his gate.

If she thought the entrance was impressive, he
couldn't wait to show her the rest of his home. Grabbing
her hand, he pulled her further inside. As they rounded the corner, it opened into the main living area and
kitchen. Peyton gasped beside him. "Oh my god, this
is unreal. This looks like something on one of those
designer shows on TV."

"I'm sure my decorator will be happy to hear that."

"Of course you have a decorator," she mumbled.

"Hey, now don't say it like that. All judgy and shit."

"Sorry I wasn't trying to be judgy." Peyton winced and
ducked her head. "I've just never really known anyone
who lived in a house like this."

"It's just a house, Peyton."

"No, Ryan, it's not." She ran her hand along the
counter and walked toward the wall of windows that
looked outside to the pool and across the valley. "This
house is amazing." She looked over her shoulder at him.
"You know when you're a kid and you have these big
dreams about what your mansion will look like?"

"Yeah." He laughed. His house was big, but it certainly
wasn't a mansion with like staff and shit.

"This is like that kind of house." Peyton sighed. "This
is truly beautiful, Ryan."

His chest tightened. This was his dream house, and
yeah, he'd had to hire a designer to get it exactly right,
but it had been worth it to him. And apparently Peyton
agreed.

"Glad you like it." He walked up behind her and
wrapped his arms around her waist as they stood and

looked out at the lights sparkling from below in the valley.

"You had a shitty day. What do you say we grab a bottle of wine and head to the hot tub to relax?"

"I didn't bring my suit."

"Peyton, there isn't an inch of your body I haven't had my mouth on. I'm pretty sure you don't need to worry about a bathing suit."

"Well, that's different. This is your hot tub. Maybe you don't want people naked in it. It's communal space."

Fuck, she was cute. He barked out a laugh. "I'm practically always naked in my hot tub."

"Ew, like with other girls?"

"Fuck no, I don't bring women to my house."

Peyton turned around to face him. "What do you call me?"

What did he call her? The best sex he'd ever had. Beyond that? He didn't know what the fuck to call her. "I'm hoping you'll be the first naked woman in my hot tub."

Peyton stepped away from him, peeled her shirt over her head, and dropped it on the corner of his sofa. "Well, what are we waiting for?"

He took a moment to enjoy watching Peyton standing in his living-room half dressed. God, she really was beautiful. "Not a damn thing," he replied as he peeled off his own shirt and chucked it on top of hers.

Unlocking the sliding door, he pushed it fully open. Loving the way Peyton gasped in appreciation when the entire wall of windows opened, making the house and outdoor space all blend into one giant room.

"Holy cow, that's outstanding."

"Agreed. It's pretty cool. That's why I hired a designer," he laughed.

"That's fair. They clearly know their stuff."

She peeled her pants down her legs, stepped out of them, and placed them with their shirts. Clad in only her bra and panties, Ryan couldn't help but stare at her. The lace cups of her bra barely concealed her nipples. As he stared at her, they beaded tightly against the fabric, standing at attention. He stepped toward her and bent down, sucking the ripe bud into his mouth.

Peyton threaded her hands through his hair and dropped her head back. "Mmm," she moaned.

"Sorry, couldn't help myself." He smiled smugly, loving that her body immediately went pliant the moment he touched her.

"You don't ever have to apologize for that. Believe me."

"Glad to hear it." He kicked off his jeans. "Why don't you get into the hot tub, and I'll grab the wine?"

"Sounds good." She reached behind her back, unhooked her bra and tossed it on the sofa. Her breasts sprang free. Ryan licked his lips as she watched her hook her fingers into the edge of her panties and push them down her thighs.

"Jesus," he muttered.

"I thought you were grabbing the wine," she teased.

"Got distracted." His dick twitched against his boxers as he watched her.

Peyton giggled. "The wine?"

"Right." He shook his head to clear the lustful fog that she'd created with her little striptease. *Fuck, she was sexy.* Peyton just naturally was seductive in everything she did. It was a part of her. And damn did he enjoy it.

"I'm going, otherwise we're never getting that wine." Peyton turned and strutted out to the pool. Her hips swayed seductively as she walked. The moonlight hit her ass, highlighting it to perfection. Fuck, he wanted to sink his teeth into it.

He stood watching her until she slipped into the water. Finally, he looked away and walked to the kitchen to grab the wine.

With glasses and bottle in hand, he walked toward the hot tub, kicking off his underwear as he passed the couch. His dick jutted out from his body as he walked. Peyton smirked when he got closer to the tub.

"Looks like someone is raring to go."

"He's always ready to go around you."

Her teeth sank into her bottom lip as she watched him climb into the tub.

"I gotta admit, Ryan, I do like the way your body moves." Peyton licked her lips. Her hand gently teased the chain of her necklace back and forth as she watched him.

"Yeah?" He leaned back, resting his arms along the top of the hot tub. And if he flexed a little for effect, who could blame him?

"Absolutely." She licked her lip. "All those workouts are definitely worth the effort, at least from where I'm sitting."

"Good to know. I'll be sure to tell the trainers."

"Whatever your team pays them, it's worth it."

He grinned and flexed his chest muscles, enjoying the way Peyton's gaze followed the movement. "So, I should stop whining when they make me up my weight?"

"Yes, you should pay them extra."

"I'll keep it in mind." He laughed. Opening the wine, he poured a glass and handed it to Peyton. She slid closer to him as she reached for the glass.

Her thigh rested against his as she sank deeper into the tub. She took a sip of her wine, then dropped her head back against the edge of the tub. "Mmm, this feels amazing. Brilliant suggestion."

"Glad it's helping." He took a sip of his own wine, then followed Peyton's lead by sinking deeper into the water and resting his head on the edge.

They sat in silence for several minutes. Then Peyton's hand touched his thigh, and instantly his dick was back at attention. He couldn't remember ever wanting any woman as much as he wanted Peyton. But he needed to rein it in. She probably wasn't even in the mood for sex, given what she'd told him in the car.

Ryan shifted so he didn't inadvertently hit Peyton with his cock since the thing was like a fucking heat-seeking missile around her. He needed to just nut up and ask her where she was at. She looked like she was practically asleep already. "You still want to stay here tonight or would you rather I took you home?"

Peyton opened her eyes and looked at him. "Why wouldn't I want to stay?"

"I don't know, I just figured after the day you had you might not be interested in having sex."

Peyton shifted her body. She sat up and turned toward him. "Are you not wanting to have sex?"

"Me? No, I wasn't sure if you would want to, and I didn't want you to feel obligated."

"Ryan, I don't do obligatory sex. If I didn't want to be here. I wouldn't be. Did my work stuff freak you out?"

"No, god, no, it's not that. I just didn't want to be an insensitive dick. Trust me, I definitely want to fuck you." He pushed his hair off his forehead. "I always want to fuck you," he uttered. "That's kind of the problem. I don't know how good I am at reading the signs at the moment because my brain isn't the one doing the thinking."

Peyton set her glass of wine on the edge of the tub and eased her leg over him, so she was straddling his lap. "Then how about we both stop thinking all together?"

He grabbed her hips and held her down on top of him, shifting his weight so his cock slid against her pussy, making them both groan. "I like the way your mind works."

Threading his hand into her hair, he brought her mouth to meet his. Fuck, nobody kissed like Peyton.

Without breaking the kiss, he reached behind him and hit the button to turn on the jets. Peyton jumped as the jets fired to life.

Ryan slid his hand under her ass, picked her up, and eased them both to the other side of the hot tub where the lounger seat was. Jets hit his knee as shifted toward the middle of the seat. He set Peyton down on the middle of the seat. She instantly jumped up, and he grinned. "What's wrong?"

Peyton glanced over her shoulder, then back at him. "Umm, nothing."

"Why don't you sit back down then?"

She chewed her bottom lip. "Umm."

"Problem?"

Her eyes flicked behind her again and back to him. "There's, umm, jets all over this seat?"

Ryan laughed. "Yeah, I know that's kind of the point of why I brought you over here."

Peyton's eyebrow furrowed as she watched him. "Really?"

"Absolutely." He dug his hands into her full ass and brought her down so he could rub her pussy along his cock. "Think of it like a giant water vibrator." He shifted her back so just the edge of her ass rested on the seat. She squirmed at the same time a little moan broke out from her mouth. "You never used a jetted tub to get yourself off, baby?"

"Umm, no, my budget doesn't exactly extend to jetted tubs."

Ryan shifted her back a little further, knowing full well it didn't matter if he moved her forward or back. One of those eight leg jets was going to hit her pussy. "You got a couple of them hitting you now?"

Peyton squirmed as her eyes closed. "Mmm hmm."

"Where are they hitting you?"

"Umm... the main part is kind of hitting my thighs but, umm," she moaned. "Some bubbles and stuff are hitting my clit."

"Just the bubbles?"

"Mmm hmm."

Ryan cupped her ass and the jet hit him on the back of hand. He firmly cupped her cheeks and changed the angle of her hips to set her ass on one of the jets. Peyton jumped.

"What about that one?" He knew exactly where it had hit her, but he really wanted to hear her say it.

Even in the hot water, he could see the blush that ran up her face. She was so sensual, but so shy at the same time. The contrast made him want to corrupt her every chance he got.

He eased her back, so the jet aimed at the crack of her ass again. Peyton tilted her head to the side slightly and cleared her throat.

"You gonna tell me where it's hitting you, Peyton?" He ran his tongue up the side of her neck and she squirmed against him. She wasn't moving away from the jet at all. If anything, she was seeking it out further.

"It's umm, kind of on my buttish area."

"Your buttish area?" He threw back his head and laughed. God, she was cute. "Do you like where it's hitting you?"

Her cheeks were now bright red as she nodded shyly. He shifted her weight so the jet shot directly on her clit.

"Oh jeez," she cried out.

"And now?"

Her nails dug into his shoulder. "Oh god," she moaned.

He shifted her off the jet and she huffed out a frustrated breath.

Grinning, he leaned down and nipped her neck. "You like that?"

"Cuz' you can't tell when I'm moaning like a banshee?"

"Oh honey, we haven't even gotten close to you moaning like a banshee. But now that I know that's the goal." He leaned in and swirled his tongue around her nipple. Peyton's head dropped back, and she threaded her fingers through his hair.

"So, which jet did you like better? Ass or clit?"

Peyton cleared her throat. "Umm, they were both very nice."

"Nice?" He snickered. "I wouldn't say me using a jet to fuck your ass was *nice*."

"It wasn't doing that." She smacked him on the arm.

"Pretty close," he murmured. He ran his teeth gently over her other nipple. "So, you liked them both, but I'm guessing by the way you moaned you liked the clit one a little better."

"Well yeah," she agreed.

"But you didn't hate the other?" He watched her to see her reaction. If she hated it, then he didn't want to do it, but if she was open to it, then man, could they have some fun.

"No, I didn't hate it." She dipped her chin shyly like she was embarrassed to like having her ass played with.

"Good." He shifted her body and felt the jet he wanted on the back of his hand. He'd spent countless hours in this hot tub after training and games to work out the knots, so he knew exactly what each jet felt like, how strong it was, how it pulsed, and he was going to put that knowledge to good use on Peyton's body.

He set her down on the jet, and her hand clamped onto his shoulder as her head flung back. "Oh, my god."

He held her in place, not allowing her to squirm away from the jet. Peyton's breathing grew more rapid. Her chest heaved to get breath. Her jaw trembled. She was so close already. He'd expected her to enjoy it, but he hadn't expected it to work this quickly.

Peyton's back arched, thrusting her breasts toward him. Not one to resist an offering like that, he sucked her nipple into his mouth. Peyton let out a deep, agonized moan. Her fingers dug into this scalp.

His dick twitched. "You are so fucking hot."

Peyton flicked open her eyes and flashed him the sexiest smile. The wanton look of a woman chasing her own orgasm. And he wanted to be buried inside her when she came.

He moved her off the jet. "No," she cried.

The look of annoyance on her face nearly made him want to put her back on. But he knew if he held her close to the edge when he did finally let her have the orgasm, it would be so fucking worth it.

"Patience." He shifted her back so the jet hit her ass again instead of her clit. She shuddered and exhaled audibly.

"I honestly didn't think I'd like that," she admitted.

He wrapped his arm around her back, cupping her waist on the opposite side to hold her in place on the jet. With his other hand, he threaded his fingers into her hair and pulled tight against her scalp, knowing how much she enjoyed the little bite of pain.

He needed to kiss her. To feel her breath shudder against his. Her breathing hitched as they kissed. She was getting close again. So, he pulled her off the jet.

"Ahh," she growled.

"Trust me, babe," he said against her mouth.

Peyton reached down and grabbed his cock firmly in her hand, and squeezed a bit harder than he'd hoped for.

"If you don't let me come soon, you won't be coming at all. Got it?" she demanded.

He pulled back to look her in the eye. "I thought we agreed you'd do what I said in the bedroom."

"One, this isn't the bedroom, and two, that was before I knew what a sadistic jerk you could be."

Ryan threw back his head and laughed. "I'm hardly a sadist, Peyton. Nothing wrong with a little edging."

"I'm definitely on edge," she grumbled.

"I didn't realize you were so impatient." He smiled at her and placed a kiss against her lips. "Let's see what we can do to help you out."

"Thank god."

He picked up Peyton and set her on the seat beside him. There was no way he was putting her back down on the jets. He didn't trust her not to finish without him.

Ryan reached over and grabbed the condom he'd set down beside the bottle of wine, just in case. He stood and quickly sheathed himself, not allowing Peyton to touch him. He hadn't just been edging her, watching her get so close, the way her breathing changed, how her body tensed. It had been a huge fucking turn on for him as well, and he was so fucking close himself.

With the condom in place, he kneeled back down between Peyton's thighs. "Now where was I?"

She wrapped her legs around his waist. Ryan leaned in and kissed her, his tongue tangled with hers as he picked her up and set her back down on the jets. The moment her body hit the seat, she tensed and her back arched, pressing her breasts against him.

Without breaking the kiss, he shifted her hips to change the angle of the jets.

"Oh god, yeah, right there. Don't you dare move me," she growled.

He sucked her nipple into his mouth. Peyton's moans grew louder and louder. Just when he thought she was about to orgasm, he shifted her off the jet.

"Noooo," she screamed.

Picking her up out of the water, he set her on the edge of the tub, lined himself up at her entrance, and drove home in one deep thrust. Peyton's nails dug into his shoulders so hard he was sure she'd drawn blood, but he didn't fucking care. Nothing had ever felt this good.

He shifted and swiveled his hips. Reveling in the way, she moaned in pleasure when he hit the right spot.

"Oh my god, Ryan."

Pleasure shot down his spine in an almost painful bolt of lust. There was no way he was coming without her, not after he'd dragged out her orgasm. He reached between them and found her clit. He stroked it at first. Peyton's pussy clamped down around his cock like a vise, greedily seeking her own orgasm.

"Oh my god, oh my god, oh my god," Peyton chanted.

He pinched her clit firmly between his fingers, and she screamed as she came. Her pussy kept contracting, pulling him deeper inside her. His balls drew up tight. He thrust harder and faster into her as he chased his release.

"Fuck," he yelled as his own orgasm ripped through him. Balls deep in Peyton, he gasped for breath. He rested his forehead against hers, unable to move.

Finally able to breathe properly, he released Peyton and slid her off to the side onto the bucket seat. He quickly pulled off his condom and chucked it on the ground beside the hot tub.

"Ew," Peyton laughed.

"I'll get it later." Yeah, that was gross, but he didn't have a lot of options. He grabbed Peyton and dropped himself onto the bucket seat, pulling her with him. The jets sprayed firmly against his back as Peyton straddled his lap. His muscles felt like melted butter, and he didn't think he'd ever felt so relaxed.

After several minutes, Peyton shifted her head on his shoulder. "Okay, so maybe there is something to be said for dragging out an orgasm."

"Glad you liked it. Guess that means I get to keep my dick for another day." He glanced down at her and smirked when she narrowed her eyes at him.

"Keep it up, mister," she said.

"Yeah? Or what?"

"I don't know yet, but I'll think of something." Her lips pursed together tightly like she was racking her brain for some kind of payback.

Ryan chuckled. "Okay, wake me up when you do." He closed his eyes and dropped his head against the seat cushion. Life didn't get better than this.

CHAPTER TWELVE

Ryan looked up at the flight board and scanned for their flight. Delayed. Fuck. He'd been planning to head to Peyton's tonight when they got into town, but the way things were heading that would not be happening.

For the past two weeks, they'd squeezed in several nights together in between his games and travel. He couldn't believe how much he looked forward to seeing her. When they'd first started this whole thing, he hadn't expected to enjoy spending time with her nearly as much as he did. Everything about Peyton was the exact opposite of his first impression.

When he'd originally suggested they hook up, he'd expected to go by her place, fuck, and be on his way. Now he found himself lingering, making up excuses to stay. He'd never met anyone else who loved spoofy horror movies as much as he did. Okay, so most people wouldn't say 80's horror movies were spoofy but come on, Jason wore a fucking paper bag over his head in the second movie. How was that supposed to be taken seriously?

Gonzo dropped into the seat beside him. "Isn't your ass numb from sitting in that chair for so long? I don't think you've moved in the past three hours."

"Eh. Misspent youth playing video games to unwind. You'd be surprised how long my ass can sit in a chair."

"That's pathetic, man."

"You say pathetic, I say hidden superpower." He stretched his arms over his head. Although now that Gonzo mentioned it his ass was a kind of numb. Flicking his wrist over, he glanced at the time, then up at the board again. "Fuck, we still have another hour before they expect to call our flight. "I'm getting something to eat. You want to come?"

"Yeah, why not?" Gonzo pushed out of the seat beside Ryan. The chair groaned from the pressure.

"Jesus, man. Easy. You're standing up, not fucking bench pressing the thing."

"Don't hate just because I can bench more than you." The cocky bastard winked at Ryan as he spoke.

"Maybe it's cuz your ass is bigger than mine?"

"Are you fat shaming me?"

Ryan eyed Gonzo. The guy was fucking huge, but definitely not fat by anyone's standards. When he'd first joined the team, Gonzo had been a bit soft, but over the past year, he'd been hitting the gym hard. The extra pounds of muscle had paid off because he now had one of the best batting averages in the league. "Yeah, Nancy, that's exactly what I'm saying. Fuck off," he laughed.

Flexing his peck muscles so they danced, Gonzo waggled his eyebrows. Ryan shook his head. "Dude, does that really impress anyone?"

Gonzo tilted his head toward a group of women sitting a couple rows away who all were raptly staring. Okay, apparently it did work.

Ryan shoved his bag toward Sims. "Can you watch our stuff?"

Sims pulled his earbud out. "What?"

"Can you watch our stuff?"

"Sure, no problem."

"You want me to bring you back any food?" Ryan asked.

Sims stretched and rubbed both hands over his face. "A smoothie or something would be sick if you can find one."

"You got it."

Ryan scanned the crowd as they walked through the airport. "Holy shit," he muttered.

"What?" Gonzo's gaze darted around as he tried to see what Ryan was so excited about.

"That dude's shirt is awesome." He changed direction and walked toward the guy. "Excuse me. Can I be total weirdo and take a picture of your shirt?"

"Yeah, no problem." The guy dropped his arms and Ryan snapped a picture of the t-shirt making sure to omit the guy's face from the shot. "Thanks, man."

"Holy shit. You're Ryan Graves."

"I am, yeah." Even after several years in the Majors, he still got a little buzz whenever someone recognized him in public. Sure it got old sometimes, but that first person in the airport or the little kid who was razzed to meet a player, it kind of still stacked up.

"Can I get a picture with you?"

"Of course." It was the least he could do for the guy letting him snap a photo of his weird swamp thing t-shirt. "Gonz, you mind?"

"Wow, you're Ramon Gonzalez. Holy shit." The guy scanned the surrounding area. "Is your whole team here?"

"Uh, yeah somewhere," Ryan replied.

"Holy shit."

Gonzo grabbed the guy's phone, snapped a couple shots, then handed the phone back.

"You can have my shirt if you want." The guy grabbed the bottom of his t-shirt and pulled it away from his body.

"What?"

"You can have my shirt. I can just buy something else there at the gift shop."

Gonzo laughed and tried to cover it with a cough.

"Nah, that's cool, man. I appreciate the offer, but you keep your clothes," Ryan told him.

"Are you sure?"

"Yeah, man, positive. A picture's cool. Thanks though."

"No problem. So where are you guys headed now? Who do you play next?"

Ryan stayed and chatted with the swamp thing fan for a bit, then finally was able to extract himself from the conversation.

"I hope that was worth it," Gonzo muttered as they walked away.

Ryan looked at the photo on his phone of the swamp thing head surrounded by the words 'I don't fucking believe it'. He pulled up Peyton's number and fired her a text.

Ryan: *Flights delayed again.*

Followed by a picture of the t-shirt. He watched as the three little dots instantly appeared.

Peyton: *Oh my god. That shirt is awesome.*
And sorry about the delay that sucks.
But seriously that shirt... so good.

He laughed as he read her replies. He'd known when he saw the shirt she'd love it.

"What's with the goofy face?" Gonzo asked.

"What?" He snapped his head up. "What face?"

"That one." Gonzo pointed at Ryan's face, then placed his hands under his own chin and batted his eyes like a besotted fool.

"Fuck off," Ryan mumbled.

"You've been saying that a lot lately, dude."

"Well, maybe you should listen." Ignoring his friend, he began walking. He was pretty sure he'd seen a smoothie place up this way.

Gonzo quickly kept pace with him. "So, you smiling about Peyton?" he teased.

"I thought you didn't want me to keep telling you to fuck off."

Gonzo held up his hands. "Alright, alright, I won't bug you about your girlfriend."

"She's not my girlfriend," he muttered. "Not for real anyways."

"But you want her to be." Gonzo's left eyebrow raised in question.

Did he? Fuck, maybe. But no. What they had worked. Peyton was a cool chick to hang out with, and the sex was unbelievable. But girlfriend? No, that just complicated everything. He didn't have time for that kind of crap. So he settled for simply saying, "Fuck off."

Gonzo, the bastard, just laughed.

It had been a long road series. They'd swept both Washington and Florida, which had them sitting pretty in the standings, but it had taken a toll on his body. His arm was tired. His teammates were getting on his nerves, and he just wanted his own bed. Thank god they had a couple days off before their next home game.

He pulled his car into the Kidsplay lot, noting Peyton's car in the parking lot. Honestly, he had no idea what he was doing here. They weren't supposed to see each other, but somehow his car had just driven here on his way home from the airport.

Not questioning it, he exited the car and made his way across the parking lot. He nodded to the group of teens leaning against the side wall.

"Nice game against Washington last night. You lit 'em up," one youth called.

"Yeah, thanks, the arm felt good. Our boys were on the sticks. It was an excellent series."

A tall boy with a hood pulled over his head stepped forward. "Peyton said you might do some pitching clinics this fall."

"That's the plan. When we start will depend on playoffs. Selfishly, I'm hoping we have to push it back because we're in the world series, but time will tell."

"That'd be cool. The clinics will be open to anyone?"

"I don't see why not."

The youth shrugged. "Sometimes those things are just open to the little guys because they actually have a chance of doing something."

"You want to learn?"

The boy shrugged like it didn't matter. "Maybe."

"You ever played?"

"Nah, wanted to but…"

"What are you doing tomorrow?"

"Tomorrow?" The boy's eyebrows rose in question as he stared at Ryan.

"I've got a couple of days off. I could stop by and throw around with you for a bit tomorrow after school. I need to stay loose, so if you're interested—"

"For real?"

"Yeah, why not?"

The boy's eyes lit up and a smile split across his face before he quickly masked it, slouched his shoulders and nodded slowly. "I could probably make that work."

Ryan smiled to himself. "Great. Say 3:30?"

He nodded in agreement.

"What's your name?"

"Slade."

"Well, Slade, I will see you tomorrow. Have a good night, boys," Ryan called to the rest of the group before walking the remaining steps toward the door. As he pulled it open and stepped in, he was met by Peyton, James, and half a dozen other expectant faces all staring at him.

"Uh hey?" he said nervously. Why were they all staring at him like that?

"Did I just hear you make plans to play catch with Slade?" Peyton asked.

"Yeah? Why? Why are you all looking at me like that?"

A smile split across Peyton's face. Her eyes shone with something he'd never seen before. He didn't know what it was, but he liked it.

"He's not much of a joiner. Mostly just hangs out front waiting for his friends to be done in here."

"Cool. Hopefully that'll change." Ryan glanced outside at the youth. The way Slade leaned against the wall, every muscle in his body screamed don't fuck with me. The kid had an edge, but the way his face had lit up at the opportunity to play catch, he wasn't completely hardened. Not yet anyway.

"So, what are you doing here? I didn't think I'd see you tonight." Peyton dipped her head and smiled. She raised her head back up and flicked her wrist toward the hall. "You want to come on back to my office?"

"Yeah." He smiled at the group. "Sorry, I'm stealing her from you."

"It's all good, honey." James waved them off.

He followed Peyton down the hall, his eyes lingering on the sway of her hips. Her fitted pants hugged her ass to perfection.

"Stop looking at my butt," Peyton said, without turning around.

"Nope, not going to happen."

He closed the door behind himself when he walked into the office. Peyton smirked and raised one eyebrow as she rested her hip against the front edge of her desk.

Ryan stepped up to her and pressed against her front, loving the way she shivered when his body came in contact with her. He grabbed her hips and hoisted her on her desk, and wedged himself between her legs.

With a little squeal, she clasped onto his shoulders. "Umm, hi."

He pulled her ass toward him and pressed his hips forward. "Damn, I missed you," he murmured when she shifted against his cock.

"Yeah, I can tell." She pressed her hand against his chest. "But as good as you feel. I'm at work and just because you closed the door doesn't mean no one will come in."

He dropped his forehead against hers and sighed. "I know. When are you off?"

She grabbed his wrist and flipped it so she could look at his watch. "Holy cow, it's already 6:00. Give me like five minutes and I can leave."

"Yeah?" This worked out much better than he'd hoped.

Well, it took fifteen minutes, but it was still a win as they walked across the parking lot. "You hungry?" Peyton asked.

"I could eat."

"Great, I've been craving a mac n' cheese sandwich all day from The Old Goat."

"There are so many things wrong with that statement. The Old Goat? That doesn't sound like someplace I want to eat."

She rolled her eyes. "Don't be a snob. It's amazing."

His mouth scrunched up. He wasn't sure he believed her. "Okay, but a mac n' cheese sandwich? That sounds disgusting."

"If by disgusting you mean you'd sell a kidney to get one because it's so good, then yeah, it's disgusting." She brought her fingers up to her mouth and kissed them. "Mmm, trust me. When you taste this, you will think you've died and gone to heaven."

"Do they sell anything else?"

"Of course, but you aren't going to want anything but this. When you bite into this sandwich, it will be like the heavens have opened up and the angels will be singing. It's a freaking masterpiece."

Ryan laughed. "Wow, that's some sandwich. The Heaven's will open up, huh?"

"Oh, absolutely." She grinned. "Follow me there, and then we can figure out whose place to go to."

"Alright."

"And don't make any snap judgments. The place looks a little rough on the outside but it's spotless inside and seriously—" She rolled her eyes back and sighed. "Per-fection."

God, the woman was adorable. Who got that excited over a sandwich? "Lead the way."

Ten minutes later, they pulled up at a rundown strip mall. Ryan winced. He didn't even want to get out of his car, let alone eat at anyplace around here. Hell, his car would probably get stolen if he left it in this parking lot.

He'd barely turned off the engine before he saw Peyton jump out of hers and beeline toward a group of people standing around with their cellphones out, filming what looked like a homeless person.

What the hell was she doing? He quickly jumped out of his car. "Peyton?" he called, but she didn't slow down. She stormed up to the group.

"Put your damn phones away," Peyton demanded as she stepped between the man on the ground and the group laughing while they filmed his pain.

"Fuck you," a man replied.

"No. Stop filming him and either offer him some help. Or walk away." Fearless, Peyton glared at the cluster of bystanders like she was ready to take on anyone. "But at the very least, be a human being and don't make light of someone else's pain."

"Whatever," another man said before he nudged the first and the group slowly dispersed.

Peyton crouched down on the ground a few feet away from the shirtless man, who was sobbing as he clutched a doll to his chest. "Are you ok?"

The man sucked in a breath between sobs and shook his head. He pressed the doll's head harder against his chest and rocked back and forth.

Ryan stepped in closer in case Peyton needed his help. What the hell was she doing running into a crowd of people and now this?

"Is that your baby?" Peyton nodded at the doll in the man's arms

The man nodded. "Sh... sh... she won't eat," he sobbed.

"You've been trying to feed her?" Peyton asked, her voice filled with compassion. She tilted her head to the side as she watched the man and his doll. Ryan stood poised on the balls of his feet in case he needed to react. He had no experience with this kind of thing, and if he was honest, it made him more than a little uncomfortable. But Peyton seemed perfectly calm and unfazed as she spoke softly to the person desperately trying to nurse their doll.

The man's stomach growled loudly. "See," he pleaded as he raised his head to look at Peyton. "She's starving, but she won't eat." He adjusted the baby's head against his nipple and cried. "My baby is so hungry. Why won't she eat?"

As he shifted the baby, Ryan got a clear view of the man's sunken stomach. The bones in his chest stood out prominently. It looked like the man had eaten nothing of substance in weeks.

"What's your name?" Peyton shifted a little bit closer, closing the space between them slightly.

"Jason."

"Jason, when's the last time you ate anything?"

"It's my baby that needs to eat, not me," Jason cried.

"I know, but it looks like you're nursing, so it's important you eat because your food is the baby's food too."

Jason stared at her for several seconds, then wiped his nose with the back of his hand. "Really?"

"Mmm hmm," Peyton replied.

She glanced up at Ryan. "Ry, can you run inside and get Jason a sandwich?"

Turning back to Jason, she asked, "Turkey? Roast beef? What do you think would hit the spot?"

"You're going to buy me a sandwich?" Jason's eyes widened as he looked up at her.

"Well, I'm not." She flicked her thumb toward Ryan. "He is. So, what'll it be?"

Jason looked up at Ryan warily, then back down at the baby. He chewed his bottom lip, then spoke so softly Ryan couldn't hear him.

"Roast beef it is," Peyton said. "And what about a drink? Milk or juice? Either of those would be good for you with nursing."

Jason wrinkled his nose. "I don't like milk."

"Juice it is." Peyton looked back up at Ryan. "Maybe grab a couple of drinks."

"You gonna be okay if I leave you out here?"

Peyton looked over at Jason. When she looked back at Ryan, her eyes were glistening with unshed tears. "Yeah, I'll be fine."

Peyton pulled her car into the second garage and parked beside Ryan. She'd never lived in a place with a garage. Heck, she'd never lived in a house. Apartments through and through.

Ryan waited on the stairs and held the side door open for her to enter his house. She rounded the corner and immediately her gaze was drawn outside. The setting sun landed on the pool, making it glisten like crystals. She'd been here several times, but it never failed to take her breath away. What must it be like to live in a place like this?

The gas fireplace and surrounding patio furniture drew her attention instantly. Ryan had created such an amazing outdoor space it would be a shame not to enjoy it. "Any chance we can eat outside?"

"Sure. You want a beer or wine? I'm not really sure what you drink with a mac n' cheese sandwich." Ryan eyed the takeout bag in his hand skeptically.

"Wine would be great, thanks." She followed him into the kitchen. Running her hand along the edge of the granite counter, she sighed.

Ryan set the bag down on the island and walked over to her. "You know you're always stroking that counter every time you come over." He pressed her back against the counter and leaned in and scraped his teeth on the side of her neck, making her shiver. "Imagine how good it would feel against your back when I lay you down on it so I can eat that sweet pussy of yours."

Her nipples beaded tightly against her bra as she bit back a moan. "Mmm, we have to eat dinner." She tilted her head to the side to give him further access to the sensitive spot on her neck.

"I say we start with dessert." Ryan bit down on her neck, and her eyes rolled back in her head.

"Dessert's good," she sighed.

Ryan's hands dipped into the edge of her pants, and he slowly lowered them down her legs, taking her panties with them. He crouched on the floor and looked up at her. "Step out," he ordered.

His nostrils flared with arousal. Peyton licked her lips and raised her foot. A shiver ran through her as her panties eased down her thigh like a gentle caress. He wrapped his hand around the arch of her foot and rested it on his knee. Gliding his hand up her calf, he pressed her knee out, opening her legs wider. He stared at her naked center, then slowly trailed his finger up her thigh.

Her knees trembled. She was sure Ryan could see how wet she was already. This man turned her on like no one else. He barely had to touch her, and she was ready to go off like a rocket. She should probably be embarrassed, but she wasn't. It turned her on even more.

He ran his finger through her slit. Coated with her moisture, he brought it to his mouth and sucked. "You always taste so fucking good."

Ryan stood, grabbed her hips, and hoisted her onto the edge of the island. She hissed out a breath at the contrast between the cool stone and her heated core. Peyton shifted her hips, loving the way her skin glided across the counter. She'd thought it felt amazing against her hand. That was nothing compared to how it felt against her butt.

Ryan pressed his hand in the middle of her chest. "Lay down. I've been picturing you spread out here since the first time I saw you run your hand over the counter."

Doing what she was told, Peyton rested her back against the granite counter. The look on Ryan's face sent a little thrill of excitement zipping through her. He really was looking at her like he'd like to feast on her body. Enjoying the surge of power she felt, she arched her back and spread her legs, encouraging him to get started.

"It's even hotter than I'd imagined." Ryan stepped between her legs. He placed his hand on her stomach and pushed her shirt up over her breasts. "The things I want to do to these tits." He roughly pulled the fabric of her bra down, shoving it under her breasts. The under wire held her breasts up, making them look perky and full and kind of hot, if she did say so herself.

She arched her back. Her nipples tightened further. "What would you do?"

"Fuck them."

That shouldn't turn her on nearly as much as it did. She'd had guys use her breasts before and it had been okay, but somehow she knew if Ryan did it, there would be no comparison.

"But tonight, I want to fuck your pussy with my tongue and feel you ride my face."

Wow, she could definitely get on board with that. Before Ryan, she'd no idea how freakin' hot dirty talk could be. "Okay."

"You like that idea, do you?" Ryan's lips curled up into a wolfish smile. Somehow that one little look conveyed all the filthy things he wanted to do to her.

"Mmm hmm." She nodded vigorously. She more than liked the idea.

Ryan kneeled between her legs. His hot breath hit her heated core, and she trembled. Her nipples beaded tighter with anticipation.

He spread her with his fingers, inhaling deeply. "Fuck yeah," he murmured a second before he ran his tongue along her seam. Peyton's back arched off the counter and she moaned. This would not take her long at all.

His tongue swirled around her clit, licking and nibbling on the tight bud. "Play with your nipples," Ryan ordered.

Peyton pinched her nipples between her fingers at the same time Ryan sucked her clit into his mouth. How could the little noises he was making turn her on so much? It shouldn't be so hot to hear someone licking and sucking her, but it really was.

Ryan inserted a finger, then another, twisting his fingers.

"Oh my god," she moaned.

She threaded her fingers into his hair. Holding his head, she rocked her hips against him.

"Yeah, that's right, baby, fuck my face," Ryan said.

Peyton moaned loudly, her hips bucking against him more knowing how much he liked it.

Her orgasm built. Ryan shifted his hand and suddenly he hit her exactly how she needed.

"Don't stop, don't stop," she chanted. Plucking her nipple with her finger, she held his head in place with her other hand. She was so close.

With one final suck on her clit, the orgasm tore through her. Her back arched up off the counter as she closed her eyes, letting the wave of ecstasy surge through her.

Ryan stood. His beard glistened with moisture as he stared down at her. Seeing the evidence of her arousal on his face was freaking hot. Boneless, Peyton didn't move, basking in the look of pure desire written on Ryan's face.

"You are so fucking sexy," he told her.

She held out her hand. "I want you."

A cocky smile kicked up the corner of his mouth. "Thank fuck." Reaching into his wallet, he pulled out a condom and set it on the island. He pushed his pants down and sheathed himself as Peyton sat up. Ryan grabbed her hips and pulled her to the edge of the counter. He pressed himself at her entrance and waited as he cupped the back of her head, threading his fingers into her hair. Peyton's eyes drifted shut.

He pulled her head toward him. His lips landed against hers, hot, hungry, demanding. Tasting herself on his lips as their tongues tangled together.

She wrapped her legs around his waist, and he drove into her in one long, hard thrust that made Peyton whimper with desire.

His tongue tangled with hers and he thrust deeper. Cupping his hands under her butt, he shifted her hips.

"Oh Ryan," she moaned. His cock hit her at a new, delicious angle. "Right there."

His fingers dug into her hips as he thrust into her. He licked up her neck and bit down on that spot above her collarbone, and she threw her head back and screamed. The orgasm she'd been chasing hit her like a freight train.

"Jesus, that was hot," he said as his hands dug into her hips, and he pulled her against him tighter. He thrust into her hard. His muscles tensed beneath her fingers as he groaned out his own release.

He rested his forehead against hers. "Shit, woman, that was..."

"I'll say," she replied with a giggle.

Ryan pulled back, separating himself from her, and smiled. "I'm never going to be able to look at this island the same again."

"Good." She smiled as she hopped off the counter. "But you should definitely wash it because that's not sanitary."

Ryan burst out laughing. Wrapping his arms around her, he pulled her into his chest. "I'll take it under advisement."

She looked up at him and wrinkled her nose. "You better do more than that."

His laughter rumbled through his chest, and she couldn't help but smile at the relaxed look of joy on his face. She wrapped her arms tighter around his waist. She didn't remember the last time she'd been this happy.

Peyton grabbed her wineglass and Ryan's beer and followed him onto the deck. She sat down and picked up her sandwich and took a hearty bite. Crispy sourdough bread, perfectly firm noodles smothered in cheesy goodness exploded in her mouth and she moaned. Even cold, these were the bomb.

She looked across the table and watched as Ryan took his first bite. "Fuck, that's good," he mumbled.

"Told ya," she taunted.

"I don't know about angels singing, but it's a damn good sandwich."

"If it had been hot, believe me, they would have sung."

Ryan chuckled. "I'll have to take your word for it." Ryan wiped his mouth and sat back. "That was pretty cool what you did with Jason today."

"Thanks. They looked like they were struggling, and I wanted to figure out how to get them to eat."

"Them?" Ryan's brow knit with confusion.

"I don't know what their pronouns are, so I'm going with them to be safe."

Ryan raked his fingers through his hair and winced. "Sorry I don't have much experience with this. Is that what you are supposed to do when you aren't sure?"

She smiled. "Normally I ask, but this situation was a bit different."

"I just would hate to offend someone by asking."

He looked so unsure of himself, which was such a contrast to the confident man he normally presented to the world. The fact that he cared enough to try to learn was a big step in the right direction. "Why would someone be offended that you are making the effort to be respectful?" she asked.

"Well, when you put it that way, I guess they wouldn't." He nodded his head thoughtfully. "Thanks. I never really thought about it that way."

"Glad I could help. I always figure when in doubt, ask."

"That's fair." He crumpled up his sandwich wrapper and shoved it back in the takeout bag. "So, how did you know what to do with Jason today?"

"I don't know." She shrugged. "It's hard not to get some mental health experience doing the work I do."

"That was more than experience, Pey, that was amazing. I've never seen anyone defend someone like that. The way you charged into that crowd, I was sure I was going to have to throw hands to defend you, but you put them in their place and then the way you were with Jason." He paused. She fought the urge to squirm as he stared at her. "That was impressive."

"Thanks. It's no big deal, really."

"The fact that you don't see that it was a big deal is kind of even more impressive." He reached across the table and grabbed her hand. His fingers slowly traced back and forth over her knuckles. "You know, you're nothing like the person I thought you were."

"Well, that's not saying much, considering your original opinion of me." She laughed.

Ryan's face scrunched up and he grimaced. "I still feel bad about that. I was such an asshole to you."

"Yeah, you were," she agreed. "But you're growing on me."

"That's good. So umm... about this weekend. I was wondering if you wanted to come to the game and meet my parents as my girlfriend."

"What?" She looked over at him, confused. Hadn't she already agreed to this? "I already said I'd go to the game and meet your parents."

Ryan rubbed his hand back and forth across the back of his neck. "Yeah, well, that was as my fake girlfriend. I'm asking if you want to meet them as my girlfriend."

She sat up straight, pushing her back against the chair. "What?"

"Fuck. Okay, clearly I'm reading things wrong here." He dropped her hand on the table and rubbed his hand across his mouth and down his beard. "Awesome."

Holy cow, was he really saying what she thought he was saying? He didn't want this thing to be fake? Sure, it had stopped feeling fake to her weeks ago, but he'd always acted like this was just a temporary fake dating, sex buddy kind of deal.

He pushed his chair back from the table. Peyton lunged and grabbed his hand. "No, Ryan, hold up. You caught me by surprise. What are you saying? No more expiration date, no more fake dating? You want to do this thing for real? Just you and me, like really making a go of things?"

"Yeah. Fuck. I'm not good at this talking crap." He sighed. "I mean, we've kind of already slipped into that anyway. Haven't we?"

Not wanting him to clam up and stop talking, she simply nodded.

"I'll admit at first the sex was kind of hot because we both didn't really like each other very much." He glanced toward the kitchen, then back at her. "But the sex is pretty fucking hot when I like you too."

She grinned.

"And I really like you Peyton. Every time I'm with you, I see these new sides to you and tonight, I don't know." He shook his head. "I'm just fucking crazy about you, and I guess I want to see where this thing can go for real. I mean, if you want to."

Her heart pounded in her chest. "I definitely want to."

Ryan's smile was so big she couldn't help but grin back at him. "Cool. So, we're doing this? You're meeting my parents as my girlfriend."

"Oh my god, I'm meeting your parents." She placed her hand against her stomach. "Are we really there? What if they hate me? What if you change your mind? This is a big deal, Ryan. Oh, my god."

His deep laughter rang across the night air. "Relax Peyton. They'll love you. You'd already agreed to meet them with them thinking you were my girlfriend. This is no different."

"Um, yeah, it is because now I am your girlfriend. So now I will actually care what they think."

Ryan snorted. "Come on, Peyton. I know you. You would have cared either way."

She pursed her lips and nodded. "Yeah, I would have cared either way." When Ryan laughed again, she smacked his arm. "Shut up, I'm a people pleaser. I can't help it."

"I know, babe." Ryan picked up his chair and slid his seat closer to hers. "Nothing has changed. This weekend will still be the same as we'd planned."

"Ryan, everything has changed."

"Really? Can you honestly tell me you weren't developing feelings for me slowly all along?"

"No, I guess not," she grumbled.

"Exactly. The only thing that's changed is we finally agreed to be truthful about what this thing really is. Honestly, I wouldn't have put in half of the effort I did if I wasn't attracted to you right from the moment I met you. Even when I didn't like you, I was drawn to you and really wanted you to be different from how I pictured."

"Me too," she whispered.

CHAPTER THIRTEEN

Peyton glanced down at the ticket in her hands and took a deep breath. Meeting the parents. Sheesh, this was a big deal. She wiped her sweaty palms on the edge of her jean shorts. Thank god she had the buffer of watching baseball. She eyed the beer vendor and chewed her bottom lip. Nope, she'd go meet them first, then decide on the beer.

She walked down the stairs toward her seat and smiled when she saw Kendall decked out in a Saunders jersey beside an older couple wearing Graves jerseys. She fingered the edge of her own Graves jersey that Ryan had given her the night before. Her nipples beaded as she remembered how much he'd like seeing her in his jersey with nothing else. She shook her head. Not smart to be thinking dirty thoughts about the guy when she was meeting his parents for the first time.

She wove past a few people and stopped at the end of her row. Kendall glanced over and smiled. "Where's your beer?" Kendall called.

"I thought I'd see if anyone needed one before I grabbed mine," she replied.

"Good answer," an older version of Ryan answered before he turned to the woman beside him. "See, I won't make a bad impression if I have a beer."

Peyton laughed. "Definitely not. What about you, Mrs. Graves? Can I bring you one too?"

"Call me Debbie, and you may as well." The woman smiled warmly.

"I'll go with you." Kendall jumped to her feet. When she got to the end of the row, she pulled Peyton into a warm hug. "Glad you made it. Prepare for the inquisition. My brother has never brought a girl to the family game day, so my parents are very intrigued."

"Oh god," she murmured. Was she ready for this? "I'm definitely going to need a drink."

Kendall laughed loudly. "I knew I liked you. Let's go."

While they waited in line, Kendall fingered the edge of Peyton's jersey. "I like the jersey. Did Ryan give it to you?"

Peyton felt the heat rising across her cheeks. Oh crap. So much for banishing the images of last night.

"Ew gross, guess that answered my question. I don't even want to know," Kendall groaned.

"Sorry," Peyton mumbled.

"Don't be. I'm glad my brother found someone he wants to have wear his jersey. Besides, I know how Pete reacted to me in his jersey, so I get the blushing. I just don't want to think about it because it's my brother and gross."

"Fair enough." Peyton laughed. "So, what kind of beer do your parents like?"

Kendall eyed the list of beers available and wrinkled her nose. "My dad considers himself a brew master so he's going to critique anything we buy. Let's go craft beer because he's more likely to want that. My mom only drinks beer because she thinks she should at a ball game, so we'll get her whatever is cheapest, since she'll hate it either way."

Peyton chuckled as she stepped up to the counter and ordered three different types of beer then turned to Kendall. "What about you?"

Kendall ordered a craft beer before reaching for her wallet.

"Nope, I've got this one," Peyton told her.

"Okay, but the next round is on me," Kendall replied.

"I don't know that I plan on having more than one. I need to keep my wits about me with your parents."

Kendall snorted. "Oh honey, you are definitely going to be having a second one. Your wits will need the moral support."

"You're not making me any less nervous about this, you know." Peyton narrowed her eyes as she looked at Ryan's sister, who just winked at her. Great, that was ominous. Peyton took a deep breath before grabbing two of the beer and leaving the other two for Kendall to grab.

They made their way back down to their seats. Kendall handed her mom the cheapest beer, then asked her dad which of the remaining beers he wanted first.

With his selection down, she took hers from Peyton, then sat down next to her mom. Peyton slid into the seat beside Kendall and scanned the field. The seats were amazing. She'd only been to a handful of games before, and she'd never sat this close to home plate. She'd be able to see every pitch clearly from here.

"What happened to the third base line?" Peyton nodded towards the vacant seats where Kendall normally sat.

Kendall shrugged. "My dad likes to sit here, so I adjust when they come to town."

Peyton scanned the crowd around them and tensed when she saw Carmella, Andy's wife, a few rows over with a group of women decked out in Hawks' gear.

Kendall leaned over and whispered. "That's the WAGS section."

"Wags?"

"Yeah, wives and girlfriends."

Peyton nodded. Good to know. The roar of the crowd announced the home team was taking the field for warmup. Kendall stood up beside her and waved her arms as Pete blew a kiss into the crowd. Several women in the nearby sections attempted to grab the air kiss, but it was clear Pete only had eyes for Kendall.

Kendall continued to stand. When Ryan walked onto the field, she grabbed Peyton's arm and pulled her up. "Stand so he knows you're here."

Ryan scanned the crowd and smiled as his parents waved their arms madly. Peyton could feel when his gaze landed on her and his smile changed. Damn, even from this distance, the man was potent.

He pointed at his back, then flicked his hand like he wanted her to turn around. She spun so he could see her back, then faced forward. The smile on Ryan's face was like nothing she'd ever seen before. Out of the corner of her eye, she saw Andy glance up at the crowd and scowl. Well, screw him. He could be as unhappy as he wanted to be about her being here. It would not dim her enjoyment of the day.

As Ryan's family sat, Peyton dropped into her own chair. Ryan's mom leaned forward across Kendall. "Well, that was interesting. I've never seen my son act like that before."

"Like what?" Peyton asked.

A snicker sounded beside her before a beer was placed against her hand and Kendall murmured. "You're gonna need that."

Smitty dropped onto the bench beside Ryan. "Nice game. You were on fire tonight."

"Thanks, the arm felt good." It was a bit sore now but nothing some ice wouldn't take care of. He rolled his right shoulder. Okay, maybe a little ibuprofen as well. That's what he got for trying to show off with his fastball. But damn, that thing had been lit.

"What are you doing now? You want to get a beer or something?" Smitty asked.

"Sorry, man, can't. My parents are in town, so we're doing a family dinner." Ryan grabbed the handle of his bag and stood up. "Next time."

Gonzo and Pete walked up with their bags slung over their shoulders. "You ready?" Pete asked.

"Big day, introducing Peyton to the parents. I didn't know you two were there," Gonzo said.

"Guess I forgot to mention it the last time you were braiding my hair." Ryan rolled his eyes. "Jesus, you guys are like teenage girls."

"Now you know how I feel." Pete laughed.

"I don't just want to hear the good stuff, I like to hear the bad too," Gonzo said. "Reminds me why I don't have a relationship." He nudged Ryan. "We can chat tomorrow when you're regretting your decision to do family dinner."

"You're an idiot." Ryan laughed before turning to Pete. "Alright. You ready to be grilled about when you're going to make an honest woman out of my sister?"

"Nope, because your mom will be too busy fawning all over her star son to even worry about what I'm doing."

"Fuck off," Ryan muttered. Unfortunately, he wasn't wrong. His mom could be a little over the top when it came to bragging about him. God, what was he thinking inviting Peyton over after a game? It was one thing to invite her over, but a whole other thing to have her around his parents after a game.

Pete nudged him with his shoulder. "It'll be fine, man. I can dive under the bus if I need to. Just give me a sign."

Ryan laughed. "Hopefully it doesn't come to that."

Rounding the corner, he scanned the crowd that filled the hallway. He spotted his dad's head above the crowd and nodded to Pete. People patted him on the back and called out congratulations to him as he passed. When he caught sight of Peyton leaning against the wall, he pulled up short. It was like his feet weren't able to move. Shit. He really hadn't been prepared for how it would feel seeing her standing there with his parents waiting for him after the game. It had been one thing seeing her up in the stands, but this, having her here with his family...

Pete clapped him on the back. "Well, enough said," Pete muttered.

"What?" he asked, turning to his friend.

"That kind of answered any remaining question I had about how you feel about Peyton."

Ryan rubbed his hand roughly across his face. "Yeah."

"Ryan," his mom called as she pushed toward him, bumping other people out of her way in her haste to grab him.

A smile split across his face. His mom loved all this stuff. "Hey." He wrapped her up in a warm hug.

His mom squeezed him tightly, then pulled back and patted his cheek affectionately. "You were amazing, sweetheart."

"Thanks." He glanced up and his dad smiled and clapped him on the back.

"Nice game, son. You too, Pete." His dad reached out and shook Pete's hand.

"Thanks," Pete replied. "Excuse me." Pete pushed past Ryan's parents and wrapped Kendall up in a hug and kiss that had his sister sagging against his best friend. A blushing Kendall peeked over Pete's shoulder, then dipped her head back against Pete's chest.

Ryan bit back a laugh at the look his mom was shooting his sister. Debbie Graves was not a fan of PDA. Especially when it involved her daughter.

Making eye contact with Peyton, his chest tightened as a wave of something he couldn't quite explain raced through him. He reached out his hand and her fingers closed around his and the feeling intensified. He pulled her toward him, cupped the back of her head with his hand, and pressed a kiss against her lips. Damn, this woman affected him.

"Nice game." She smiled up at him, her blue eyes twinkled mischievously. "You looked hot."

Momentarily forgetting where he was, he stepped closer to Peyton and tightened his grip in her hair. "Yeah?"

"Ryan," his mother's stern voice behind him broke through his haze and dumped a bucket of ice water on him. He shuddered. What guy could feel anything but a little creeped out about lusting after a woman with his mom right there?

Why did his parents have to be here? This was the first game Peyton had come to as his girlfriend. Not the fake shit like last time, but honestly his and wearing his jersey to prove it. It was stirring up all kinds of shit in his mind. He really didn't want to have to do family dinner. All he wanted to do was take her home and fuck her until she looked at him the same way he was feeling right now.

He placed a kiss on her forehead. "To be continued," he whispered.

"Count on it."

Ryan wrapped his arm around her shoulder and turned to his family. Kendall smirked at him, and he couldn't help but laugh at the knowing look on Pete's face. Okay, maybe he understood a little better where they were coming from. It didn't make it any less gross that it was his sister, but it made more sense now, how when you were really into someone it kind of took on a life of its own.

"So, who drove?" Ryan asked, looking at his parents and sister.

"I did," his father replied. "Your sister said she wanted to ride home with Pete."

"What about you?" He turned to Peyton.

"I left my car at home as discussed." She rolled her eyes dramatically.

"Good girl." He smiled to himself when her eyes narrowed at him.

Ryan turned to his family. "So, I'll see everyone at my place." Grabbing Peyton's hand, he squeezed gently. "Ready?"

"I think so."

Inside the car, Ryan fired it to life. Music blasted through the speakers, and he winced. "Sorry, it gets me in the right headspace to play."

"Really? I would never have pegged you for a death metal guy. You are just full of contradictions, Mr. Graves."

"What kind of music would you have pegged me listening to?"

"I don't know, maybe country rock."

He flicked to the chart hits channel. "I'll listen to pretty much anything, but weirdly before a game I like thrasher music. It gets me all pumped up."

Pulling into traffic, he flicked a glance at Peyton. "Okay, so how was the game with my parents?"

"It was good. I'm glad I had your sister there as a buffer. Kendall definitely made things easier on me. But your parents are nice."

"We'll see if you still think that after dinner," Ryan said.

"Why wouldn't I like them still?"

He sighed. "They're pretty invested in my games. I know it always drove Kendall crazy, so I'm hoping they chill out tonight."

Peyton shifted in her seat, pulling her leg up so she could sit sideways and face him as he drove. "How do you feel about it? You said it drove Kendall crazy. What about you?"

He tightened his hand around the wheel. "I don't know, it depends."

"On?"

"On whether they think I'm living up to my potential or not, I guess. When they think I'm doing great, it's awesome. I mean, who doesn't enjoy having people tell them how amazing they are? But when I'm not living up to potential, it can be a bit... annoying I guess is the best word."

"Well, based on how you played tonight, I can't imagine they would think you are anything but amazing."

"Here's hoping." He reached across the console and put his hand on her thigh, enjoying the way she shifted into his touch. "Thanks for coming today. I liked having you there."

"Good, I liked being there." Peyton ran her fingers gently up and down his arm.

He shifted in his seat. When she touched him like that, he could imagine exactly what her hand would feel like on the rest of his body. *Fuck, why did his parents have to be here?* He'd much rather be celebrating by christening a few more surfaces with Peyton instead of having dinner with his family. "Did I mention how hot you look in my jersey?"

"I think you mentioned something about it the other night, but I don't mind hearing it again."

"You're planning on staying over tonight, right?"

"If you want me to."

"Oh, believe me, I do." The sappy side of him was looking forward to waking up with her in the morning. Not that he'd ever admit that out loud if anybody asked.

CHAPTER FOURTEEN

When they walked into his kitchen, Ryan's mom was in full swing. The blender roared on the counter with some kind of fruity concoction.

"Oh good, you're here." Debbie looked up from where she was slicing a lime on the counter. "Where are your margarita glasses?"

He eyed his mom standing at the kitchen counter and winced as he remembered what he'd done to Peyton on that same surface. "Make yourself at home, Mom." Ryan placed a kiss against the side of her head as he slid past her. Reaching into the cabinet, he pulled out a couple of glasses and set them on the island.

"Shrek cups?" Debbie arched her brow and picked up the offending glass.

"Oh my god, I can't believe you have those." Peyton picked up the glass with the characters on it and smiled.

"I had these glasses when I was a kid, but they all broke. I can't believe yours didn't."

"Probably because he wouldn't let anyone else drink out of them when we were kids," Kendall mocked.

Ryan narrowed his eyes and pretended to glare at his sister. "Well, come on, can you blame me? You were like a baby giraffe. Nothing was safe around you."

"That's true, babe." Pete wrapped his arm around Kendall and pulled her to his side. "Remember that time you fell out of the tree when you were spying on us in the pool?"

"I wasn't spying. I was studying and lost my balance," Kendall said.

"Studying, Pete maybe," Ryan teased.

"Can you blame her? I was hot."

"You certainly thought you were." Debbie looked at her husband. "Do you remember how he always walked around with no shirt on that entire summer?"

"Of course I remember. I nearly went broke feeding every teenage girl in the neighborhood."

Peyton watched the interplay between the family and Pete. It was nice to have that kind of history with people. She'd moved around so much after her parents split up it had been hard to have friends through high school, let alone beyond that. Rayne had been her only constant. That was probably why she'd gone into the field she had. No matter what city she'd moved to, there was always a community center where she'd been able to go to play sports and meet people.

"So, about those margarita glasses?" Debbie asked.

Ryan leaned back against the counter and stuck his hands in his pockets. "I don't have margarita glasses. You're stuck with Shrek."

"Yes." Kendall's fist pumped in the air. "I finally get to use the glasses."

"Good point." Ryan reached up into the cupboard and pulled down a tall plastic poolside tumbler. "Put Kendall's in this." He pushed the blue cup toward his mother.

"You're an ass," Kendall muttered.

"Kendall." Debbie's stern voice brooked no argument from either of her children.

Debbie poured margaritas into the glasses and passed them around. "Peyton, we didn't really get a chance to talk too much during the game. Are you from San Diego?"

"Umm, sort of. I was born here, then moved when I was thirteen. We lived all over the west coast, and then I moved back here for my degree and never left."

"What about your parents? Where do they live now?" Debbie pulled out a barstool and sat down across from Peyton.

Peyton took a sip of her margarita to wet her mouth. Debbie stared at her with that inquisitive mom look that let her know she was in for a long night of getting to know you grilling. Fantastic.

"My mom lives in Seattle."

"What about your dad?"

Peyton shrugged. "No idea."

"You don't talk to you dad?" Debbie asked.

"No."

"Well, that's a shame." Debbie shook her head.

Shifting uncomfortably on her chair, she looked down at her glass on the counter. "I guess."

Ryan placed his hand on her back for support. "Mother," he growled in warning.

Peyton couldn't see what Ryan's face looked like behind her, but his tone clearly told Debbie the discussion was done.

"You said you moved around a lot as a child. Where else have you lived?" Debbie pressed.

Ryan's body tensed behind her. She could practically feel the annoyance coming off him. "Jesus, Mother. Maybe let her finish her first drink before you start in on the inquisition."

"I'm just trying to get to know her," Debbie muttered. "You never let me meet your girls, so I'm curious that's all."

"I didn't think the object was to freak her out in the first five minutes." Ryan sighed loudly. Peyton bit back a laugh. If a sigh could sound annoyed, his did.

Debbie rolled her eyes. "Don't be ridiculous. You wouldn't be dating her if she scared off that easily."

Peyton laughed and then smiled reassuringly at Debbie. She had expected nothing different. She was just as curious about Ryan's family as they were about her. "It's fine."

"What do you say I put these ribs on while the ladies get to know each other better?" Pat said, grabbing the platter out of the fridge.

Ryan reached into the fridge and pulled out three beers and handed one to Pete. "I've got your beer, Dad," he said. He paused next to Peyton and leaned down. His warm breath brushed against her neck and goosebumps pooled on her skin. "You gonna be okay if I head outside with my dad?"

"She'll be fine, Ryan," Debbie scoffed. "I'm not going to rip out her fingernails to get information out of her."

"You better not," he replied.

Peyton put her hand on his arm. "Go, I'll be fine." If Ryan's family were anything like hers, Kendall would be the one in the hot seat any minute anyway.

With the men outside, Debbie fired the blender to life again. "Was this your first time watching Ryan play?"

"No, I went to the game where Tommy threw in the first pitch, but I've also seen him play a bit at the center."

Debbie's spine stiffened. "Play at the center? What do you mean?"

"I work at a youth community sports program."

"Oh, that's right, that's how Ryan said you two met, because his team is volunteering there. He was very impressed with your work."

"Right." Peyton bit back a smile. He certainly wasn't impressed with her when they'd met that was for sure.

Debbie's brow wrinkled. "Surely Ryan doesn't play though when he's there."

"Sometimes he does. It depends on which kids are there and team dynamics."

Debbie's gaze snapped outside to where the men were standing around the barbecue. "What if he gets hurt?"

Kendall snorted. "He's a professional athlete mom, I'm pretty sure he can hold his own with a bunch of six-year-olds."

"It's not the six-year-olds I'm worried about. Ryan doesn't know how to do anything halfway. What if he rolls his ankle running or falls down? I can't imagine your fields are in very good shape. I don't like that at all."

"Ryan is perfectly safe. He doesn't usually do much running." There was no way she was telling Debbie that so far Ryan had mostly been playing with teenagers. The woman would lose her biscuits.

Kendall leaned over and poured another margarita for herself and topped off Peyton's. "Mom, seriously, he's a grown ass adult. He could stub his toe getting out of the pool too. You want to line that in bubble wrap?"

"I know that, Kendall, but he's worked really hard to get where he is in his career. I don't want him doing anything to jeopardize that."

"Oh my god, Mother, if he can't handle it then maybe he's in the wrong field."

"How you can you say that? Ryan has a *gift*."

"Yeah, I'm aware," Kendall growled.

Peyton watched the byplay between mother and daughter. She didn't know what the story was, but she'd have to be an idiot not to sense the undercurrents floating around the kitchen. "So, how long are you and Pat in town?"

"Just for the weekend. We are flying out to Greece on Monday and then going on a cruise for the next month."

"Wow, that sounds amazing."

"We can't wait." Her shoulders bounced with excitement as she wiggled her arms in front of herself. "I still can't believe Ryan remembered me telling him how I wanted to go to Malta."

"Geez, Mom, I booked the damn tickets. It wasn't all Ryan," Kendall muttered.

Debbie reached over and squeezed Kendall's arm. "I know, sweetie. Both of my children are fantastic. Your dad and I appreciate this gift so much. I'm just telling Peyton how thoughtful your brother is."

"So the cruise is a gift from Ryan and Kendall?" Geez, her mom usually got a gift certificate for the spa and a card.

"Yes, it was supposed to be for our thirtieth anniversary, but we were still working and couldn't get the time off. Now that we have retired, we can finally do it."

"Oh, that's very sweet. I'm sure you'll have a fantastic time." Peyton glanced out to the barbecue where Ryan was in deep conversation with his dad. Even from here, she could see the tension on Ryan's face. What was that about?

As she watched, Pete said something and suddenly everyone was laughing. Whatever the moment Ryan had been having with his father was gone. Turning her attention back to Kendall and Debbie, she listened as the two women discussed the itinerary for the trip. It sounded amazing.

Ryan popped his head into the kitchen. "Two minutes on the ribs, Mom."

Several hours later, Peyton pulled her feet up onto the daybed that overlooked the valley while Ryan walked his family to the door. After several minutes, he returned and dropped into the seat beside her. He shifted her so she was forced to curl into his chest. Smiling to herself about what a snuggler he was, she placed her hand on his stomach and absently rubbed her hand back and forth.

"I love my family, but they can be exhausting."

"Well, it must be exhausting to never do anything wrong."

"What are you talking about? I can't do anything right."

Peyton shifted on the daybed so she could look him in the face. "Your parents are obviously incredibly proud of you."

"Oh, absolutely they are." He dropped his head back onto the pillow. "I don't really know how to explain it. They wanted me to reach my goal so badly that it kind of became their whole world, and the idea of anything fucking that up is unthinkable for them both."

"But you're living your dream."

"Yeah, but it could all be taken away in a heartbeat. So, I can't rest on my laurels." His chest rose and fell on a deep exhalation. "My dad was on me tonight about how my pitching seemed off today and how you—" He glanced down at her. "Need to either come to more games or no games because having you in the stands was a distraction to me, or some such bullshit."

Peyton's stomach clenched. "Your parents hated me then?"

"What? No, they loved you. My dad was just worried that I'm in too deep with you. I'm going to get hurt, and it'll fuck up my game."

"Why would he think that?"

"Probably because I never introduce them to anyone for this exact reason. They analyze every little thing. I glanced up in the stands today, so I was distracted because you were there." He snorted. "I look up in the stands every game. I love seeing the crowd wearing our jerseys, and when I'm at away games, I scan the crowd looking for the splash of a Hawks jersey in the stands. The fact I knew you were there wearing my jersey wasn't a distraction. It was fucking fantastic. If I seemed nervous at all, it was probably because they were there." He laughed. "Not that I could ever tell them that."

"Well, if it's any consolation, your sister did a good job telling your mom to chill about her sweet, sweet boy," Peyton teased.

"Shit, sorry about that."

"Nah, it wasn't too bad. She didn't have any baby photos to pull out, but I will say it was a bone of contention that she couldn't find a photo album in your living room. She knows she made one for you."

"Jesus," he muttered. "She means well, but I think sometimes she forgets I'm a grown-assed man."

Peyton snickered. "That's exactly what you sister said."

"The grown-assed man part?"

"Yep, direct quote."

"Should have known." He sighed and pulled her tighter against him. "Thanks for being here tonight. It was nice."

"It was yeah." Peyton snuggled in and let her mind replay over the evening. "It was nice being with a bigger family. Growing up, it was just my mom and I, so I didn't get to experience having a sibling and the rivalry and memories that go along with that. It was nice to watch."

"Anytime you want my sister, you're welcome to her."

"I might have to take you up on that. She's pretty awesome."

Ryan made some weird noise in the back of his throat that could have been agreement or the exact opposite. She couldn't tell.

"So, you have a couple of days off before you head to New York?"

"Yeah, leave Thursday morning. New York then Detroit, but after that we're home for eight games, which is unheard of then LA and San Fran. Lots of downtime, which will be nice."

He slid his arm down her hip and hoisted her, so she was lying on top of him. Peyton laughed and sat up, straddling his lap.

Ryan's hands rested on her hips, and he shifted his own. The movement brought her down right on top of his cock. She bit back a sigh as he hardened beneath her.

"You gonna miss me while I'm gone?"

"Eh." She shrugged.

Ryan flexed his hips, pushing his hard cock against her core, and she dropped her head back. *My god that felt good.*

"You sure you won't miss me?"

Peyton ground her hips into him. "I'll miss this."

"Good thing I've got a couple days to fuck you then. By the time I leave, you'll be so sore you'll need the reprieve."

Peyton peeled off her shirt and tossed it to the side. Loving the way Ryan's eyes darkened as he stared at her chest. "Coach better not work you too hard at practice if you're going to live up to that promise."

His hand slid up the leg of her shorts. "Don't you worry about me."

CHAPTER FIFTEEN

Ryan slung his bag over his shoulder as he walked across the stadium parking lot the next morning. "Yo Pete," he yelled when he saw his best friend exiting his own vehicle.

"Hey, you all recovered from family dinner?" Pete asked.

"I should ask you the same thing. If you don't put a ring on my sister's finger soon, I swear to god, my mom will make your life a living hell."

Pete grimaced. "Debbie definitely made it clear she feels her daughter should be married rather than living in sin." He hoisted his own bag onto his shoulder as they walked toward the player entrance. "But after last night, I'm not sure your sister would agree."

"What do you mean?"

"Ken went on a pretty good tear last night after we got home about how this isn't the middle ages where she needs to be defined as some man's wife or some such shit. I don't know with those two." Pete rolled his eyes.

"I kind of thought she was going to throw something at my mom when she started talking about you getting the milk for free."

Pete laughed. "No shit, but I hate to break it to your mom—I was getting the milk before we moved in together."

"I'm just going to forget you said that and pretend it never happened," Ryan muttered.

"I'm not." Pete waggled his eyebrows.

"Ah fuck, gross. Stop talking." Ryan shoved Pete's head, then pushed open the door to the locker room.

The second he stepped in, the place went silent as all eyes turned toward him and Pete. A couple of guys stood around Andy with guilty looks on their faces.

"What?" A feeling of dread knotted his stomach. Something about the way the guys were looking at him did not sit well.

"Nothing," Andy replied.

Johnny glanced at Andy and smirked, then looked back at Ryan. "Yeah, nothing."

Henderson looked down at his feet, then shuffled toward his locker.

"Obviously it's not nothing. So what?" Ryan demanded.

Chase stood up from the bench where he was lacing up his shoes and glared at Andy. "You're showing the video in the fucking change room, dude. You should at least have the balls to show it to him."

"What's happening?" Gonzo's voice chirped as he pressed into the locker room behind them.

"No idea. That's what I'm trying to find out," Ryan said.

Andy stared back at them, not saying a word.

"Andy here was just showing us how lucky you are, Ry. And why you seem so chill lately. Your girl..." Johnny brought his fingers up to his mouth in a chef's kiss. "Damn."

Ryan's spine stiffened as every muscle in his body went on alert. "My girl, what?"

"I was just showing the boys a little home movie Peyton and I made," Andy said.

"A home movie?" Fuck, he didn't like the sound of that.

"Yeah," Andy replied. "The lighting isn't the best, but the content is top shelf."

"Fuck yeah it is," Johnny agreed, and threw his hand up for Andy to smack.

Ryan strode across the locker room. "Show me," he demanded.

"I don't think you're gonna want to see it, Ry," Sims said from his locker. Ryan snapped his head toward the rookie, then looked around the locker room at his teammates. Fuck, almost half of the team was already here and other than Andy and Johnny, none of them would make eye contact with him. "You've all seen it?"

"Not everyone. Baby Sims didn't think his virgin eyes could handle it," Andy jeered.

"Or maybe I just have more class than you assholes," Sims snapped. "Seriously Ry, you don't need to watch that. Andy's just being Andy."

"Yeah, that's kind of the problem." Ryan stood in front of Andy and held out his hand for the phone. "Show me the fucking video."

Andy chuckled, then hit play on his phone. Instantly an image of Peyton on her knees giving a blowjob to Andy filled the screen. Ryan stumbled back, bumping into Pete. He dimly registered Pete's hand on his shoulder as his mind reeled.

"What the fuck, Andy?" Pete snarled.

Ryan couldn't even form words. He looked around the change room at his teammates. His supposed friends. Nausea twisted his gut. Why would Peyton not have told him about the video?

"What? Your boy can't handle seeing proof of how much Peyton liked sucking my dick?" Andy taunted.

Ryan saw red. He lunged at Andy. The other man jumped away at the same time Pete's arm wrapped around Ryan and yanked him back. "Ryan, don't. He's not worth it," Pete growled in his ear.

He glared at Andy. At this particular moment, he didn't fucking care what the consequences would be for him. Andy was dead.

Gonzo grabbed him on the other side and together they dragged him into a treatment room.

Ryan paced around the room. "He's fucking dead."

"You gotta relax, Ry," Gonzo said.

"Relax? He just showed the entire team a video of my girlfriend sucking his dick. I'm not going to fucking relax."

"You freaking out, or worse, doing something stupid and getting suspended is exactly what Andy wants. Don't give him that?"

"Why the fuck would he want that?" Ryan looked around the room for something to take his anger out on. Of course, they'd chosen this room with the fucking ice-bath and massage table. There wasn't a goddamn thing in here that would help. "Fuck," he yelled.

"Who knows? It's fucking Andy. He's jealous, I don't know." Pete picked up one of the resistance bands and chucked it at Ryan. "Pull on that or something."

Ryan shot his friend a withering stare. A resistance band was not going to do jack shit in helping him release what he needed to release. The only thing that would was smashing Andy's smug face.

Pete hoisted himself up on the edge of the massage table. "That video was taken before you guys got together. It's not like you didn't know they had a past," Pete said calmly.

"Big fucking difference between knowing and seeing it in technicolor." Peyton had said she hadn't had sex with Andy. That video said otherwise. What the fuck was going on? Why did she lie to him?

"I'm sure there is, but it doesn't change anything, Ry."

"You can't be serious?" This changed everything. How the fuck was he supposed to trust her when she'd lied?

"Most of the guys on the team didn't even see the video," Gonzo said.

"Whether or not they saw it, they'll all fucking hear about how it exists."

"And what they do with that information will be determined by how you react. So calm your shit down," Gonzo told him.

That was a whole lot easier said than done. He paced around the room, yanking and pulling on the resistance band as he walked. This whole thing was so fucked up. It was like rookie year all over again. He couldn't do this again. It had been bad enough when his college girlfriend had cheated on him with a teammate and the shit he'd been put through, but this? This would be so much worse. He kicked the garbage can, sending the metal bucket launching across the room. It hit the wall and slid to the floor.

A light knock sounded, and Ryan snapped his head toward the door. Smitty gave a small wave through the door, then stepped in.

"Hey sorry to interrupt. Coach wants everybody on the field. I thought it'd be easier if it was me that came in rather than him." Smitty gave Ryan a tight smile. "Sorry man, I heard. Andy's a dick."

"Hmm, that's one word for it." Ryan pushed his hand through his hair roughly. His hand trembled with residual adrenaline, and he flexed his fingers, opening and closing his fist to gain control of his body. Pete was right, he would not give Andy the satisfaction of fucking with his game. He glanced through the window at the empty locker room, then at his friends. "Thanks guys."

"Anytime," Pete said. "Get changed and let's get out there."

Ryan walked onto the field. Every muscle in his body vibrated with rage as he stood on the practice mound.

He took a deep breath and exhaled slowly as he tried to center himself. Andy gave the sign for a slider and lined up his mitt. Ryan eyed the glove, then Andy's face. The urge to ignore the call and whip the ball at Andy's head as hard as he could instead was strong. If he thought the guy would miss the catch, he might actually follow through on the urge.

Fuck. He wanted to kill him. Screw what was best for the team. The guy needed to be tuned up and he was just the person to do it.

"You gonna throw the ball or what?" Andy yelled.

"I'll throw it when I'm good and fucking ready," he snarled. Ryan was holding on by a thread and this piece of shit didn't know how close he was to getting his teeth knocked out.

He closed his eyes and took another deep breath. *Focus on the glove.* That was all that mattered. Not who was holding it, but where the glove was placed. There was nothing else. He breathed slowly in and out, then finally opened his eyes. Like looking down a tunnel, his vision focused on the mitt, and he didn't see anything else. He wound up and launched the ball. The glove didn't even have to move to catch it.

"That was a little outside, Ry," Coach Gill called from his place behind Andy.

What the fuck? That pitch was perfect.

"Try a fastball this time," Coach yelled.

Andy shifted his body and held his glove up. Ryan lined up, visualized the pitch, and launched. Motherfucker. Once again, he'd thrown the ball perfectly where the glove was and once again, the pitch was wrong. This time inside.

Five more pitches all the same. Andy wasn't holding his glove where it needed to be to give him the proper marker. How many times had they gone over where he liked it held for each pitch? Andy had one fucking job. Hold his glove where Ryan needed it held and then catch the goddamn ball. Andy was no fucking good to him if he didn't hold his mitt in the right place.

Coach and Andy walked out toward him on the mound.

"What's going on? You seem a bit off today," Gill said.

"I'm not off, your boy here—" He pointed his finger at Andy. "—Isn't holding the fucking sequence right."

"Fuck you, Graves. I'm holding my fucking mitt exactly where it's supposed to be. You just can't hit the target."

"Is that why the pitch lands in your glove without you moving a fucking muscle?"

"Keep telling yourself that, superstar," Andy mocked.

"Do your fucking job and hold your goddamn glove where it's supposed to be," Ryan snarled.

Coach Gill stepped closer to Ryan. "Ryan?" Coach's brow knit with concern.

Ryan took a deep breath to calm himself down. This wasn't him. He could always separate life from baseball. What happened in the locker room was left in the locker room. The field had always been his sanctuary, like going to church. While he was on the field, the rest of the world ceased to exist. So why the hell was he struggling to do that today?

"Sorry," he muttered to the pitching coach. It wasn't Coach's fault Andy was an asshole.

"You got your pitcher all sorted, Coach?" Andy's eyebrow cocked up, taunting Ryan.

Gill turned and poked Andy in the chest. "That's not helping. You do your job and hold the glove where you know Ryan likes it, and Ry will do his job and get it in the fucking pocket."

"His shitty attitude has nothing to do with my glove. He's just sour cuz he realized he's snacking on my sloppy seconds," Andy taunted.

Ryan saw red. He lunged toward Andy who stumbled back. If the coach hadn't grabbed hold of Ryan's waist, he would have sent Andy on his ass.

"Ryan," Coach snapped. "What the fuck?" Gill pointed at Andy. "Get the fuck back to your spot. Ryan, my office. Now."

Ryan glared at Andy, who gave Ryan a taunting salute before he turned and walked back toward home plate.

Ryan followed the pitching coach as he walked down the tunnel toward his office. Neither of them spoke a word. Once inside the office, Ryan closed the door behind himself and paced around the room.

"Sit your ass down," Coach snarled.

Ryan dropped into the chair on the opposite side of the desk.

"You mind telling me what the fuck that was out there?" Coach demanded.

"Not really." He was pissed, not only at Andy, but at himself. He knew better than to let someone get in his head. Andy was an asshole. He'd always been an asshole.

"Not an option, Ryan. If you want to see the field tomorrow night, you better start talking."

Defiantly, he widened his legs in his seat, leaned forward, and rested his elbows on his knees as he pinned his coach with a stare. "You wouldn't bench me. You know I'm the best pitcher to line up against New York."

"Watch me," Coach growled. "You're a great pitcher, Ryan. We all know that. But what I saw out there on the field was some bush-league shit. And that kind of bullshit is how you lose games, not win them." Coach leaned back in his chair and crossed his arms over his chest. "So, start talking if you want to play."

Unable to continue sitting in his chair, he pushed up and walked around the confined space on his side of the office. "I'm sorry about losing my cool." He angrily scrubbed his hand across his face. "I wasn't making excuses. Andy wasn't holding the sequence right, but I could have handled it better."

"You think?" Coach rocked back and forth slightly in his chair, never uncrossing his arms as he watched Ryan. "I'll deal with Andy later. But we both know he's a jealous little shit, and he always tries to fuck with you and make you look bad when he thinks you're getting too big for your britches. You normally rub it in by making the pitch despite where he holds his fucking glove. That's the thing that makes you so great, Ryan. You know your body and what you can do. You can visualize better than anyone I've ever seen."

Ryan dropped back down into his chair. "I know. I couldn't get out of my head like I normally can, so I needed the fucking glove to be where it was supposed to be today to hit it."

"Why?" Coach rocked again. The squeaking of the seat set Ryan's teeth on edge and, from the look on Gill's face, he knew it. "Talk to me, Ryan. I gather it had something to do with Peyton."

Ryan ground his teeth together as he remembered what he'd walked in on today when he'd arrived at practice. He nearly cracked a tooth as he clamped his mouth tighter.

"Yeah, you could say that."

"Talk, Ryan." Coach leaned forward and rested his hands on the desk. His posture left no room for argument.

"Peyton briefly dated Andy. That's kind of how we met."

"Fuck."

"Yeah, umm." Ryan rubbed his fingers back and forth over his brow to ease the tension that was throbbing behind his eyes. "Things with Peyton and me have gotten more serious, and Andy didn't like it."

"What did he do?"

"When I showed up at practice today, Andy was showing his buddies a video of Peyton and him, umm..."

"Jesus," Coach muttered.

"Yeah." Ryan drew his hand down over his mouth, smoothing out his beard.

"Sorry, son, that's messed up."

"It's not great."

"Makes that showing out there a little more understandable. But you've got to be able to leave that shit off the field. You know that."

Coach was right, he knew that. But how the fuck was he supposed to leave it when he looked across the plate at the piece of shit who'd done it?

"Take the rest of today to get your head on straight. Talk to your girl. Because I can promise you if don't have your shit together tomorrow when you board that plane, I'll bench your ass."

"Yes, sir."

"And Ryan. You can bet your ass I'll be talking to Andy."

"Thank you."

"Whatever shit is happening between you two needs to stay off the field. It was a dick move on Andy's part, for sure. But we both know there are guys who are team first, and there are guys who are me first. Andy is me first, always has been. He's never been good about losing the spotlight."

"This was never a fucking competition," Ryan growled.

"Easy for you to say when you're the winner."

"Fuck."

"Leave it off the field, Ryan. I'll talk to Andy and he'll catch the sequence properly or his ass will be benched. And believe me, he doesn't want that any more than you do."

"I'll do my best to leave it off the field, but any chance Patel can catch for me the next game? Give me a chance to figure my shit out. I wouldn't normally ask, you know that but..." Ryan exhaled. "I appreciate you giving me time to figure out everything with Peyton, but I also have to figure out my teammate, my catcher, trying to fuck with my head. I'm not sure I trust he can leave things off the field, and I need to know he'll hold the sequence properly or he's no fucking good to me."

"Leave it with me." Coach pushed back in his seat. "If I don't trust that Andy will put the team first, Patel will catch for you. I can promise you that. Now get your shit figured out so that I can count on you to win the next game."

Easier said than done. He didn't have the first clue on what to do to get his head on straight. Jealousy wasn't something he knew how to deal with. Seeing Peyton sucking off Andy was burned into his brain. He didn't know if he could get past it.

Shit, this was why he never got seriously involved with women. Everything about this situation was messing with his head.

He sure as shit wasn't in the right space to talk to Peyton. Fuck, he needed a drink.

CHAPTER SIXTEEN

Peyton kicked off her shoes at the front door and made her way to the kitchen.

God, days like today sucked. She hated when she had to call DCFS about one of the kids in her program. Pulling a bottle of wine from the fridge, she poured herself a hefty glass. As she took the first sip of icy cold wine, she closed her eyes and sighed.

Images of the burns on Billy's ribs flashed before her eyes, and she took another sip. Please let this time be different for him, she prayed. Billy had been bounced back and forth between home and foster care so many times already, and each time the situation seemed to get worse and worse for him. Not only was he getting harder to place in foster care, but each time he went home the secrecy grew. If his shirt hadn't gotten ripped during football today, who knows how long it would have been before he ever talked to anyone? She understood the law around reporting, but each time he was sent back home, his faith and trust in the staff at the youth center diminished.

With a glass of wine in hand, she made her way down the hall. She needed a hot shower to wash the day off her. The sound of her doorbell ringing pulled her up short. She debated ignoring it, but on the off chance it was Ryan, she turned and made her way toward the front of the house. With them heading out-of-town tomorrow, she doubted it would be him, but a girl could hope.

She pulled open the front door and smiled when she saw Ryan standing there in his sweats. His hair stood up on end like he'd had the windows down while he drove. "Hi, what are you doing here?" she asked, stepping back to allow him to come in.

"We need to talk."

"Okay," she murmured hesitantly. Anxiety danced down her spine. Why? She couldn't quite say, but something about his tone was off. "You want some water or anything?"

"Why didn't you tell me you'd made a sex tape with Andy?"

She reared back like she'd been punched. "What?" What the hell was he talking about, a sex tape?

"You fucking lied to me. You said you never had sex with him and today I had to walk into work to see a fucking video of you two together."

"Back up. I never had sex with Andy." Her mind reeled as she tried to catch up with what he was talking about.

"Well, you sure as hell gave him a killer blowjob. And now all the fucking guys on the team saw it."

She dropped onto the couch. Her stomach lurched. He'd filmed her? Her mind raced. How had he filmed her? Oh my god, who else had he shown?

"There's a big fucking difference between we started messing around and we made a fucking sex tape. Jesus Peyton. Do you know how embarrassing that was?" Ryan demanded.

"Oh, it was embarrassing for you?" she scoffed.

"Yeah, Jesus, it was bad enough when the guys bugged me about taking his sloppy seconds. Now I have to deal with them knowing what you look like when suck cock. Fuck, Peyton. I didn't sign on for this shit." He angrily shoved his hand through his hair.

Humiliation warred with the rage burning in her chest. How dare he be mad at her for something outside her control?

"Sloppy seconds, huh? Well, god forbid *you* be embarrassed about me."

He stared at her like he'd never seen her before. Then shook his head. His gaze ran up and down her body, and his lip curled in disgust. "I have to play with these guys, Peyton. You could have fucking warned me. If you had told me the truth, I would have been prepared for this kind of thing."

"Prepared for this?" She scoffed. "How do you prepare for a sex tape you didn't know was made? My god, you're a jerk. Get over yourself, Ryan." She laughed, sounding harsh even to her own ears. "Do you honestly think I'd agree to some douchebag showing everyone a video of me?"

"I don't even know anymore." He shook his head. "I bought all the shit you spewed about not being some kind of groupie. That you were different from those other girls. And yet you're the worst of them all. Making your little sex tape to secure the deal."

"Fuck you," she snarled. "I didn't know about the god-damn tape."

"Yeah right," he scoffed. "The angle of that camera was pretty fucking good for you to not know it was there." He glared at her like some piece of trash. "You played me, and I was too fucking stupid to see it."

"Well, now that you've seen the light you can get the fuck out," she yelled.

"I can't believe I was so wrong about you," he said before storming toward the front door.

Tears burned behind her eyes. "You and me both," she whispered to his receding back.

The front door slammed shut behind him, and she dropped back onto the couch as pain ripped through her body.

God, how could she have been so stupid? Did she learn nothing from briefly dating Simon? How had she not seen that all professional athletes were the same? They were all a bunch of entitled assholes. She'd stupidly believed Ryan was different, but he wasn't. Hell, maybe he was worse. At least with Simon, what she eventually saw was what you got. He was a rich, egotistical asshole. But Ryan? He'd acted like he was so sweet and caring when really, he was just the same.

It had only taken a handful of dates with Simon for her to realize he wasn't for her. But with Ryan, she'd thought they had what it took to go the distance. That what they'd been building was real. That he respected her, cared for her. Clearly, she'd been so wrong about him. Her chest tightened as she tried to swallow past the pain. She'd been in love with the jerk and now—.

She sniffed and wiped the tears that streamed down her face. Reaching behind her, she grabbed the couch pillow and clenched it to her chest before curling into a ball on the sofa. She let the tears flow.

After her brutal day, she'd been so excited to see Ryan on her front doorstep. And it had all fallen to dust. How could she have been so blind? How could he believe she was that kind of person?

She jackknifed up. Oh my god, there was a tape out there with her giving Simon a blowjob. Who else had he shown? How the hell had he taken it in the first place? How had she not known that he'd videotaped her? Ryan said the angle was good. How was that possible? Her mind played back and forth over that evening. To the hotel room out by the airport where he'd been staying the night before the team had left on the road.

Like a movie, she went over and over that night. Oh my god, she was so naïve. Clearly, he'd planned it all along. He'd been the only one on his team to be staying there. He'd said it was so he could sleep later. After finding out about his wife, she'd realized he'd done it so he could get away with cheating on her, but obviously there'd been more to it than that. He was a bigger piece of carp than she'd ever imagined. How could she have not seen that? So much for always priding herself on being able to read people.

She angrily wiped the tears from her face.

There was no way she was letting him get away with this.

CHAPTER SEVENTEEN

This had been the longest five days of her life. Waiting for them to get back from their road series to talk with Simon had been almost impossible. But she needed to confront him face to face and not on the phone.

All week at work, she'd been a mess, waiting for the other shoe to drop. She had to get Simon to delete the video. If her employer found out there was a sex tape out there of her, she'd lose her job. The Hawks could pull their contract. Who would hire her to work with at risk youth with something like that out there? Simon needed to fix this.

Peyton sat in her car, anxiously drumming her hands on the steering wheel as she waited for Simon to arrive for practice. She prayed she didn't run in to Ryan while she was here confronting Simon. The last thing she needed was to deal with him too. Finally, she saw Simon's Tesla pull up. As he walked across the parking lot toward the entrance, she got out of her car. Conscious of the other players who also were arriving for practice, she squared her shoulders and called his name. His head turned and when he saw her, a smirk split across his face. How had she found him attractive? Now, looking at him, it was so obvious what a snake he was. How had she not seen that before?

"Well, well, well, if it isn't the beautiful Peyton Sharp. To what do I owe the pleasure?" he asked loudly as he walked toward her. High-fiving one of his teammates as he walked past him.

He stopped in front of her and scanned her face before wrinkling his nose. "I'm guessing by your face, Ryan talked to you."

"You took a video of me?"

"Yeah, so?" He shrugged.

"Yeah, so?" she yelled. "Are you fucking kidding me with that?"

"Hey, now, what happened to the girl who didn't swear?"

"She had a fucking sex video taken of her without her consent, asshole," she snarled. "How the hell could you take that video without my permission?"

"What's the big deal?"

"Are you kidding me?" Peyton stared at him. His brow knit with confusion. Was this guy for real? "You took a video of something intimate without my knowledge, Simon. That's not okay."

"Come on Peyton. There was no way you would let me film it."

"EXACTLY! Then you shouldn't have done it," she growled.

"But that's what made it so hot. When a good girl like you gets all down and dirty sucking cock. There's nothing sexier than that. I wanted to remember it."

A disgusting, cocky smirk slide across his face and his leer scanned down her body like he was remembering every filthy detail.

"You're disgusting. Delete the video. It's bad enough you took it without my permission, but you showed it to your teammates. I don't deserve that."

"You might not have, but Golden Boy needed to be taken down a peg."

Peyton reared back. "You did this to get back at Ryan?"

"Yeah, he was just supposed to pretend to date you, so Carmella didn't find out. He wasn't supposed to fuck you himself. You were mine."

"I was *never* yours, asshole."

"Well, that video says otherwise, now, doesn't it?" He waggled his eyebrows at her, then licked his lips. "You were really fucking good, Peyton. I might just have to watch it again before practice."

"Delete that video, now, or I tell your wife." Peyton fought to stand tall, despite wanting to cover her arms over her chest to stop him from looking at her.

"What do you think my wife will do?" He laughed. "My wife knows how good she has it. She's not going to care that I hooked up with some little groupie for a BJ."

Peyton gritted her teeth. Asshole. "Well, I guess we'll see about that won't we?" she challenged.

He stepped in closer to her. Every survival instinct in her body went on high alert. She should be safe in this parking lot in broad daylight. But she didn't know what kind of guy he really was. Was he the kind to hit her? Maybe.

"What's going on here?" A deep male voice called from behind her, and she breathed a sigh of relief. She glanced over her shoulder and saw Smitty and Gonzo walking up toward them.

"Nothing," Simon said.

The two men stopped just behind Peyton. Their presence letting her know they were there and it felt like they had her back.

"Doesn't look like nothing to me. Does it look like nothing to you, Gonz?"

"Nope, doesn't look like nothing to me either," Gonzo replied.

"Mind your business, boys," Simon told them.

"I don't know, Andy, this here is our boy's girl and she doesn't look too happy with you, so since Ry's not here that kind of seems like our business," Smitty said.

"Something we can help you with, Peyton?" Smitty asked her.

She winced. God, this was so humiliating, but needed to be done. She took a deep breath and looked Smitty in the eyes. "I need him to delete that video."

Smitty winced and she glanced over at Gonzo, who didn't meet her stare. Their expressions making it clear they had both had seen the video in question.

"I don't have to delete shit," Simon growled.

"You do when I didn't give you permission to make the video."

Gonzo stepped closer to Andy. "You took that video without her knowing?"

"Who cares? She's a fucking groupie. We've all made videos, man."

"Not without permission, we haven't," Smitty replied.

"Delete it," Gonzo snarled.

"Fuck you." Simon puffed up and stepped into Gonzo, challenging the other man.

A slow mean smile curled up the corner of Gonzo's lips and he stood tall, the move emphasizing the size difference between them. "Trust me, little man, you don't want me to make you."

When Simon glanced over at Peyton, he didn't look quite as confident as he had a moment ago.

Peyton squared her shoulders, pulling on all of her strength and confidence and maybe stealing a little from the men at her back. "Delete the video or else."

"Or else what? Like I said, Carm's not going to care."

She chewed her bottom lip. How was she supposed to make him do the right thing?

"Or else she goes to the cops," Smitty said.

Peyton's stomach dropped. God, she knew that was an option, but could she do that? The idea of going to the police made her feel sick. Going to the police would ensure everyone found out about the video. Her employer would fire her for sure. Yes, she didn't know about the video, but there was no way they would want her to work with the youth when she had a sex scandal attached to her name. It was wrong, but that's what would happen. The Hawks would likely pull their support because of the scandal. What a mess.

"Yeah, on what charges?" Andy scoffed.

Peyton squared her shoulders. How could she tell the kids to stand up for themselves when she wasn't willing to do it herself? "I didn't know about the video, Simon, and it's illegal to show anyone."

Andy stared at her and she shifted her weight, forcing herself to stand strong. Could he tell how much she didn't want to have to go to the police? She hadn't done anything wrong and yet she'd never felt so much shame in her life. It was humiliating to have to face Simon, to know Ryan's friends and teammates had seen something so intimate.

"Whatever Peyton. You're not gonna do shit and we both know it. Walk away." Andy stared at her with cruel eyes. It was like he got some kind of charge out of seeing her humiliated like this.

"I'm not leaving until you delete the video, Simon."

"Fine, stay." He turned on his heel and started to walk away.

"Do you not listen to any of the PR lectures they make us attend? California has laws around revenge porn and video consent, asshole. With all the shit in the media right now, this is not a scandal you want to have," Smitty called after him.

Gonzo gripped Andy's shoulder and he winced. "Delete it. Now."

Andy pulled his phone out of his pocket and unlocked it.

"Angle your phone so she can make sure you're deleting the right thing," Gonzo ordered.

"Jesus." Andy angled his phone toward Peyton and with a couple of swipes he deleted the video. "Happy?"

The knot in her stomach eased slightly as he deleted the first video. "Getting there. Delete the one on the cloud too," she demanded.

"Fuck." Andy pulled up his cloud account and deleted the video from there too while Peyton watched.

"Are those the only copies?"

"Yeah," he grumbled.

"It better be because otherwise I'm not kidding about going to the police." She glanced behind her at Ryan's friends and Simon's teammates. The outrage on their faces steeled her confidence. "You were dumb enough to show the whole team the video, so you gave me some witness's the police can call upon."

"We'd be more than happy to talk to them," Smitty replied.

Andy's mouth tightened into a hard, sneering line. "You seriously would side with her over your own team-mate?"

"We happen to be on the same team, but we sure as hell aren't friends, asshole," Smitty snarled.

"Whatever. Should have known you two were so far up Golden Boy's ass—"

Gonzo pressed his chest against Andy's, bumping the smaller man back. "You want to finish that sentence?"

"No."

"Didn't think so," Gonzo replied.

Andy turned and stormed off toward the entrance to the stadium.

Peyton hated to admit that she wasn't sure Simon would have deleted the video without their backup. His ego wouldn't let him be pushed around by a woman. He would have forced her hand. "Thanks, guys. I really appreciate your help." Her cheeks burned with humilia-tion as she looked at the two men and pasted on a small smile. At least these two weren't douchebags.

"No problem, Ryan would have our ass's if we let that asshole talk to you like that."

If only that were true. The man at her apartment the other night was not the man she knew. She wasn't sure which one was the real version. At this moment, she wasn't sure she cared. Everything in her hurt. This entire incident was too raw, too painful, too real. "I'm not sure Ryan would care all that much."

"What are you talking about? Of course he would," Smitty replied.

"Maybe you should talk to him about that," she told them.

Gonzo stuck his hands in his front pockets and looked down at his feet. "We heard you broke up."

"It'll blow over." Smitty said.

"No chance of that." The things they'd said to each other couldn't be unsaid. He hated her, thought she was a whore. And honestly, he wasn't who she thought he was either.

"That your doing or his? Because I know the video was a bit of a shock, but Ryan is crazy about you."

"Not crazy enough, apparently," she replied. The pain of admitting that out loud slicked through her chest and tears welled up behind her eyes. "Shoot," she mumbled as she blinked rapidly to quell the tears from sliding down her face.

"Ah geez, Peyton, don't cry," Smitty groaned.

"I'm not." She sniffed. "This has all just been a lot." She looked at Ryan's two friends and smiled sadly. Humiliation weighed heavily in her gut. What must they all think of her? How was she supposed to work with the team when they'd all seen her like that? It didn't matter that she hadn't been aware of the video that didn't change the fact that they had all seen her. It would have been one thing if she had Ryan's support, but she didn't. To the team, she was just some groupie. So much for keeping things professional. What if someone stupidly said something in front of the kids? What if they leered at her in that slimy way Simon had just done? God. The video might be gone, but it wouldn't be forgotten. Why had she thought getting rid of the video would fix everything? This wasn't over.

Her ears buzzed and her heart pounded in her chest as panic set in. There was no way she would spiral out of control in the parking lot. She took a deep breath. "Thanks again, you guys. It means a lot to me."

The sound of a car pulling into the parking lot drew her attention. Ryan's SUV slid into a stall. She didn't have the energy to deal with that today. Peyton flicked her hand toward her car. "I'm going to get out of here so you can get to practice. Thanks again."

"You don't want to stay and talk to him?" Smitty asked.

"Nope. Not a good idea," she replied before bolting to her car. Once inside, she quickly threw the car into gear. She caught sight of Ryan staring at her with a look of confusion on his face as she fled the parking lot.

Today had been hard enough without adding a confrontation with Ryan into the mix.

CHAPTER EIGHTEEN

Ryan stared after Peyton's car as she fled the parking lot. What had she been doing here? And why hadn't she stuck around to talk to him?

He made his way over to Gonzo and Smitty. "Was that Peyton?" he asked.

Gonzo scratched the back of his neck before finally answering. "Um yeah."

"What was she doing here?"

"When we got here she was giving Andy hell," Smitty replied.

"Because he showed the video?"

Smitty shifted from one foot to the other. "Yeah, that too, but I think mostly she was pissed that there actually was a video."

Ryan pulled up short. "What do you mean, actually was a video? She honestly didn't know about it?"

"Didn't seem to, no. She was pretty upset that he'd taken the video without her knowing."

"What did Andy say?" Ryan asked. His mind raced as he tried to process what this all meant. "How did he take a video if she didn't know?"

"No idea, but he didn't seem too concerned about it, even when Peyton threatened to tell his wife he got all douchey and told her Carm wouldn't care. Apparently, his wife is just happy to be along for the ride, however that looks," Smitty said.

"Yeah right," Gonzo scoffed. "If Carm knew he had a video of him with some other girl and he was showing it around the locker room that would be the last BJ he ever got because I'm pretty sure she'd do a Bobbit on him."

"No shit," Smitty laughed. "Whatever agreement they might have between them, she doesn't strike me as the kind of woman who would be okay with her husband publicly showing a video of him with some other girl."

"Guys, can we focus here? So Peyton was here to call Andy out on the video. What happened? Did she get it resolved? I mean, she left and you both seem chill, so I'm hoping she did but..." Fuck. Why didn't she ask him for help?

"Yeah, we helped set him straight. No worries," Smitty said.

"What does that mean?" Ryan's body tensed. Jesus, normally you couldn't shut these two up, and today it was like pulling teeth to get them to give him any information.

Gonzo's lip curled as anger radiated off him. "It means we helped him realize he should delete the video."

"Helped him how? Fuck, would you two just fucking explain?"

"What? I thought you broke up and were done with her. You didn't want to talk about it, blah blah blah." Smitty rolled his eyes.

Ryan clenched his jaw so hard he was surprised his teeth didn't crack as he bit back the urge to grab his teammate by the neck and force him to talk. "Just because we broke up doesn't mean I don't care if she is treated well. And if Andy took that video without her knowing then he fucking needs to pay for that."

"Chill dude, we explained it to him and he saw the error of his ways and deleted the video." Smitty glanced at Gonzo and smirked as the two men exchanged a look.

Gonzo snorted. "Yeah, threats of jail will do that to you."

"You threatened him with jail?" Ryan let out a harsh breath. How the hell had it come to that?

"Well sort of. We mostly just backed up Peyton. Asshole needed to be reminded about California law on taking and distributing video without consent." Smitty shrugged. "He was being a dick."

"He's always a dick," Gonzo muttered.

"Yeah, what the hell did Peyton see in him anyway? I mean seriously, look at her and then fucking Andy... Shit, he was swinging way outside his weight class on that one."

"Fuck focus, you two, Jesus." Ryan gave an exasperated sigh, desperate to get all the information his friends were being so stingy about relaying.

"What? We told you everything. Peyton didn't know about the video, Andy didn't care. We helped convince him otherwise."

"I'm going to fucking kill him," Ryan growled.

"We dealt with it, man. You guys broke up, not your problem anymore." Gonzo waved his hand dismissively.

"Are you trying to piss me off?"

"What? I thought you didn't want to wreck the team vibe and you needed to focus on your career and all that drama wasn't good for your game." Gonzo mocked.

"It's different."

"What's different?" Pete stepped up to the group in the parking lot.

"Dipstick just learned that Peyton didn't know Andy had taken the video."

"Shit, seriously? He took a video of her doing that without her knowing?" Pete's eyes widened. "What a fucking piece of shit. Who does that kind of thing?"

"I know, right? I knew I wasn't friends with him for a reason," Smitty replied.

"No shit," Pete agreed.

Gonzo turned back to Ryan and pinned him with a look. "Ok, so back to Peyton. How is it different now that you know for sure she didn't know about the video?"

"It just is," Ryan grumbled.

"It just is?" Gonzo shook his head. "Are you seriously saying now that she didn't know about the video you'd be with her, but not when you thought she did? You aren't that guy, are you?"

"What guy?" Ryan stood taller and stepped toward his friend.

"That judgmental asshole. No woman of mine ranh ranh bullshit. Seriously, dude. Even if she knew about the video, it happened before you were together, so who the fuck cares? She didn't know he was married. Once she found out she couldn't be done with him fast enough, that's all that should matter."

"Yeah, easy for you to say. You try telling me that when you see a video of the woman you love sucking off some other guy."

"The woman you love?" Pete asked.

His chest tightened like there was a vice wrapped around him. Christ, did he love Peyton? Maybe? Yeah. He rubbed his hand against his sternum. His throat closed, making it hard to breathe. Fuck.

"You okay, man?" Pete clapped him on the shoulder.

He rubbed his chest again and took a deep breath and let it out slowly. "Yeah, fine. Let's get to practice."

"Avoiding the question doesn't change the answer, just so you know," Pete told him.

Didn't it? Maybe not, but that didn't mean he had the first clue what to do about it.

Ryan walked into the change room surrounded by his best friends. Andy looked over at them as they walked in and smirked. Rage flowed through Ryan.

Pete placed his hand on his shoulder and mumbled. "Don't. That's what he wants. Don't let him."

"Morning boys," Andy mocked.

"Fuck off," Pete replied. Before nudging Ryan on the arm and pushing him toward their lockers.

Ryan forced himself to take a deep breath and ignore the other man. Now was not the time to have it out with him. But if his friends thought he was letting this go, they were kidding themselves. There was no way he wasn't having words with the asshole. Ryan dropped onto the bench in front of his locker and kicked off his shoes.

After he was dressed, Ryan made his way out of the locker room. "You want to warm up?" Andy asked him as he came up behind him in the tunnel.

"No thanks, I think I'll see if Patel wants to catch a few."

"Patel, what the fuck? I'm the starting catcher," Andy growled.

"And?" Ryan shrugged. "I'll chuck at you when coach tells me I have to. Until then, stay away from me."

Ryan walked onto the field and yelled. "Yo, Patel, you want to warm up?"

"Uh, yeah," the other man stammered.

"Ryan, hold up," Coach Gill called out.

He wandered over to the pitching coach. "What's up, coach?"

"Why aren't you warming up with Andy? He'll be catching for you tomorrow night?"

"Honestly? Because he's an asshole, and I need to throw a few to blow off some steam before I have to deal with his shit, otherwise my game will be crap. And I'm not giving him that."

Coach stared at Ryan, assessing him. Ryan stared him straight back in the eye. He had done nothing wrong, and he wasn't backing down on this. "Fair enough. Anything I need to be aware of?" Coach asked.

Ryan glanced over at Andy, who stood glaring at them. *What an asshole.* How the fuck was he supposed to play with him?

"Son, you don't have to be friends with every one of your teammates."

"We are definitely not friends," Ryan snarled.

"But you do have to be respectful because you're teammates."

The muscles in his jaw twitched as he clenched his teeth together, trying to get a handle on his anger. "And what happens when there's nothing about the guy that deserves respect?"

Coach shifted his hat off his forehead, moved it around a little then put it back in place. "No one is all good or all bad, Ryan. Everyone has something about them that is redeemable."

"Not everyone," he mumbled. He looked over at Andy again. He could still picture the way Andy had sneered at him with such cruel glee when he'd shown the video of Peyton around the locker room. Now that he knew she hadn't agreed to the video, Andy showing it was even worse. Shit, who was he kidding? Even if she'd agreed to the video, she didn't agree to have it shown around a locker room. He dragged his hand through his hair. And he was an asshole for not realizing that before. Fuck.

Coach glanced over at Andy, then back at Ryan. "You sure you don't need to talk?"

"Yeah, I'm fine." Was he? Who the hell knew? But he'd worked his entire life to make it to this point in his career, and he would not let some piece of shit on his team fuck things up for him. He needed to get his head straight. Block out everything but the game. He looked at his pitching coach and gave him a tight smile. "Thanks, Coach."

"Ryan, if there is something I need to be aware of, talk to me. You're the best pitcher in the league. Our team needs you. But the thing about pitching is you need someone to catch the ball. This is a team sport, kid. Get your head in the game."

"Yeah." He took a deep breath and exhaled.

Ryan walked toward Patel to warm up. He rolled his neck and tried to calm his breathing. Over the years, he'd practiced every technique known to man to calm himself, relax, and shut out the noise. Once a pitcher got in his own head, his game could quickly go to shit. And when you're throwing a hundred-mile-an-hour-fastball, a wild pitch could seriously hurt someone. Sighing deeply, he picked up the ball and ran it through his fingers. The feel of the stitching and the leather against his palm instantly calmed his nerves. He tossed the ball lightly to Patel, who caught it and threw the ball back. After several more throws, his mind cleared, and the tension eased from his neck.

This made sense. Baseball, he knew. He understood the rules. No emotions, just him and the game he loved.

After several minutes of playing catch, Coach Gill called Ryan over to the pitcher's mound with Andy behind the plate. Fantastic. He rolled his shoulders several times as he took the mound. He was a professional, he could do this. And if he imagined it was Andy's face in the center of the mitt, then so be it. He smirked to himself, lined up and let it rip.

"Jesus, Graves, that ball is still smoking," Coach Gill whooped. "How's the hand Andy? You got any bones left in there?" Coach laughed.

"My hand's fine," Andy grumbled.

"So much for warming up slowly. Don't think we need to work on the fastball today," Coach told him before turning to the catcher. "Andy let's work on varying the sequence a bit. Get in a few more splitters and forks to mix things up. Let's take advantage of what our boy can do and keep 'em on their toes."

For the next forty minutes, Andy called pitches and Ryan riffled them at him with laser-like precision. His game was on fire, and he had to admit Andy matched him and set up the catch perfectly. Maybe coach was right, and everyone had something redeemable about them. Andy could catch a ball. Too bad he was such a waste of space everywhere else.

"That's good for today, boys," Coach called. "I want your arm fresh for tomorrow. Ry, go hit the gym and cool down."

Andy jogged up to him as he left the field. "Nice job out there today."

"Thanks," Ryan replied.

"So we good?" Andy asked.

"We're fine on the field, but outside of that I have nothing to say to you, man."

"Jesus, get over it. It's not like I did anything to you."

"It's not about doing anything to me. What you did to Peyton is messed up."

"She loved every minute of it."

"Yeah? She loved having you take video without her consent? Oh wait, it was having you show a private moment to the entire fucking team that she loved. *Right*."

"Come on, man, girls like her? They know the score."

"Girls like her?" Ryan's shoulders tensed. "I don't care who the woman is, asshole. There's a reason what you did is illegal. Because it's fucking wrong, and if you can't see that, then there is something seriously wrong with you."

"You're just jealous that she never enjoyed sucking your cock as much as she did mine and that video proves it."

Rage unlike anything he'd ever felt before surged through his body. He punched Andy square in the face. The other man stumbled, righted himself, and charged at Ryan. Pain lanced through his face as Andy's fist connected with his cheek. Ryan swung and swung, connecting his fists with any part of Andy he could. Arms wrapped around his waist, pulling him off Andy. Blood covered Andy's face, his nose pushed off to the side, and Ryan couldn't help the smile that spread across his face. Good, he was glad he'd broken the fucker's nose.

"What the fuck, Ry?" Pete's voice growled in his ear, and he realized it was his best friend who'd pulled him off the other man.

He shrugged Pete off. "It's fine, I'm good."

"You're good?" Coach Gill yelled. "You're good? What the actual fuck you two?" Coach stepped in so close Ryan could feel him vibrating with anger. This would not be good. His hot breath hit Ryan in the face a moment before he poked him in the chest and yelled, "Did I not just ask you if you needed to talk? If there was anything I needed to know, and you looked me in the eye and said everything was fine. And now this?"

Out of the corner of his eye, Ryan saw the manager, Cal Schneider, storming onto the field.

"You two, my office, now," Cal growled.

"Yes sir," Ryan mumbled.

"Be repentant," Pete whispered.

Ryan scowled at his best friend. "That asshole deserved it."

"Not the right answer if you want to play tomorrow, dude."

Ryan rubbed his eyebrow and winced. He scrunched up his face, noting several more sore spots. Guess Andy had tagged him more times than he'd thought. He peered over at Andy as he gingerly moved toward the locker room area. By the way he was moving, he was hurting a lot more than Ryan was.

Good.

Asshole deserved it.

Ryan followed Cal and Andy inside the office. "Close the door, Ryan," Cal ordered.

He shut the door and sat down in the vacant seat beside Andy.

"Alright Simon, Ryan, does one of you want to explain to me what happened out there?"

Ryan gave his hands a once over, taking note of the large split across his knuckles on his right hand. He flexed his fingers. Shit, that hurt.

"Is one of you going to answer me?" Cal pressed.

"Just a difference of opinion, sir," Andy mumbled.

"A difference of opinion? That's your story? Just a difference of opinion?" Cal stared at them both. Ryan kept his head down not wanting to see the disappointment on the team manager's face.

"Ryan?"

He glanced up at the man who had the ability to change the trajectory of his career in a heartbeat. The disappointment on Cal's face hit harder than any punch Andy had landed. Shit.

He couldn't say he was sorry for hitting Andy. The asshole more than deserved it. And he'd do it again in a heartbeat. But he could have chosen a better time and place to have their discussion. By letting Andy goad him into fighting at practice, he'd let the asshole win. He knew better than that kind of thing. He'd spent his entire life working hard to be the best, to be respected, to be controlled, to be admired, and in one afternoon he'd thrown it all away.

"I expect better than this from you, Ryan. Some of the other guys? Smitty, Sanchez, Reed, sure, but not you. You won MVP of the league for a reason, Ryan. What the hell? Difference of opinion? That's all you two clowns will give me."

"I'm sorry I disappointed you, sir," Ryan replied.

"Sorry you disappointed me. Not sorry you fought, but sorry you disappointed me?" Cal replied.

Shit, he'd been hoping he wouldn't catch the distinction in that apology. He glanced up at Cal who sat waiting expectantly. He looked over at Andy. Was he sorry for fighting? No. Andy deserved to be tuned up. Just thinking about it now and he wanted to hit him again for what he'd done to Peyton.

"Yes, sir." Ryan sat up straight and met his manager's stare head on.

"Care to explain?" Cal asked.

Ryan looked over at his teammate. He didn't feel connected to the other man at all. He no longer had those feelings of camaraderie that he normally felt with the guys he played with. Everything about the guy made him angry. Andy had no remorse for what he'd done to Ryan, to Peyton, to his own wife. What kind of person was like that? How could he ever trust him to have his back? And wasn't that something he needed in his catcher?

"Let's call it irreconcilable differences, sir. I think with our history it would be difficult for us to trust each other on the field. Given that I'd like Patel to catch on my days. You have Andy playing DH quite a bit lately, so it'd be easy to line that up with my pitching days."

"You're trying to get me fucking benched, you pussy," Andy yelled. "Over some bitch?"

"Stop fucking talking about Peyton, Andy. I'm not fucking kidding."

"Enough," Cal yelled.

Ryan pushed back in his chair. He needed to chill out if he had any hope of this turning out in his favor. He took a deep breath.

Cal leaned back in his chair and crossed his arms over his chest. "So let me get this straight. You two are fighting over a woman?"

"Yeah, basically," Andy replied.

Ryan's jaw flexed. It was a little more than that.

"Ryan?" Cal said.

He glanced up at his boss. "It's a little more complicated than that."

"If you expect me to separate my best pitcher and my best catcher. I'm gonna need a little more than that."

"We don't need to be separated. Ryan is upset because I had a relationship with Peyton in the past, and he just found out some details about how close we had been," Andy said.

"Are you fucking kidding me?" Ryan growled. Hell no, there was no way that little asshole was playing the victim in all of this.

"I think he's a bit surprised by his feelings for Peyton, and he got jealous. But it's all good on my end, honestly," Andy said.

"No." Ryan shook his head. "No... fuck no... you don't get to do that. You don't get to be a complete sleazy degenerate and try to play it off like I'm just a jealous lover. No."

"Come on, Ryan, you're jealous." Andy leaned back in his chair and hooked his arm over the back of his seat.

Ryan's hands clenched around the arm of the chair. It was taking everything in him not to knock the cocky little shit out. "The reason we got into a fight is because you're a piece of shit who can't keep his mouth shut. I tried to put the team first, like I've always done. But fuck that, you're not worth it, Simon," he snarled out the name, making it clear they weren't buddies.

Ryan turned to the team manager. "Okay, cards on the table here. Simon cheated on his wife with Peyton. She didn't know he was married. When she found out, I stepped in to help her save face at the team party and we hit it off. Andy was a non-issue. Honestly, when I hooked up with Peyton, I assumed she'd slept with Simon, so I had no reason to be jealous about anything."

"Okay, so what's the problem?" Cal leaned forward, resting his elbows on the desk.

"You want to tell him, or you want me to tell him?" Ryan turned to Andy and pinned him with a glare. The little fucker better own up to his shit.

"You're blowing this whole thing out of proportion," Andy mumbled.

"No asshole, I'm not," Ryan replied. "The problem we are having is because he took a video of Peyton and him together without her knowledge and showed it to the team."

"I deleted the fucking video," Andy snapped.

"Yeah, after fucking Gonzo and Smitty made you because you wouldn't do it when Peyton asked."

Cal held up his hand. "Hold up, let me get this straight." He turned to Andy. "You videotaped yourself in an intimate situation with a woman without her knowledge. Is that right?"

"Yeah," Andy mumbled.

"Then not only were you dumb enough to do that, you decided to be the big man and show the team this video?"

"Yeah."

"Holy fuck you're stupid," Cal muttered. "So not only did you open yourself and this team up to a sex scandal, but because you were jealous, you made it fucking public knowledge." Cal rubbed his head. "Jesus," he muttered and turned to Ryan. "Is she going to the police?"

"I don't know, but she should."

"She wo—wouldn't," Andy stammered.

"For your sake, you better hope she doesn't. Fuck," Cal roared. He grabbed the phone and pressed a number. "Yeah, I need legal in my office ASAP."

"Legal," Andy whispered.

Cal dropped the phone back on the receiver. "Get comfortable boys, because neither of you is going anywhere."

CHAPTER NINETEEN

Peyton glanced at her front stoop and sighed when she saw Ryan sitting on her step, playing on his phone. As she walked closer, he lifted his head. The bags under his eyes were visible from where she was. He looked like she felt.

She squared her shoulders. Well, good. She was glad he was suffering. He should be.

"Why are you here, Ryan?" she asked as she walked up the steps to her front door.

"Can we talk?"

"I'm pretty sure we said everything that needed to be said last week." She opened the front door and stepped inside.

"Please." His pained voice cut into her like a dull butter knife, ripping and gouging her insides as it broke the skin.

Crap, why was she so soft? "Fine." She left the front door open and walked into the living room, waiting for him to follow.

She dropped into her favorite chair and pulled the fuzzy blanket off the back of the couch to wrap around herself for protection. Her fingers dug into the plush fabric, and she squeezed while she waited for Ryan to speak.

"I'm sorry, Peyton. I was an asshole."

"Yeah, you were." She pulled the blanket further up her lap as a shield.

"I didn't handle things very well when I found about the video. The guys told me you showed up at the field and confronted Andy."

"I'll just bet they did."

"Gonzo and Smitty felt awful about what happened."

"Tell them thanks for their help. I'm not sure Andy would have cooperated if they hadn't stepped in."

"You shouldn't have needed their help. He should have done the right thing."

"Sadly, there are always guys like Andy out there."

"But there are also always guys like Gonzo and Smitty too, and I'd like to think I fit in that boat as well." He rubbed his hands nervously against his legs. "I probably should have talked about it with you first but I..." He sighed. "I talked to Cal about everything."

"You what?" Her heart beat erratically as adrenaline surged through her blood. Her brain racing about what to do next. Why would he make this worse by telling the team's manager?

Ryan reached out and placed his hand on her knee like he was trying to soothe an injured animal. His voice dropped lower. "I didn't make this worse for you, I promise.

Her bottom lip quivered as she fought to suck in air. "Why would you tell him?" she whispered.

"Because Andy can't get away with doing what he did."

"Right. Like the team is going to do anything," she scoffed.

"I don't know what they are going to do. They're still discussing it." His leg absently jiggled up and down. "I wanted you to know that I realize I reacted poorly and I'm trying to fix it."

"Yeah. Can you guarantee the team isn't going to pull their support at Kidsplay now that you brought this to their attention? What's going to stop them from getting me fired?"

"I'm not going to let that happen."

Peyton's eyes widened. "Really? How are you going to stop it?"

"They wouldn't want the bad press that would come along with you losing your job over this when Andy is in the wrong. The bad publicity you could create for them would be a nightmare. The team wouldn't want that to happen."

"I hope you're right." Peyton fidgeted with the strap of her watch. Even if she didn't lose her job over this, she still had to figure out how to work with the men who'd seen her in that position. "How are you going to make your teammates unsee the video?"

Ryan pushed his hands roughly through his hair. "I haven't figured that part out yet." He exhaled and rubbed his hand roughly against his beard. A gesture she'd noticed he did whenever he was feeling stressed. "I fucked up, Peyton, and I'm sorry." He leaned forward and rested his elbows on his knees as he stared at her. "Tell me how to fix this."

"You can't, Ryan. I'm always going to be the girl who gave your teammate a blowjob, and the rest of your team is now along for the ride. And now management knows. I have no way of knowing how this is going to play out at my work." Her stomach turned at the idea of that video being seen by her bosses or the kids at the center. How was she supposed to explain it? "You had no right to tell them, Ryan."

"I didn't know what to do to help. I can't sit back and do nothing. I fucked up. I know that." He rubbed his hand across his beard.

She wasn't proud of what happened with her and Andy. She couldn't think of him as Simon anymore. That person didn't exist, he never did. Now he was simply Andy, the narcissistic athlete.

She hated that she'd been the other woman with him, but she hadn't known, and yes, she needed to take some of the blame for that because she absolutely should have searched him online.

But it was the video she couldn't get over. How was she supposed to face any of those people ever again? She'd been a joke, a freakin' baseball groupie meme.

She'd seen how Ryan had reacted. He might say he could get over it, but they both knew he couldn't.

Sadly, she looked at Ryan, wishing things were different, but they weren't. "What about when one of your teammates makes a dumb comment?"

"They wouldn't."

"Yeah right, that might be true until they get a few drinks into them and then stupid stuff flows out of their mouth."

"Then I'll shut their mouth for them," he growled.

"Really? You're just going to fight your teammates?"

"I don't know, maybe. It wouldn't be the first time," he mumbled.

"Come on, Ryan. We both know you are team first. You always have been. And I get it." She fiddled with the fringe on the edge of the blanket. "You can't fight your teammates and we both know it, or you'll have no cohesion on the team."

"Then I'll ask for a trade, and we could move someplace else, and I'll get a new team."

"So I should move? Screw that." She swallowed past the lump in her throat. "I didn't do anything wrong, Ryan. I didn't make a sex tape. I didn't consent to that video. I'm the one who your friends laughed about and demeaned while they joked about my dick sucking abilities." She angrily wiped the tears that streamed down her face. "It's not okay." She wiped her nose on her sleeve and shook her head. "And I can't be with someone who thinks it is."

"What the fuck? I never said it was okay. I talked to the coaching staff about him because I thought what he did was wrong, Peyton. How can you say I'd condone that?"

"That's great, Ryan, but it doesn't erase what you said before you knew I didn't consent to being recorded." She pushed her hair off her forehead and took a deep breath. "When you think about that video, you're still embarrassed by it. Not for me, but for yourself and how it affected you. How it affects your relationship with the team. You wouldn't be fighting your teammates to defend my honor, Ryan. You'd be fighting your teammates to defend yours."

His eyes narrowed and he bristled at what she said. "How would I not be defending you?"

"How would it be defending me? You go off throwing punches at your teammates. Who's standing beside me? Protecting me?" She raised her eyebrows in question. "No one." She shook her head as she imagined how that scenario would play out. "And when team dynamics get destroyed over it, who gets blamed? Me."

Swiping the tears streaming down her face, she smiled sadly. "I appreciate you coming by, Ryan, but it doesn't change anything. Until you can realize that nothing about what happened is about you, there's not much more to say."

"How can you say this wasn't about me? The whole reason Andy showed the fucking video was to hurt me."

"Hurt you? When your teammates look at you, what do they see?"

"What do you mean?"

God, men could be so obtuse sometimes. "How did that video change the way they see you?"

He sat silently for several seconds, then finally spoke. "It didn't."

"Right. How did it change the way they'll look at me?"

Ryan rubbed his hand over his mouth. When he looked at her, his eyes were red from holding back tears. Seeing the emotion he was trying to restrain caused more tears to flow down her face. Her chest pulled tight.

"Exactly," she whispered. "That's how it's not about you, Ryan." She sniffed. "I can't be with someone who condones that kind of behavior."

"I don't condone it."

"But you do, Ryan. Every man in your sport does when he turns the other way and ignores behaviors, so you don't damage the team. I need someone who will stand by my side and put my team first. And unfortunately, with you, baseball will always be your number one team."

She looked at him and her heart broke at the resigned look of sadness on his face. She could see from the emotion in his eyes that he knew she was right.

Sure, he might claim to care about her, but nothing was more important than the team and his teammates.

"I appreciate you coming by, Ryan, but nothing has changed."

"I'm not letting you go without a fight, Peyton," Ryan said.

Pain ripped through her chest. If only it were that simple. "I don't know that this is a fight you can win."

Ryan stood up and squatted down in front of her. "Haven't you realized I always win, Pey?"

"I wish that were true but..." Unable to stop herself from touching him, she cupped the side of his face, then pulled back when he leaned toward her. "No, Ryan. That's not going to help."

His blue eyes filled with emotion as he stared at her, encouraging her to reconsider. "I think it would help a lot."

"Ryan, I think we both know this isn't a good idea. There are just too many obstacles in our way. You're heading into a playoff run and my work is crazy busy with all this Hawks' programming coming up. Assuming that doesn't get pulled."

"They aren't pulling the program. I told you I won't let that happen."

She chewed her bottom lip. As much as she wanted to believe him, she wasn't sure he had that kind of pull. "Look Ryan, it was fun while it lasted, but let's be real. This was never going anywhere. We didn't even really like each other." Maybe she was being a coward and chickening out before she got even more hurt. But the school of hard knocks had taught her she needed to protect herself because nobody else would. "I think the cost of this relationship is outweighing the benefit."

It was like a shutter slammed shut over his eyes. The warmth that she'd grown to expect when he looked at her was gone. Once again, she was looking at the cold, detached, judgmental ball player she'd first met. The same one who reappeared when he saw the video. "God forbid I stop being useful," he growled. Ryan pushed to his feet and stormed toward the front door.

That wasn't what she meant at all. But with time, he'd see she was right. Some things were just too hard. Unfortunately, that didn't stop her from wanting to stop him. But that wouldn't solve anything. Instead, she let him go.

CHAPTER TWENTY

Ryan waited for the receptionist to hang up the phone before stepping up to the desk.

"Hi, you're Ryan, right?"

"Yeah. Hi Simone, any chance my sister is available?" God, he hoped he got her name right or he'd never hear the end of it from Kendall about how he doesn't pay attention to anything that isn't baseball.

"She just finished up a team meeting, so let me check if she has time to see you."

He leaned back on his heels. "No problem." Scanning the empty waiting room, he couldn't help but smile. His sister had done well for herself. When she'd taken over as manager of the design agency, it had been floundering, and in a year it was one of the up-and-coming firms in the city. But then he wouldn't expect anything else from Kendall. She made him seem like a slacker, and that was saying something.

At the sound of heels clicking on the floor, he glanced up as his sister strode toward him. "To what do I owe this pleasure?" Kendall asked.

"You got a minute?"

Kendall's eyes narrowed as she assessed him. "You okay? You look like crap."

"Gee thanks." He rubbed his hand roughly against his forehead then pushed his hair back. "I wanted to talk to you about something." He shifted uncomfortably. This wasn't really a conversation he wanted to have in the waiting room.

"Sure, come on back." Kendall turned and led the way to her office.

He walked over to the window and peered down at the view below. "Who knew my little sister would have a swanky corner office one day?" He smiled when he saw the picture of Kendall and Pete on the corner of her desk.

"Sit, do you want coffee or anything?" Kendall asked.

"Nah, I'm good."

"Spill, what are you doing here?" Kendall leaned back in her office chair and crossed her arms over her chest.

Was he dreaming too big? He didn't think so, but who the hell knew? His sister had been a huge help to Pete in getting his non-profit up and running smoothly. Ryan was really hoping she'd do the same for him.

"I was uh..." He cleared his throat. "I was hoping you could help me with a project. Point me in the right direction, maybe help me write up a pitch or whatever."

"What kind of project are we talking about?"

He tried to swallow, but the spit stuck in his throat. He should have taken her up on the drink. Why was he so nervous? This was his sister. She'd seen him icing his nuts and crawling from room to room because he couldn't walk after taking a ball so hard it broke his cup. And she'd barely made fun of him despite how ridiculous he'd looked. He could certainly talk to her about this.

He cleared his throat. "What would it take to start a... I'm not sure mentorship is the right word? More like a public speaking program to talk to youth at schools and stuff."

"Well, that depends on who's speaking? What are they talking about? I kind of need more to work with here, Ry."

"I wanted to figure out how to go about pitching the idea of having professional ball players go into schools and talk to the sports teams. At this point I'm thinking the boys, eventually I'd like to expand out to all the kids but for now I'm thinking student athletes and talk to them about being better men."

Kendall leaned forward and rested her elbows on her desk. "What do you mean better men?"

"I don't know, just talking to them about consent and treating women, fuck, people in general with respect."

"Go on," Kendall pressed.

"What I'm picturing is talking to groups of guys about being better. Don't ask a girl for nudes, don't slut shame her when she does. If she's been drinking, don't be dick and take advantage of that."

"I like where you're going, but don't they do that already in school?"

"No idea. I'm sure some schools do, but clearly the message isn't getting across based on what I see and hear. We have this platform as athletes. We should use it."

"Why don't you talk to Kirsty about this?"

He shrugged. "I don't want it to turn it into what always happens where the guys who are the biggest fuckups are the ones who get the most opportunity to contribute because they need the good PR. The last thing I want this to be is some fuckwad like Andy telling guys to be better when he's the biggest culprit of doing shit like this."

"So this is about Peyton?" Kendall flashed him a sad, supportive little smile. "Pete told me you broke up."

"No... yeah... maybe..." He leaned his elbow on the arm of the chair and wiped his face. "Not really. I mean yeah, what happened with her and me wanting to make things right started me down this thought process. But then I got to thinking about one of the girls at the center who was sexually assaulted by a group of boys from another school when she was drunk at an after party. They think because they're athletes and rich the rules don't apply to them. She was barely conscious for fucksakes." He stood up and walked over to the window. "There's this culture that guys. Athletes. Are above the law and it's fucked up. The only way that it'll change is if athletes make it change."

"Have you talked to Peyton about this?"

"No, I mean yeah, she's kind of the reason I'm wanting to do this, but I was a dick athlete too. I didn't have all the details before I jumped right in, judging her for what happened. I'm no better than the other guys."

"Oh my god, Ry, there is no comparison between you and someone like Andy. You would never do something like that."

"No but, how many times have I looked the other way when my teammates cheated on their wives, or took drunk girls home from the bar to celebrate? We've all had a guy on the team who we wouldn't let the women we cared about go near because we didn't trust him, and yet we sat by because the team is the most important thing." He rubbed the tension in the back of his neck and turned around to face his sister. "I feel like we need to do better as men, be better. Hold each other accountable for how we treat women because I don't know, shouldn't that be the standard we hold our teammates to and the kind of thing that truly puts the team first?"

Kendall got up from her desk and walked over to Ryan, and threw her arms around his neck. "You're a good man, Ry."

He squeezed her back and sank into her for a moment. "Thanks."

Kendall pulled back. "I knew the pressure from dad growing up and coaches and teammates to win at all costs had left a mark on you, but I thought that's why you were such a perfectionist. I didn't know it affected you this way too."

He pressed his tongue against his front teeth, then let out a breath. "I didn't really think so either until I started thinking about the thing with Peyton and Andy."

"You should talk to Peyton about this."

"She's not really interested in anything I have to say, and I don't blame her."

"Maybe you were just saying the wrong things before." She squeezed his arm. "She'd want to hear this. You're a good man, Ry. Yeah, you can be a jerk like anyone else, but at your core you're a good person. Talk to her."

He shook his head. "She deserves better than a guy like me."

Kendall's eyes filled with tears as she looked at him. "There's no one better than you, big brother. You made a mistake. You aren't perfect, no matter how hard you try to be. Show her this side of you. Be vulnerable."

"Or I need to practice what I preach and listen to what she's saying. She told me to fuck off, Ken, and leave her alone. I have to respect that as much as I don't want to. This isn't about me. I'm the one who hurt her. I don't get to decide if or when she'll forgive me."

Kendall wiped the tears that leaked down her cheek. "This sucks. Are you still volunteering for your shifts with the kids?"

"I am. She never seems to be there when I come, so I think it's pretty clear she'd rather not see me. I'm hoping with time she'll change her mind, and we can talk, but until then, I have to respect her wishes." His eyes burned with his own unshed tears, and he pinched the bridge of his nose. "So, about this program idea. Any thoughts?"

"Let me sit on it for a few days and see what I can come up with. We're going to have to talk to Kirsty about it because you'll want some guys on board and then extend it out to the league. But if we do the pitch properly, we should be able to come up with something that will ease your concerns. Possibly keeping it totally separate by creating your own non-profit. All proceeds go to sexual assault centers in each city or something." Kendall's pen flew across the notepad on her desk as she wrote ideas. Her hand zipped across the page in an effort to keep up with her brain.

Ryan smiled as he watched his sister work. He'd known coming to Kendall about this was the right decision. If anyone could figure out how to make this fly, it was her.

After several minutes, Kendall blinked at him like she hadn't realized he was still in the room. "Sorry, I got in the zone. Give me a couple of days, and we'll chat after you get back from this next road trip."

"Sounds good." He walked over to her desk and bent down and kissed the top of her head. "Thanks, sis. For listening and doing this."

"Of course."

As he walked toward the door, Kendall said, "What are you thinking for the name?"

"Do better, be better."

Kendall smiled and nodded. "I like it. Good luck at the games."

"Thanks," he said as he walked out of her office. Now he just had to get his head on straight so he could actually play. Falling in love fucking sucked.

CHAPTER TWENTY-ONE

Tuesday evening after a long day of work, Peyton kicked off her shoes and walked to the kitchen. She opened the fridge and pulled out a beer, cracked the top and took a long, slow pull. She was just about to take a second when the doorbell rang. Who the hell was that?

She padded across the floor, stopped at the front door, and peeked through the peephole. Shoot, why was Kendall here?

Taking a deep breath, she exhaled then opened the front door. "Hey Kendall."

"Hi, sorry to just stop by unannounced." Kendall smiled and pulled a takeout bag from behind her back. "I brought provisions. Any chance I can come in?"

"Sure." Peyton stepped back to allow the other woman in. "You want a beer?"

"Love one, thanks." Kendall followed Peyton into the kitchen and peeked around. "Your place is cute."

"My place is a dump," Peyton replied.

"No, the building is a dump, your place is cute. You've got a good eye for decorating. It's homey. I like it."

"Thanks." Taking the takeout bag from Kendall, Peyton emptied the contents on the kitchen counter.

"I didn't know what you liked, but I figured you can't go wrong with grease after a breakup."

"Why are you bringing me breakup food? Aren't I like enemy number one now?"

"God, no." Kendall leaned against the counter. "My brother is an idiot."

"True," Peyton agreed.

"If it's any consolation, he knows he was an idiot."

"Why do you say that?"

"Because he's all mopey and doesn't want to do anything. His game has gone to shit." Kendall paused and watched Peyton, scrutinizing her for so long Peyton wanted to squirm. "I've never seen my brother like this. Even when he broke up with Denise, he wasn't like this."

"Who's Denise?"

"Umm." Kendall looked down at her feet and slowly crossed one foot over the other. "Crap. He never told you about her?"

"Nope."

"He's going to kill me but—" Kendall picked up her beer and took a sip. "Maybe we should sit down, eat and the story can kind of roll out of my mouth that way it won't really be my fault that I spilled my brother's secrets because we were telling war stories over drinks and well...what can you do?" Kendall chewed her bottom lip. "That sounds believable, right?"

"Definitely," Peyton agreed. She grabbed a couple of plates and started dishing up the fried chicken, fries, and gravy that Kendall had brought. Plate in hand, she led the way into the living room and dropped onto the couch. After several minutes of eating in silence, she pressed Kendall. "Denise?"

"First, how are you doing with everything? I haven't really talked to you." Kendall's eyes softened with compassion as she looked at Peyton. "I'm sorry about the video I can't even imagine."

Peyton's stomach knotted. Even just thinking about it made her feel sick. "I'm okay, about as good as you'd expect."

Kendall leaned back in the chair and curled her right leg underneath her, shifting her weight until she seemed comfortable. "How's work?"

"It's good. Thankfully, no repercussions from the video." Peyton still couldn't believe she'd dodged that bullet. And so far, none of the kids had heard about the video. Thank god, because that was not something she wanted to explain to them. When everything first happened, she'd been sure the Hawks' would pull their contract and she'd lose her job. That hadn't happened. Kirsty had come in to talk to her about everything and reassured her the Hawks' management was doing everything they could to make it disappear. They'd been worried she'd make a public issue for Simon and the team, which was laughable. All she'd wanted was for it to go away. The last thing she wanted was to make it public. Not a chance.

"I'm glad. I know Pete and Ryan both said it wouldn't affect your career, but I was worried."

Her chest tightened. Ryan had talked to his sister about his concerns for her career. Why had he done that? She chewed her bottom lip. "What did Ryan say?"

Kendall looked down at her beer and slowly peeled the label down the glass. "He was pretty tight-lipped other than saying he wouldn't let it affect you. Pete said Ryan's been in several meetings with management but other than that I don't know much They just said it wouldn't affect your career. Sorry I don't know more than that."

"That's okay." Her heart thumped in her chest. Had Ryan really done meetings with his team to protect her? He'd said he wouldn't let anything happen to her, but things change. She pursed her lips. No, that wasn't fair. Ryan knew how important the program was. He wouldn't let anything happen to it. Peyton took a sip of her water and set the glass back on the side table. "So Denise?"

"Right." Kendall set her plate on the coffee table. She leaned back in her chair, pulled her knees up to her chest, and wrapped her arms around her legs. "So, Denise was my brother's girlfriend in college. They were pretty serious, or at least we all thought they were. I'm not sure. She was one of those girls, you know." Kendall took a sip of her drink.

"What kind of girls?"

"Gorgeous." Kendall rolled her eyes. "We're talking like one of those women who makes other women feel instantly insecure about their appearance because she's that freaking beautiful."

Peyton's gut churned. That's the kind of woman Ryan normally went for? She knew she was attractive, but the only reason traffic stopped when she walked by was if she was at a crosswalk. "Why'd they break up?"

"In hindsight, she was drawn to Ryan because everyone knew he was going to be drafted. Don't get me wrong my brother is amazing, but that's not what Denise liked about him." Kendall picked up her plate and took a bite of food, then sank deeper into the chair. "Ry was a big shot on campus and together they were this power couple. When the draft came up, we all knew he was going to Chicago. He'd been down there multiple times to meet with the team. The contract his agent landed him was amazing, and they were willing to have him go straight to the majors. Which is unheard of. It was everything he'd ever dreamed of.

"Two weeks into training camp, he dumped Denise. He got into a huge fight with my parents because he wanted to leave Chicago and go to Philly's farm team instead, which seemed ridiculous."

Peyton sat forward in her chair. "What happened?"

"Denise slept with one of the players in Chicago. The guy wanted her to dump Ryan and be with him."

"Oh my god," Peyton gasped. How awful. "He wanted to go to a different team so he didn't have to see Denise?"

"Sort of." Kendall sat quietly for several seconds. "Denise didn't want to break up. She wanted to work it out. It was just sex, after all, and could he blame her? The guy was like a fucking rockstar in the league. Married but who cares, right?"

"He was married?" Peyton covered her mouth with her hand as she processed the information. From everything she knew about Ryan, that wouldn't sit well with him. "And of course, Ryan cared."

Kendall nodded. "Ryan cared. Denise isn't the one who told Ryan, the guy did. Bragging about it to let Ryan know his place." Kendall's shoulders dropped and she sighed. "Given Ryan's unprecedented contract, I guess the guy thought Ryan needed to be knocked down a few and this was the way to do it."

"Ouch." Peyton could only imagine how much that must have hurt Ryan.

"Yeah, Ry could either dump Denise or this guy would make sure everyone on the team hated Ryan." Kendall's mouth tightened. "There was no way my parents would let him walk away from everything he'd worked for over a girl. My parents rode him hard to get him to follow his dream and not let what happened hold him back, so he stayed in Chicago. But how could they have a cohesive team when that's what he was walking into? Those guys were merciless. It was brutal."

"Hang on I thought he broke up with Denise."

"Oh, he did. There's no coming back from that one." Kendall sighed. "But that didn't stop the guys from ribbing him and talking about him. Like I said, the guy felt Ryan needed to learn his place on the team. Ryan might have been a big shot in college, but this was The Show and he better not forget it." Kendall set her plate down and leaned forward so she was facing Peyton. "My brother has always been this black and white thinking perfectionist. In his mind, you always put what's best for the team ahead of yourself. No matter what. Even at the expense of yourself. So he put up and shut up." Kendall smirked. "And became Rookie of the Year just to prove a point to everyone on the team."

"That's messed up," Peyton replied. But it explained a lot. Why his initial reaction was all about himself and the team instead of her.

"Yeah, it is," Kendall agreed. "But that's what's been drilled into his head since day one. Team first, no matter what. My dad always disliked those players who thought they were bigger than the team. There was no way he was letting my brother become one." Kendall shook her head. "This one time in high school, Ry got lippy with my dad about how he was going to The Show and what his life was going to be like. The endorsements he'd have, how he'd be the hot shot on the team. My dad marched him outside in the pouring rain and made him run while dad drove the car behind him to light the street so he could see." Kendall smiled sadly. "He looked like a drowned rat when he got home, but he was a whole lot easier to be around."

Peyton winced. "Well, I'm glad he was easier to be around at least." She took a sip of her beer as she pictured Ryan as an up-and-coming player with the beautiful girlfriend and the world at his feet. What must that have been like for him? The rookie on the team with everyone talking about him, gossiping? It broke her heart.

Somehow, despite all that, he managed to win Rookie of the Year on a team that made his life miserable. It spoke volumes about the man he was. And explained a little why he had such an adverse reaction to her when he thought she'd chased after a married teammate. She sighed. And why he was having such a hard time with the idea of the guys talking about him again.

"My brother isn't perfect, but when Denise cheated on him, and the entire team knew about it and talked about him behind his back. That changed him. Not only did it divide the team, but it broke something in him when he felt like he was forced to pick the team over himself especially when his teammate was in the wrong." Kendall put her feet on the ground and sat up straighter. "I know this changes nothing, but I'm just trying to help you understand why my brother was dick when you first met and then again when that video came out. To Ryan it felt like everything was happening all over again. That first year was rough on him, but it's nothing compared to how this is affecting him."

"But don't you see, Kendall, that's why this would never work. How can it? Especially given what you just told me," Peyton asked.

"But that's where you're wrong. When shit went down with Denise, my brother won Rookie of the Year. With you, his game is shit." Kendall stared at Peyton. Her eyes imploring her to listen. "My brother punched a teammate, Peyton. He went to the coaches and told them what kind of man Andy is knowing full well that Andy could get suspended or traded which would hurt the team, and he didn't care because Andy had hurt you. You came before the team. Ryan doesn't put anything before the team, not even himself, and I just wanted you to know that."

Peyton's head whirled as she tried to process what Kendall was saying. "I appreciate you telling me all this."

"I'm just going to tell you one more thing, and then I'm going to leave so you can think about all this. Ryan came to me about doing an educational campaign with youth sports."

"What do you mean?"

"He doesn't like the way athletes feel like they are above the law and can treat people however they want. So, he wants to go into the schools and talk to the male athletes about how they treat women. Really hitting them about respect, consent, and just being better."

Peyton reeled back in her chair. "What? He wants to do that?"

"He does and all the money raised will be donated to sexual assault centers in the area."

"Why would he?" Peyton's eyes burned as she fought to fight the tears that threatened to fall.

"Because of you. Because he told his coach about Andy expecting him to be suspended and knowing that might screw up their team. But the coaches did nothing other than switch Patel to catch for Ryan and it pissed him off."

"Did he really expect them to suspend Andy over a sex tape that no longer exists?"

"Not really, no, but for the first time in his life it pissed him off the team was put first before what was right." Kendall set the plate down on the table. "My brother is crazy about you, Peyton. When Pete and I were having some issues early in our relationship, my brother sat me down and explained Pete's history, and it really helped me to understand Pete a little better. I thought it was important you had a clearer picture of Ryan. Falling in love with you threw a curveball at him he didn't know how to handle. He fucked up, I know that, and so does he. But when you love somebody, you love all of them, Peyton, even the fucked up pieces."

Kendall stood up and set a ticket on the coffee table. "Tomorrow is the last regular season game. Ryan's pitching. I know it would mean a lot if you were there."

"Did he ask you to come here?"

"God no, he'd shoot me if he knew I was doing this. He was pretty adamant when we talked that I should leave it alone. He was respecting your wishes and giving you space." Kendall pushed the ticket closer to Peyton. "I'm asking you to think about coming, so at the very least you can talk. You don't seem over him, Peyton, and I know he's definitely not over you. Don't you think you owe it to yourselves to talk?"

"He hurt me, Kendall." She absently brushed away the tear that dripped down her cheek.

"I know he did, sweetie. And he deserves to have his ass kicked. But you can't kick it if you don't talk to him."

Peyton wrapped her arms around herself, her brain swimming with emotion as she tried to process everything Kendall had said.

"I'm going to get out of here and let you think." Kendall stood up, and Peyton followed.

At the front door, Kendall leaned over and pulled her into a hug. "Just think about it, please."

"I will." Peyton returned the hug, then opened the front door and shut it behind Kendall.

She walked back to the living room and sat down on the chair. Her eyes were immediately drawn to the ticket on the table. Could she go to the game? Could she open herself up to that kind of hurt again?

Picking up the ticket, she ran it between her fingers. They'd only been together a short period of time and already they'd had so many bumps. Maybe that was a sign they shouldn't be together. She stared down at the ticket and remembered what it had been like watching him play. Bumpy or not, she'd never felt about anyone the way she felt about Ryan. That's why this all hurt so much because she'd fallen in love with the idiot.

God, what should she do? Go? Stay?

Ugh, she dropped the ticket on the table and stood up. She didn't have to decide tonight.

CHAPTER TWENTY-TWO

The locker room buzzed with energy the way it always did before a home game. Being the home team was an advantage for a reason. The chants and cheering when their team did something great. Booing at the away team. It all rocketed up the energy he normally felt before a game.

So why the hell couldn't he get himself out of this funk? It had been weeks since he'd broken up with Peyton, and still he couldn't stop thinking about her.

Normally, when he hit the field, everything else immediately fled from his mind. Nothing mattered except the batter in front of him. He'd spent more hours on training his brain to block out the noise than most people did earning a degree. And it had worked. He was the best in the league at what he did for a reason. But when things fell to shit with Peyton, it was like all of that work was for nothing. He couldn't get his head on straight.

The chatter in the locker room instantly died the second Cal walked into the room. "This is a big game, boys. We're number one in the division, but Houston is only one game back, so if we want to keep our spot heading into playoffs we need a win tonight."

Cal scanned the room, finally homing in on Ryan. He pinned him with a stare before continuing to scan the room. "Everyone needs to focus tonight. I know we all have other things going on in our lives. Wives, girlfriends, sick kids at home and what not. But honestly, I don't fucking care. When you walk onto that field nothing else matters but this game. You got me?"

It felt like the entire team looked at him when Cal spoke. Fuck, he needed to grow a pair and get his shit together. Things with Peyton were messed up, but baseball—that made sense. This team made sense, and there was no way he could let these guys down. Being number one going into the playoffs was huge. It set the tone for the series, reminded the other teams who to fear. Not only did it give them a bi in the first round, but home team advantage when they did play. And if he didn't want the coach to bench his ass, he needed to focus and pitch.

When their little pep talk wrapped up, Ryan continued to sit on the bench. He closed his eyes as his teammates moved around him. He knew they were all there, but he blocked it out, using every technique he'd been taught to clear his mind and focus on the task at hand. After several minutes, he opened his eyes. The locker room was empty except for Pete.

"You good, man?" Pete asked.

"Yeah, I think so." At this particular moment he was. Now he just needed it to stick.

"Good." Pete clapped him on the shoulder. "You got this. Even when you're off your game, you are still one of the best in the league. Remember that. Stay out of your fucking head. There is no one who can take us all the way better than you can."

"NLS champs then World Series, baby."

"You know it," Pete agreed. "Let's kick some ass and get them the fuck out of our house."

"Ryan, hold up," Coach Gill called.

"I'll see you out there," Pete said before he jogged out of the room, leaving Ryan alone with the pitching coach.

"What's up, Coach?"

"How you feeling?"

"Good." Ryan smiled, hoping he portrayed the confidence he wanted to be showing to his pitching coach.

"You fix things with your girl?"

"Not yet, sir. That part of my life is still fucked up, but I've got my head on straight for the game."

"Nothing can fuck up your head like the right woman."

Wasn't that the truth? No woman had messed with his head like Peyton. No one else had really mattered enough since Denise and even she hadn't come close to the way he felt about Peyton, and it clearly showed in his game.

"Look, son, when it's the right woman, you know. And judging by where your head's been at, you clearly know. You'll figure it out. Give it time. But you know what will help get your head right about her?"

"Not a clue."

"Getting your head on right about baseball. You gotta compartmentalize, you know that. Once your love life bleeds into the game, everything gets muddy, and you can't tell what's important anymore. It's all important. But when it's muddy, you do a half-assed job on it all, and that's not what you want. Let's fix the game, then we'll fix the love life."

"I got the game locked down, Coach."

"Good, now get out there and warm up."

Ryan jogged out of the locker room toward the field entrance. The crowd roared as he ran onto the field. Once he got to the mound, he stopped and scanned the crowd for his sister. They'd started the tradition when baseball had taken him away from home and he'd been nervous about the crowds. It had started as a joke between them. Scanning for his sister's goofy face had instantly calmed him down. Somehow they'd just kept doing it over the years, and now it had become one of his rituals. When he knew she was there, he had to find her or they'd lose the game.

He looked over the third base line when Kendall liked to sit so she could see Pete better. He smiled when he spotted her waving her arms.

Holy shit.

Peyton.

What was Peyton doing with his sister?

Peyton gave a small shy wave. He raised his arm back.

What did this mean? Did she forgive him? Did she want to work things out? What the fuck? His mind raced.

Pete jogged over. "What's up?"

"Peyton's here."

"Yeah, I saw. You cool?"

"Not really. Did you know she was coming?"

"Ken said she was going to try to get her to, but I didn't really think she'd come, so I didn't mention it."

Pete glanced up at the women, turned back to Ryan and grabbed his arm, pulling his attention away from Peyton. "It doesn't matter. Right now, you need to focus on the game. After you can figure out why she came."

"No, fuck that." Ryan pulled his arm free and took off in a run.

"Ryan!" Pete yelled.

Ignoring his teammates and coaches, he jogged toward the third base line. There was no way he could pitch until he talked to her. She knew how important baseball was to him. She wouldn't have come if she didn't want to work things out. Peyton wouldn't mess with his head like that.

He vaulted over the rail that blocked the fans from the field and dashed up the stairs to Peyton's seat. Fans reached out to touch him and yelled as he pushed past. Nothing was going to stop him from getting to her.

By the time he got to her row, Peyton had pushed her way free, meeting him at the edge of the seats.

"What are you doing here?" he asked.

Peyton spoke just as a man thrust his hat toward Ryan for a signature. "Dude, seriously?" Ryan glared at the guy with the hat and the group of people gathering around him. He took Peyton's arm and pulled her to the side so the middle walkway railing was at her back to protect her in case anyone pushed her. He turned to the crowd. "Hi, can you all just give me a minute please?" Ryan turned back to Peyton.

"You're here." He drank her in, taking note of everything about her. Loving the way her eyes warmed as she smiled back at him.

"I'm here," she whispered.

He stepped closer to her. When she didn't back away, he stepped closer still. "What's this mean?"

Peyton looked at him, then nervously at the surrounding crowd. "It means I talked to Kendall and actually listened to what she had to say, and here I am."

Ignoring the crowd, he pressed, "So you forgive me?"

"I wouldn't say I forgive you. But we can talk about everything after the game," Peyton told him.

"Fuck the game," he growled.

"Whoa, dude," the male behind him chirped.

Ignoring signature dude's attempt to interrupt, he focused on the amazing woman in front of him. "You are more important." He clamped his hand into a fist to stop himself from reaching out to touch her until he knew why she was here for sure.

Peyton's eyes filled, and she gave him a watery smile. "Ryan, I wanted to be here for you, so go play. I'll be here when you're done, and we can talk."

Screw it. He cupped the back of her neck and pulled her closer to him and held her, so she had to look him in the face. "Peyton, nothing is more important to me than you. Why are you really here?"

"Because I love you so..." She shrugged like that said it all.

And it did.

A smile split across his face. "You love me?"

"Yes, you idiot, I love you."

"Thank god." He crushed his mouth to hers. Cheers erupted around them, reminding him exactly where he was. "I love you too," he whispered against her mouth before he pulled back.

Peyton's cheeks were a bright red as she tried to duck her head and hide. He put his finger under her chin and lifted her head. "Don't. I want everyone to know you're mine."

She narrowed her eyes at him, and he laughed. "We'll talk," she said. "Now get back down there. You've got a game to win."

"Yes, ma'am." Unable to stop himself, he leaned in and placed another kiss on her lips. "I'm going to kick some major ass down there," he told her. And the crowd around them erupted again. Definitely no such thing as privacy in a stadium full of people.

"Good. Now go." She pushed against his chest.

"Love you," he called as he turned and jogged back down the stairs. Security waited at the railing and ensured no one got in his way as he climbed back over the railing onto the field.

"I know, I know." He held up his hands to hold the coaches off from speaking. "But trust me, my head is on straighter than it has ever been." He made eye contact with Cal. Hoping the manager didn't toss him on the bench. "I got this." He looked at Coach Gill and tried to relay with his expression that he'd heard him earlier, and he was in the right head space. Finally, the pitching coach nodded in understanding.

Turning to the manager, Ryan said, "Cal, I know I shouldn't have run into the stands. But I am going to pitch the game of my life today. You will not regret leaving me in."

Cal rested his hands on his hips and looked at Ryan for several seconds, then gave a head tilt to Mark. The two stepped away and spoke quietly while Ryan watched on anxiously. There was a very real possibility he was benched for what he'd done.

Mark spoke while Cal listened. Man, he hoped his pitching coach was going to bat for him. He glanced up at the stands and instantly saw Peyton in the crowd of people. Regardless, it had been worth it.

Finally, Cal and Mark stepped back to him. "You better pitch the game of your life." Cal reached out and pressed the ball into Ryan's chest.

Taking the ball, Ryan squeezed it tightly in his hand and let out the breath he'd been holding. "Absolutely. Thank you, sir."

"Get warmed up." Cal shook his head at Ryan like he couldn't even process what had happened. He probably couldn't. It wasn't like players ran into the stands every day.

Ryan watched as the two men walked back toward the dugout, then turned to look at Pete. His best friend shook his head and laughed. Gonzo flashed him a thumbs up from his place near third. It was going to be a great game.

He turned back around and gave the signal to Patel to toss him the ball so he could warm up. After a few warm-up pitches, the ump stepped up to the plate and called for the game to start. Ryan had never been more ready in his life.

Peyton stood beside Kendall in the hallway after the game as they waited for their guys to come out.

A pretty teenage girl stepped away from the group and walked over to Peyton. "You're the girl from the stands, right?"

"Um, yeah." Peyton glanced around, taking note of several people looking her way.

"I thought so. That was the most romantic thing I've ever seen," the teen gushed.

"I agree." Peyton still couldn't believe Ryan had left the field and run into the stands to talk to her. He'd said she was more important than baseball.

"Can I have your autograph?" the girl asked.

"What? Why would you want *my* autograph?"

"Because you are total goals. Not only are you dating the hottest guy in baseball, but he like totally claimed you on national television. It was hot," the teen spouted. "I want to be you when I grow up."

Peyton looked over at Kendall for help. How did she politely decline giving a signature for something as ridiculous as who you fell in love with?

Thankfully Pete and Gonzo walked out of the change room, and the teen's attention was pulled to them instead, and Peyton was able to slip back against the wall as a rush of fans moved forward to get autographs from the players.

After the fans moved away, Pete walked over to Kendall, gave her a kiss, and wrapped her under his arm. "Ryan is going to be a bit still. He got called into a press conference."

"I'm not surprised. He was the shit," Kendall replied. "Wasn't he amazing, Peyton?"

"Unreal. I don't think I've ever seen a no hitter on tv let alone in real life. It was pretty awesome."

"Seems you're good luck," Gonzo said to her.

"I don't think luck had anything to do with it. He's an outstanding pitcher," Peyton replied.

"Yeah, but he doesn't pitch too many no hitters. No one does and they sure as hell don't usually do it in the final game of the season." Gonzo high-fived the first baseman as he walked past.

"Div champs," Hernandez yelled, and the group of waiting fans roared, engulfing the player into the crowd.

Pete leaned against the wall with Kendall resting against his chest and looked at Peyton. "So you came."

She knew Kendall wanted her here, but did Pete agree? Or did he think his best friend was better off without her? Peyton steeled her shoulders and looked him in the eye. "I did."

A smile curled up the edges of Pete's mouth. "Thank god because my boy's been a bit of wreck without you. I'm glad you decided to give him another chance."

"We've still got some stuff to figure out, but yeah, me too."

"He's been an idiot, but he's a fast learner, so he'll be worth the trouble. It won't take too long to get him housebroken," Pete told her.

Kendall snorted. "I still don't have *you* housebroken."

Pete kissed the side of Kendall's neck. "Yeah, but I don't have a big fancy degree like your brother, so you gotta cut me some slack."

"You're an idiot." Kendall laughed.

"I know, babe, but I'm worth the effort too."

"Some days," Kendall teased.

Watching Kendall and Pete together gave Peyton hope that she and Ryan really would be fine. Maintaining a relationship with a professional athlete had its challenges, as they'd already learned. And the way some of his teammates cheated scared the crap out of her. But Ryan wasn't Andy, and he wasn't her dad.

On that front, she knew she could trust him 100%. Yeah, they had stuff to work through, but what they had was worth fighting for.

Finally, Ryan exited the change room with Brandon Sims, and the remaining fans erupted with cheers as they swarmed the two men for autographs. Ryan's gaze found hers over the crowd, and he smiled before mouthing sorry as he gestured toward the fans.

She waved off the apology. After the amazing way he played tonight, she had expected nothing different. He'd been amazing.

After several autographs and photos, he pushed through the crowd and made his way over to the group. "Hi." He placed a kiss on her lips, then rested his forehead against hers. "I'm so fucking glad you are here," he whispered.

"Nowhere else I'd rather be," she told him and wrapped her arms around his waist as he pulled her tighter against his chest. She'd missed this. The way he held her against her body, how safe she felt.

"So, where are we going to celebrate?" Sims asked.

Ryan's arms tightened briefly, then he released her from the hug. She'd expected him to step away, but he simply wrapped his arm around her and pulled her against the side of his body as he turned to his teammates. "I'm gonna pass."

"What do you mean you're gonna pass? We just won the division." Smitty raised his palms up, his brow knit with confusion as he stared at Ryan.

"I know. It's awesome."

"So, we have to celebrate," Gonzo agreed.

"I plan to celebrate. Just not with you assholes." Ryan looked down at her. His blue eyes blazed with emotion. How had she ever thought they were cold? Peyton's stomach flipped. Was he honestly picking going home with her over celebrating his win with his team? This was a huge night for them all. He should be with his teammates.

"I don't mind if we go out. We can talk after." Peyton squeezed his arm in reassurance.

"See your girl doesn't mind if you come out for a drink," Sims said.

Ryan's eyes warmed as they lingered on her face. No one had ever looked at her like that before. Like she truly mattered.

"Peyton, I don't want to go out with the team. I want to go home with you. So unless you had your heart set on celebrating with the team, I'd rather skip it and take you home."

"Home's good."

A slow, carnal smile slid across his face. His tooth bit into his bottom lip as he watched her. God, that was sexy. She definitely wanted to go home, like immediately. They could talk after the makeup sex, couldn't they? That wouldn't be wrong. Actions do speak louder than words after all.

Ryan arched his eyebrow as he looked at her. "Oh crap, did I say that out loud?" Peyton slapped her hand over her mouth.

He barked out a laugh. "No babe, you didn't say anything out loud, but you have a very expressive face."

Heat rose up her neck and across her cheeks. "Oops," she whispered.

"I like it." Ryan turned to his teammates. "Congrats on the win, boys. Thanks for helping me have a no hitter, couldn't have done it without you."

"You seriously aren't coming out for even one drink?" Sims shook his head as if he couldn't fathom anything making him want to miss out on the party.

"Nope, I've got a better offer." Ryan reached out and tucked a lock of hair behind her ear. The feel of his fingers against her neck made her shiver involuntarily.

"Fair enough." Smitty shifted his bag on his shoulder. "Great game, Ry. Peyton, I couldn't be happier to see you tonight. I'm glad you came."

"Thank you." She smiled warmly at him. Ryan's friends were good guys. He was lucky to have them.

Ryan looped his arm around her shoulder

She was glad she came too.

EPILOGUE

Energy buzzed all around them as Peyton gripped Kendall's hand from their seats on the third-base line. Game five of the World Series. The Hawks were up three games to one against their rivals from Detroit. A win tonight would make them world champions. To say Ryan had been edgy the past couple of days was putting it mildly. But who could blame him? Winning the World Series would be huge.

She smiled to herself as she remembered how she'd helped him burn off steam last night and then again this morning. That playoff beard was growing on her. Sure, it looked a little ragged, but the things he could do with that scruff more than made up for the appearance. And after breakfast with his parents this morning, Ryan had more steam than usual to blow off.

Thank god, Ryan's parents were sitting somewhere behind home plate. She had to admit she was kind of glad they weren't all sitting together. The pressure Ryan's parents put on him to stay focused and win was intense.

She wasn't proud of herself and some might say it was petty of her, but she still wasn't over what Pat had said about no woman being worth hurting his career or the team. The right woman was definitely worth it, and in her mind, the right woman wouldn't make him pick. The fact she'd been willing to sacrifice being with him, so he didn't have to choose didn't make her any less valuable.

Kendall peeled Peyton's fingers off her hand. "Girl, I know you're nervous, but we're going to need the medics down here in a minute if you don't ease up on the death grip."

Peyton looked down at Kendall's hand and winced when she saw the deep crescents in her friend's hand from Peyton's nails. "Sorry."

Kendall flexed her hand. "It's all good." Picking up her beer, Kendall took a sip. "My nerves are shot."

Peyton eyed the scoreboard. Top of the ninth. The Hawks were up by one. One away. Two more outs and they were done. She couldn't believe Ryan was still pitching. He'd been on fire tonight and as a result, he was still in the game. The closer hadn't been brought in. She prayed the team pulled out the win. If they didn't, Ryan would blame himself despite how phenomenally he'd pitched all game.

"I will be so glad when this series is done," Kendall said. "If Pete's lucky underwear has to go one more game, his bag isn't coming inside."

"I'm sorry, what?" Peyton shifted in her seat to look at her Ryan's sister.

"They're his lucky underwear. Don't want to wash the luck out. It's ridiculous." Kendall rolled her eyes.

"I'm sorry, are you saying Pete wears the same un-derwear every game?" Peyton giggled, then mentally ran through the number of games in the series. "Ew, he hasn't washed his underwear for *five games*."

"Oh no, these are playoff underwear. He hasn't washed these bad boys since they played Philadelphia."

"Ew, gross. That's disgusting. Why?" Peyton cringed as a shudder ran through her body.

"Stupid baseball superstitions. My brother isn't any better."

"Yeah, but Ryan just won't touch his facial hair. It's a scraggly beard, but it's clean."

"Ew, nope, nope, nope." Kendall shook her finger in front of Peyton's face. "Wipe that look off your face, gross, I don't want to know and if you keep smiling like that, it'll make me picture things and no, ew." She pointed her finger sternly. "So stop."

"Yes, ma'am." Peyton snickered.

The sound of the bat cracking against a ball pierced the air and the crowd was on their feet. Smitty backed up and caught the ball at the top of the fence, stealing a home run from Rodriguez. The crowd roared.

Ryan lifted his hat and held it against his chest as he saluted Smitty, who did the same thing back.

"Holy fuck, that was close," Kendall said.

Peyton snorted. "You swear like your brother."

"I know, it's awful. Pete isn't any better." Kendall rubbed her palms nervously against her thigh like her palms were sweating. "I'm surprised it hasn't rubbed off on you."

"Honestly, me too." Peyton bounced in her seat as the next batter walked up to the plate. "Of course it has to be

Simpson," she muttered as she looked at his .354 batting average as it flashed up on the screen.

Two down, one to go. She stared down at Ryan, sending all her positive vibes his way. "You got this, baby," she murmured.

And as if he heard her. Ryan turned and looked into the stands. A slow smile spread across his face that she could see from her seat. If she didn't know better, she would have sworn the cocky bastard winked at her too. Whether or not she imagined it, a calm slipped over her. They were going to win. Ryan had this in the bag.

Strike one.

The crowd roared and began chanting.

Strike two.

The crowd erupted to their feet. Peyton and Kendall stood. Their hands clasped together as they waited for the next pitch.

One more. Just one more.

Ryan shook off the first call from Patel, shook off the second before finally seeing what he wanted in the third. Peyton held her breath as Ryan wound up and launched a missile of a pitch. At the last second, the ball dipped, leaving the batter holding his bat in his hands as he watched strike three sail cleanly over the plate. He'd thrown a freakin' curve.

Peyton screamed. Holy crap, they'd won the world series.

She threw her arms around Kendall and the two women jumped up and down. After several moments, Kendall grabbed her arm and pulled her into the aisle and down the remaining few stairs to the railing. Security held up his hand to stop Kendall from trying to climb over.

"We're with players," Kendall told him.

Peyton dug around in her bag to try to find her pass. Her fingers hooked on her car keys instead of the ring of the pass. God, you'd think in a clear bag the stupid thing would be easier to find. In the excitement of getting onto the field, she'd forgotten all about having her pass out.

"Sure you are, honey," the guard said. He pointed at a group of women waiting along the railing. "So are they."

Peyton looked over and didn't recognize any of the women. "No, but we actually are dating players."

"Like I said. Sure you are."

Peyton's fingers connected with the lanyard in the bottom of her bag, and she pulled it out victoriously just as a security guard from the field tapped their guard on the shoulder. The big man turned and looked at them, then winced. "Sorry," he said.

"No problem," Peyton answered. "You're just doing your job."

"Thanks," he replied as he stepped aside and opened the small gate to allow them onto the field. Behind them, the group of women swarmed the guard, groaning when he closed the gate behind Kendall.

"Why do they get to go on the field?" a woman's voice whined. Peyton didn't wait to hear the answer. She scanned the crowd of players, staff, spouses, and media as they swarmed all around the field cheering.

Kendall grabbed her arm and pulled her toward the home team dugout. Finally, she spotted Ryan standing off to the side with a group of reporters, microphones shoved in his face. Gonzo ran up behind him and dumped the Gatorade container over the top of Ryan's head. He jumped but the liquid soaked his head and shirt, making the jersey stick to his muscular body.

Kendall slapped her hand over her mouth and laughed. It was like Ryan could sense she was there because his head snapped up in her direction. His gaze landing on hers.

He said something to the press, then jogged toward her. The reporters all turned. Their cameras trained on him as he ran toward her. Normally she would be embarrassed that the cameras were aimed her way, but all she cared about was getting to her man. A cameraman stepped in front of her, his camera aimed at Ryan. She'd barely stepped around the man when muscular arms banded around her body, and she was picked up into the air. His wet jersey soaked into her shirt, pulling her into the celebration with him.

Ryan's lips crashed down on hers, his tongue tangled in a hungry, adrenaline-fueled mass of teeth and lips and tongue. It was dirty and messy and the best kiss of her entire life.

The kiss broke, and she held Ryan's face in her hands. His smile was so big she was surprised his face could contain it.

"Holy fuck, Pey," he yelled.

The noise on the field was deafening. Even with Ryan right against her she could barely hear him. "Congrats, baby," she yelled to be heard over the crowd.

His energy and excitement were contagious. He stared at her. His eyes heated. Her man was riding the adrenaline high and horny as hell from it.

Too bad the media had other ideas for him.

Cameras shuttered around them. Reporters called out his name. Ryan rested his forehead against hers. "I gotta talk to the press," he groaned.

"Do your thing. I'm not going anywhere."

Ryan gave her a quick kiss, then pressed his lips against her ear and said, "I'm counting on it. I fucking love you, Pey."

"I fucking love you too," she said, smiling to herself when he stared at her lips and arched a brow. It was so weird to her how much he loved when she cursed.

"I'll be quick."

"No rush. We've got all night to celebrate."

"And I'm going to use every minute of it." He pressed a quick kiss to her lips. "Get ready." After setting her down, he turned toward the press.

"Ryan, tell us about that curveball," a reported called.

It seemed fitting that Ryan had thrown a curveball to win the game. Because the man had thrown her life for a curve and she wouldn't have it any other way.

THE END

Want a bonus scene? <u>Subscribe to my mailing list and you'll get instant access to an exclusive Throwing the Curve Bonus scene!</u>

Get ready for more ballers in the next Playing for Keeps series book. <u>Jeff and Saskia's book Sliding into Home is up next!</u>

<u>Grab a copy now</u> or keep swiping for a preview.

SNEAK PEEK AT SLIDING INTO HOME

Kia looked down at her shaking hands and took several deep breaths. She could do this. Everything would be fine. So why did she feel like she was going to throwup?

She stopped at the edge of the ball diamonds and scanned the fields to look for Jeff or Smitty as her son had affectionately been calling him. Peyton had said he was working with the older kids today but every diamond had teenagers on it. Which one would he be on?

Drawn to the far diamond she watched as a group performed an elaborate celebratory cheer. The volume and enthusiasm growing with each chant. When they parted she instantly saw Jeff standing with the teens. At the first sight of him, her heart did a little stutter step that she quickly tried to squash. She could do this.

Slowly making her way down the sideline toward the far diamond she tried to quell her nerves. When she'd seen him two days ago it had been a shock. She'd been blindsided but today? Whole other ballgame. Today she was purposefully seeking him out after all this time. God what if he didn't believe her, or didn't care. She didn't think he was that kind of guy but how the hell did she know? She'd spent one night with him six years ago. She didn't know anything about the guy.

One of the teens pointed in her direction and Jeff's head turned toward her. A smile split across his face and he lifted his hand in acknowledgement. He said something to the teens then the group disbanded and the youth began gathering up their supplies. As Jeff walked towards her, Kia's heart pounded in her chest. The closer he got, the more her heart thumped.

Jeff smiled when he got close to her. "Hey Saskia."

"Hi, how are you?"

His brow wrinkled, confusion evident on his face. "I'm good, what are you doing here? Where's Max?"

She took a deep breath. "He's at daycare. I was hoping we could maybe talk."

Jeff glanced behind him at his group then at the surrounding fields. "Yeah, sure. We just finished up our game so I'm done for the day."

"Oh that's good." Was it? Shoot. She wasn't ready to talk now. When she'd come here she'd been expecting him to be busy and need to schedule something on another day. She wasn't prepared. They couldn't have this conversation here, but it's not like she could explain why it would be best to go elsewhere. Shit, shit, shit.

Jeff cocked his head to the side as he studied her. "What's up? Something going on with Max? Is he having troubles?"

"No, no, not at all. He loves everything about coming here." She smiled as she thought of her son. To most people she was a screwup, but no one would say that when it came to her son. Max was the best thing she'd ever done in her life. Nothing was more important to her than his happiness which was why she needed to do this. Now. "He's been talking about you for weeks. Smitty this, Smitty that. I didn't realize he was talking about you until the other day I had no idea."

"He's a cool little guy."

"Yeah, he is." She smiled at a couple of teens who eyed her as they walked past.

"Thanks coach," the taller of the two youth said.

"No problem. Good job today, guys. Thanks for putting the stuff away. Appreciate it."

Jeff turned back to her. "So you want to talk here or did you want to grab a coffee or something?" He paused to study her. "You sure you even want to talk to me. You're kind of freaking me out with how nervous you are."

She laughed and okay yeah, even to her own ears she sounded nervous. Real smooth.

"Saskia talk to me, what's going on?

"I go by Kia now."

His smile ticked up in the corner of his mouth as he watched her. "Kia, I like that, it suits you."

Her heart thumped again. Damn it. She wasn't supposed to still be attracted to him. She had a boyfriend. A great one. Well good. Ok, at least. This was about Max, nothing else mattered. She took a deep breath. "I wanted to call you after the seeing you the other day but obviously I didn't have your number. I came by here to ask for it but the staff wouldn't give it to me. I guess they thought I might be some crazed fan or something."

He laughed. "You do look a little sketchy."

A overly loud, uncomfortable laugh burst out of her. God she really was a hot mess. So much for being calm and relaxed. She glanced at him, heat rose in her cheeks.

Jeff stepped a little closer to her. His gaze slowly swept down her body. "What'd you want my number for?" His tongue dipped out swept across his bottom lip like he was imagining doing all kinds of things to her.

"Oh god, not that." She held up her hand. "I have a boyfriend. But um..."

"Just thought I'd check. With how nervous you are this felt like some weird booty call or something."

"God, no, definitely not." With a shaky hand she pushed her hair back from her face. She eyed the empty bleachers and flicked her wrist toward them. "You want to sit?"

"Yeah sure." Jeff walked beside her. "It's wild how quickly this place clears out at the end of the games. Considering how many kids are always running around her doing stuff you'd think they'd linger more on the fields."

She scanned the now empty diamond. "I'm sure the little guys take longer to clear out."

"Sometimes."

Kia could feel him watching her, waiting for her to talk. This was so much harder than she'd anticipated. She dropped down onto the vacant bleacher and Jeff sat down beside her. He turned toward her. "So you gonna tell me why you're here?"

"Umm yeah." She clasped her hands together in her lap. Took a deep breath and blurted, "Max is your son."

Buy Link

ABOUT AUTHOR

Lauren Fraser resides in British Columbia, Canada, with her husband, two children, and two dogs. When she's not busy writing, Lauren loves to spend time with her family outside—camping, hiking and paddle boarding. Lauren writes about love and relationships in many different forms, but in the end, she's a sucker for a happy ending. She is multi-published and loves to hear from her readers. For the latest updates, visit her website.

Website http://www.laurenfraser.com/
Newsletter http://www.laurenfraser.com/newsletter-
Receive a free ebook for newsletter subscribers only

Also By

Playing for Keeps

Too Far   Prequel

Everything to Me   Book 1

Throwing the Curve   Book 2

Cowboy Code

Rode Hard Book 1 Cowboy Code Series

Rough Stock Book 2 Cowboy Code Series

Round Up Book 3 Cowboy Code Series

Standalone Books

Letting Go

The Geek Next Door